STORY OF THE BRETHREN 1

dragon's HEART

LaVerne

USA TODAY Bestselling Author

THOMPSON

Lavernethompson.com

isisindc@msn.com

First Editor- Lara Parker

Line Editor- Zena Gainer

Cover illustration by Fiona Jayde

Print ISBN- 9780-9859646-610

This one is for all those who dreamt of dragons. Not just owning one, but being one. Let there be dragons. Can you hear my dragon roar?

ACKNOWLEDGMENTS

This story was a long way in coming to this point. I have so many to thank for pushing me on, but I have to give shout outs to my RPW writers' group: Eve Tesoro, E. W. Walsh, Scarlet Hunter, Tess Black, and my Strydie. Also, to my sometimes partner in crime, Stephanie Williams. And last, but so not least, VR. Love you all.

From fire we're born,
from fire we thrive,
from fire we breathe,
by fire we die.

LEGEND

Once, these majestic beasts soared through the heavens at will. Masters of wind, rain, thunder, and lightning. Favored by Mother Earth and ruling over her domain. But all that happened before man embraced the coming of the one God and Earth magicks slowly disappeared. Or so legend had it.

Once, dragons numbered in the hundreds of thousands, but only a handful of hatchlings had been born in a thousand years. Their number slowly dwindled.

Once, predators now prey. With their magic weakening, humans—with the help of one of the brethren's own—hunted and killed dragons, their mates, and any offspring. The survivors of the purges had to leave Mother Earth or die. Earth was no longer safe. Only one place left they could go.

The brethren had to return to the lost land of their beginning by opening a gateway to another realm. Earth was merely one of many worlds existing on parallel planes. Those with the knowledge and the power could travel through gateways connecting them, but at a great risk. They were unsure how to open such a gate or where they would end up if they succeeded. Memory said it could be done. They had to try or die.

Still, some decided to stay. Earth was home. To remain behind and survive, they would willingly forgo their birthright. Forever shed their dragon skin, drain their remaining powers, and become fully human.

Some simply wanted to die as dragons in this world. They were too old for change. Dragons had roamed Earth's skies for ten thousand years. The brethren could not imagine a sky without dragons in flight. Some would not surrender this heritage. They refused to live as anything other than what they were on the planet of their birth.

Just before the first of the sun's rays crested the eastern horizon, dragons gathered at their sacred place high in a remote, hard to get to area in the Sperrin Mountains of Erin. An area few humans had ever seen, but every dragon knew. It was a special place, a circle of power controlled by a ring of stones with no name where the first dragon appeared.

Those who would journey in search of the world from whence they began formed a circle around one dragon. The strongest amongst them stood in the center of the stones, his massive twelve-foot frame dominating the area. Like the first dragon who opened the portal, a Dark Dragon Lord led them. As dark as the deepest night, as memory said the first Dragon Lord to have been. Unlike other dragons, whose scales shimmered with a spectrum of colors, his scaled massive form seemed to absorb light. No color whatsoever reflected off a hide appearing as smooth as silk but impregnable as a diamond.

His raised majestic head showed a spiked ridge running from the bridge of his nostrils over his skull down the length of his body. Green slitted eyes—the only color on him—filled with emerald fire looked around at the dragons gathered just within the circle and outside it. He turned so he could survey them all. No great number remained.

His father—their leader—dead, killed by treachery. His mother's dying roar of rage still echoed in his blood, but before she died, she destroyed the one who killed her mate.

2

Draakar had come to their aid too late. He was young for a dragon, but as their son and the most powerful among them, he led now as their Dark Lord, and he would not let the brethren down. But so few of them were alive to lead. So many dead or their magick weak. He could wait no longer.

He'd mated last night, joining with the strongest female amongst the remaining brethren, a mate who could call forth his powers. Draakar hoped it would be enough. He would make sure of it. In one last effort to save their race, he would use his powers to open a portal to another world.

The Dark Lord turned to look down at the smaller golden dragon standing at his side. The realization of what he had done fractured his heart. This pain something he would have to endure for the rest of his long life. The golden dragon was now his mate for life, but not by choice. His sacrifice for the brethren. Their needs over his own.

The dragons gathered, channeled all their power to him, helping him open a gate to the beginning world. It had not been done in the time of any dragon alive. There had been no need, but it had been done in the long ago past, and dragons were long-lived with boundless memories. Need drove them to attempt it now. The memories in their blood, passed down to them from the first ancestors, promised it could be done. The first dragons, the forbearers, the ones who came from another place, showed them the way. To a place not of this earth, not of this world.

Now the Dark Lord and his remaining brethren used those memories as a guide to their realm of origin. They dug deep within themselves to the part of their souls still binding them to a past left behind. From a time so long ago, no dragon living remembered this place, yet no living dragon could forget its existence. Time to go home, back to their beginnings. Home to the birthplace of fire, the birthplace of the heart of the dragon—Akgon. They had to return home to survive. The time of dragons on earth was over.

As the sun glistened high in the sky, above the Dark Dragon Lord the very air trembled, a swirling gray cloudy mass appeared. They had done it, created a portal, but the Dark Lord had to maintain it. The only one strong enough to do so. He had to hold it open until all who wanted to go crossed over. One by one, the dragons flew through and disappeared within the cloud until he remained the last of those who wanted to leave. Before leaving, he tried one last time, sending a mental plea to his brethren who watched from the ridge. His great body shuddered with exhaustion from using such strong magicks, but by will alone, he would hold the gate open a while longer.

Come with us. It is not too late.

A unanimous response to his plea floated into his consciousness. *No. But we wish you all a safe journey.*

The Dark Dragon Lord had no choice. Even his great strength could not hold the gate open much longer. *Then I wish you speed beyond the wind. Goodbye.*

With a heavy heart for those electing to stay, for the life they left behind, Draakar raised his wings and followed his remaining brethren through the gate. A bright flash of silver lightning appeared to swallow him as he crossed over. The swirling cloud folded in on itself, forever closing the gateway behind him, leaving a faint scent of smoke in the air.

The ones staying behind had little time for regret, much too late for that. Their combined strength would not equal the power of a Dragon Lord, and rarer, even those magicks available to the Dark Dragon. Only three had been born in their thousands of years on earth. Two were dead and the last survivor now gone.

With the sun hovering above the other horizon, casting the sky in a purple haze, the day ended. Tomorrow would be a new beginning. Those who chose to forsake their brethren heritage and become human shed their dragon skin for the last time. They changed as they turned, walking away from the stones on human legs, using the last of their magic to get down the mountain. A few others spread their iridescent wings and took to the heavens one more time. For a short time, for the last time, dragons rode the currents in the night sky until those too were gone.

Gone to die.

Those who chose life joined with humans and never passed down the secret of their dragon ancestry to their offspring.

The dragon blood lay dormant. Even those with great promise of magicks were never taught. Those brethren now lived human lives, with human life spans. They had given up their magic. Finally, all who remained to teach their offspring and to show them the way of the dragon passed from life. And while the blood passed from generation to generation, weak in some, strong in others, it did not stir. There was no one left to call to it. Dragons became a thing of myth and legend. A fairytale.

Yet the dragon blood waits…it sleeps…

Waiting.

Waiting.

Dragons are known for their patience.

CHAPTER ONE

"Oh no! Not again." Maya rolled over and buried her face in her pillow. "Aargh!"

For the third night in a row, she'd had the same dream. *Dragons!* Well, one dragon. A black dragon with emeralds for eyes. Consuming her, drawing her into their fiery depths. A fire, while dreaming, in which she gladly and willingly burned. After the first dream, she'd awakened in a cold sweat and checked her skin for burn marks, only to find her body unblemished.

For the hundredth time, she wondered why had she taken the tour of the dragon stones? It had sounded so exciting when the hiking guide told her and a few other people in the lounge about it. Something different and not on the listed hiking tours of the Sperrin Mountains, but as he'd claimed, more interesting.

In truth, the hike itself was quite amazing and the stones magnificent. According to the guide who described them, the stones were not as tall as Stonehenge, only about half their size but older and all preserved in a perfect circle. These stones had also been polished by the elements until they not only looked like marble, but appeared as smooth.

The guide didn't know how they had gotten there or who put them there. He told some local story to the group about druids and the harvest, most of which Maya ignored. She was too busy rubbing one of the stones and getting an electric shock for her efforts.

"Ouch!" she cried, rubbing her fingers and glancing at some of her fellow hikers who stared curiously at her. "I could swear there was an etching of a dragon carved into that stone a second ago."

The guide, James, came over to where she stood and looked. He brushed his hand over the unblemished, once again smooth, surface. "Nothing but dirt," James assured her.

"Why are they called the dragon stones, anyway?" Maya had asked.

James shrugged. "Not sure."

Her dreams had started later that night. It's strange she'd never heard of the standing stones before. No one had warned her for days after her visit she'd have nightmares about being burned by a dragon. *And aching for the feel of his fire on her skin.*

Oh, why hadn't she just gone to Paris on her vacation, like originally planned? She had no idea what possessed her in the first place to come to Ireland. Her grandfather on her mother's side was Scottish, not Irish, and the rest of the family consisted of African descent. She should have gone to Africa or Scotland. No, she should have gone to Paris. Maybe it wasn't too late. She had eight days of vacation left; she could still go.

That's it! Just what she needed, a change of scenery. All this green—the land of leprechauns, dragons, and fairy princesses—made her loopy. No need to go looking for problems. Enough sat on her plate, so she didn't need any more restless nights because of weird dreams. Her conscious mind held enough to keep her awake at night. She didn't need her subconscious interrupting her when she did get to sleep. Feeling better after making up her mind to cut her trip to Ireland short, she went back to sleep.

The shrill ringing of her telephone jarred her awake. "This had better be important," she said groggily into the receiver. Funny, she could see emerald eyes in the still place between sleep and wake. Someone spoke, but she couldn't seem to focus her mind away from those mesmerizing eyes.

"Hello. Who is this? What did you say?"

A gruff voice she hadn't expected to hear for at least another couple of weeks spoke into her ear. "I'm sorry, hon, but I missed you, so I took a chance."

Not a voice she wanted to hear. "Justin? Is that you? I thought we agreed you would wait for me to call you."

"I know. But I just missed you so much. I couldn't help myself. Do you miss me? I could be on the next plane out."

She must still be dreaming. The trip had given her time to think and to put a little—well, all right, a lot—of distance between herself and Justin. For the past three years, everyone had been expecting them to get married. Frankly, they'd never really gotten past the 'dating friends' stage. She'd never been intimate with any man. Never been tempted. Her relationship with Justin had simply been convenient—for her. Probably because he never pushed for anything more physical than kissing and touching, making him the perfect boyfriend. A sure date whenever she needed one and good eye candy. But when he'd finally asked her to marry him, she couldn't say yes. Instead, she faced the truth about her feelings for him.

Justin continued to speak into the tense silence. "I know it's still too soon after your grandmother's accident for you to go off by yourself. Let me help you get through this."

At first, she'd blamed postponing her decision about Justin on the death of her beloved grandmother. She couldn't think about marriage so soon after Nana's death. It had only been six months since she'd stood by her grandmother's graveside. The woman who helped raised her. Who meant as much to her as her mother did. She'd needed to get away by herself for a while. Take a much needed break from running the marketing firm her grandmother had started over ten years ago at the age of seventy.

Never one to let a little thing like age slow her down, it took a drunk driver to take her life. Before Nana died, she swam every morning and wore a perfect size six. Nana would still be alive but for a harsh quirk of fate or a shortage of angels in heaven.

Maya forced her attention back to the conversation. "I'm sorry, Justin. I didn't sleep well. And no, you can't join me. I need to be by myself. Anyway, I'm not sure where I'll be."

"What do you mean, you're not sure where you'll be?" Justin asked, with the slightest hint of desperation in his voice.

"Just what I said. I've had it with the Emerald Isle. As soon as I can get an internet connection, I'll be making arrangements to leave. Don't expect me back home until the tenth."

"What? But where are you going? How will I be able to get in touch with you?"

"This is just something that I feel I have to do. I need this time for myself. I don't know who I am anymore."

"You are my future wife. That's who you are."

"No, Justin. I'm not your future anything." She sighed, tired from the last few nights of restless sleep and now having to deal with Justin. "I never told you I'd marry you. I need to figure myself out."

"I don't understand you."

At twenty-eight, she didn't understand herself, but she

took pity on him. He cared about her, even loved her, but he wasn't *in* love with her or she with him. Friendship and convenience were no longer enough. "Listen, if you need me, just send me an e-mail. I have my laptop and cell with me and I'll check in with you after I get settled." Before he could voice any further protest, Maya said goodbye and hung up the phone.

She reminded herself to call her parents after she got up to let them know her change of plans. If she didn't, Justin would call them and upset them needlessly. Ever since Nana died, everyone had been worried about her. They had been so close. Her parents kept waiting for her to do something rash. Like take this trip alone to Europe, the one they'd planned on taking together.

"We have no choice. I am sorry, Your Majesties. I have done the scrying an unprecedented three times. And I have confirmation from my sister seers. If the dragon brethren are to survive, we must renew the blood. Talon must go back."

"No," the Dark Lord growled at his trusted advisor.

Three dragons stood on pebbled ground in the open arena, making up the heart of the palace, surrounded by the sacred circle of standing stones. The circle of power. The runes cast within always cast true. Anyone else would have backed down at the sound of the Dark Lord's displeasure, but the chief advisor held his ground and did not move as his Lord continued to rant.

"This makes no sense. I will not have it. I will not accept this."

The Lady Sierran placed a golden claw on her mate's dark

scaled shoulder. "Draakar, we have no choice. Valour speaks true and you know this."

Draakar, the Dark Dragon Lord, spread his wings, a span as long as a seven-foot man and so thick and dark they appeared like black velvet. The surrounding air vibrated from the draft. He raised his mighty head. A roar emerged from the depths of his soul, bellowing out his rage. Crimson fire stretched toward a purple heaven. No, brethren in the land missed hearing the cry of pain and rage issuing from the depths of their Lord's throat, and none existed who did not share in his pain. Thousands of dragons answered with roars of their own and crimson, green, gold, and blue fires blazed across the skies, turning it a kaleidoscope of color.

"I did not open that gate over a thousand years ago to condemn my only son to death," the Dragon Lord roared.

A dragon with golden glittering scales stepped in the circle and faced his sire. The image of his mother, though not as large as his father Draakar.

"Sire...Father. I must go. I am ready and I will survive. With your help, I will do what I know I was born to do."

The great dragon looked into eyes of emerald fire matching his own. "Oh my son, would that it were not so. Do you really understand what is being asked of you?"

"Yes, Father, I do. I must relinquish my birthright, but only until I return. Make no mistake, I will return. By the claw of the First Dragon Lord, I will find my mate. I must. We all know she is not here. She is one of the Forgotten Ones. One left on earth."

The Lady Sierran rubbed her head against her son's shoulder. "Ah, Talon. We know you must go, but it is so hard for us. Your father's power is waning. The power sustaining our life energy here is tied to his and is also weakening. We do not quite understand why. We do know you must mate in order for you to come into your full powers and become the Dragon Lord you were meant to be."

"With respect," Valour spoke up. "No, Your Majesties, not just mate. He must find his truemate. I am convinced she is the key to unlocking his full powers."

No one refuted his words.

"Only with a true mating could Talon hope to sire a Dark Dragon Lord. We must restore the balance of this world," Valour continued. "Too late. We have come to understand one of the reasons the brethren abandoned this world to begin with. The power of a Dark Dragon Lord is required to sustain it. As we all know, the temperature of this dimension fluctuates between extreme cold and extreme heat. While we can survive in a form of hibernation in extreme cold, we dragons need heat. As we've come to understand, there must be a balance. The Dragon Lord provides the balance, because too much heat is also our weakness."

Talon scoffed. "Too much heat means death. From fire we're born, but by fire we die."

Draakar nodded. "Some of the old memories make more sense now. Akgon is a land of fire and ice. Since our return, the temperature throughout the land has gradually changed and affects our connection to the magicks of the land."

Valour bowed his head, acknowledging his words. "All you say is truth, but the brethren are weakening, Lord, along with you," Valour stated as fact. "The periods of extreme temperatures are getting longer and more intense. In time, dragons will start dying. Even though we're long-lived, most of us are old."

Yes, most of the brethren were older than Sierran and Draakar. Some like himself, Valour thought, old even for dragons. While dragons had been born in the thousand years since Draakar opened the gate to Akgon, the home world, they still only numbered a few thousand. Not the hundreds of thousands they should have been.

"Talon is one of the last born among us," Valour continued. "And while at four hundred years he is young for a dragon, he is also one among a rising number, only willing to mate with their truemates." Most of the dragons were not mated to truemates, including his Lord and Lady, but Valour kept those thoughts to himself.

Sierran's quick glance at Draakar did not go unnoticed by Valour. Sierran and Draakar did have an inkling of why his powers were waning. She was not his truemate. Although they were joined and Talon their offspring, their mating had been done of necessity.

Their great powers enabled them to maintain the illusion of truemates. Only Valour knew the truth—he had realized long ago—but no one else knew, not even their son. He also suspected his Lady realized the price she would now pay for forcing Draakar's hand so many ages ago. Nonetheless, it was worth it and necessary, and why he'd aided her. While they may not have been truemates, Valour knew their hearts. Sierran did love him, and Draakar loved her. Together, they had saved the brethren—for a while.

Now she had to face the harsh reality of the truth. She could no longer help her mate sustain his powers. She could only enhance it and not for much longer. Her life energy, her power drained fastest of all. Only Draakar's truemate could sustain him now. Sierran turned her head to look at Valour, knowing he read some of her thoughts, and confirming for him her awareness of the situation. She would tell Draakar none of these things. She nodded slightly at him and he nodded back to let her know he understood. As always, she kept her own counsel.

At first both Sierran and Draakar thought to convince Talon to take one of the stronger females as his mate, a gold or a bronze, and had come to Valour to get his support. They'd had it once before, but Valour told them this time things were different. He would not pressure the boy. Besides, Talon absolutely refused. He wanted his truemate or he would have none at all. Not even for his race would he sacrifice his mate.

"I have always known she is not of this world," Talon said. "I have simply been waiting for her to be born, for her life energy to grow strong enough to call to me so I would be able to find her. For a short while, from time to time, I can sense her, but only for brief moments." *Like a passing caress across his heart whenever he caught just the right wind current.*

Valour caught Talon's last thought and smiled.

"I need to go to Terra now," Talon continued. "I must be ready when it is time to claim her, and it may take a while for me to find her. The sooner I can begin my search, the sooner I can return to Akgon with my mate. I have no doubt I will find her and bring her back with me."

DRAAKAR'S SIGHED and faced his son. "I am proud of you, you know."

Talon did what he himself had not, so long ago. Draakar had known once he stepped through the gate on Earth he had left his truemate behind, sacrificing them both, but the brethren needed him. Unfortunately for the dragons, he realized too late they would also need his truemate.

"I am not even sure we have enough strength amongst us to reopen the gate," Draakar said.

"I have faith in you, Father," Talon replied. "I will help. All of Akgon will help, and when I cross over, I will shift."

"Yes," Valour agreed. "You will not be able to hold your dragon form for long on Terra. You will revert to human form, although you will still be stronger than humans, and you will have some powers."

"Do you know how much of his brethren powers he will retain?" Talon's mother asked.

"I'm not sure," Valour replied. "I suspect Earth magick has changed, but he should still be able to wield it. Once he is joined with his mate, he will come into his full strength and she should be able to help sustain him."

"But will it be enough?" Draakar asked.

"It must be," Talon replied.

"It required thousands of dragons to help me open the portal the first time."

"Yes," Talon said, "but once opened you were able to hold it on your own."

"Just barely," Draakar said.

"But you had to get us all through and then yourself also," Valour said, his wide snout flaring even more. "This will be easier, the energy output required would be less, and there might be others on earth who may be able to help Talon reopen the gate."

"I thought the dragon magick had been purged from Terra," Sierran stated.

"Not really," Valour replied. "The dragon bloodline is still there. Talon will have to find a way to tap into it."

"How, Val?" Talon asked.

"Blood will call to blood," Valour answered, nodding his head. "Not all will answer, and not all will be able to be trained. Next to your father, you will become the most powerful dragon ever born, and your son has the potential to be even stronger than your father. But any son you have must be born here. If he is born on Earth, his powers may be lessened."

"Why?" Talon asked.

"I'm only guessing, but from the ancestral memories we gained when we returned to our home world. Akgon, as the land of our birth, accesses the strongest of our magicks. The stronger the magicks, the stronger the births, and Earth magicks were weak when we left."

"What if he has a daughter?" Draakar's tail whipped up with his irritation.

"You know Dragon Lords only have sons, Highness."

"But the blood has been changed on Earth. The Earth magick had been tampered with when the brethren drained theirs into it. What if the change affects the gender of the child? What if he has a female child?" Draakar persisted.

Valour bronze spiked tail twitched in irritation now, too. "The prophecy says the child of the Dragon Lord will be the next Dark Dragon. The prophecy refers to Talon; he is the heir. Only males can hold the power of a Dark Dragon. His son will be a Dark Dragon. It is why we are risking opening the gate. Only a Dark Lord can save us and rebalance the magicks of our realm."

"You are right, Valour," Sierran agreed.

"It will take time and the strength and will of all brethren to hold the balance until another Dark Lord can come into his own," Valour continued. "A mated Talon will allow us time. He and his truemate would provide the necessary strength."

Draakar sighed painfully; the knowledge Valour spoke true burned in his heart. "I know. Call the brethren to the circle. If I must do this, let it be done now."

"Majesty, I think all already know your decision. Look."

"So it seems." If he hadn't been such a loyal adviser, Draakar would have been irritated, which he was, but not with Valour.

Draakar looked to the sky and, as far as he could see,

17

dragons were in flight headed toward them. He glanced over at his mate. While not his truemate, he had come to love her, and she had given him his beloved son. Whom he must now send back to Terra. She nodded her head to him to show her support. She didn't realize what opening the gate again would cost her. Her strength was weakened already, and enhancing his for this task would sap most of her remaining reservoirs.

Draakar gazed at his son, sure love and pride shone in his eyes for all to see. Still, he said the words, "I am proud of you and I love you. This is your time. As it was mine to lead the dragons through the portal, it is your destiny to return. Come back to us. Return to your mother and me."

"Fear not, Father. I will do what must be done."

Valour stepped from the center of the circle of stones to stand with the other brethren. They began to form an even larger circle around their Dark Dragon Lord, his mate, and his heir. As one, as many of them had done so long ago, they channeled the power of the brethren to their Dark Lord, who harnessed it and opened the gate he'd once sealed.

A hint of smoke carried on the air, while above the head of the golden male dragon, a swirling gray cloud appeared. Without glancing at his parents standing behind him, Talon spread his wings and, in one great sweep of air, flew through the cloud. Blood red tears fell from Draakar's eyes as he watched the gray cloud fold in on itself and disappear. He looked down to see the red drops solidify into two rubies laying on the pebbled tiles, and his mate Sierran in a crumpled heap at his feet. Bending down, he gently lifted her within his great forearms. When he saw Valour step forward to help, Draakar shook his head, stopping him in his tracks.

"Do not fret, mate mine," she said. "I am not dead yet. I just need to rest."

Without saying a word, Draakar leaped into the air and

flew to one of the more comfortable regions of the realm. Finally arriving at his destination, he set down with his mate beside a waterfall surrounded by pink crystal rocks. He carried her beneath the fall, allowing the healing water to bathe her. Sierran's scales slowly lost their dull sheen and glowed golden again. After a while, she stood on her own. They both knew she would not live to see many more risings.

"For the last time, beloved." Sierran changed to her human form. Golden scales shimmered and blurred until a perfectly shaped naked human woman form appeared.

Draakar watched her change and changed, too. Where once stood a dark dragon, there now stood a pale-skinned man. He gathered his wife to him; her ankle-length golden tresses draped over his arms as he kissed her. A kiss of peace.

"I release you," Sierran said. "Your truemate is also one of the forgotten ones, the ones left behind. I know you have to go, too."

"I made my choice long ago," Draakar stated. "I cannot leave you." The words "not yet," lingered between them.

"You don't. It is I who leave you. I am sorry I was not the one. She is out there, and you must find her. Go to her and watch over our son."

"I love you."

"Then you must do this for me, for the brethren, and for yourself. You have suffered enough. You have never come into your true strength. With it, we would not be in this predicament. I love you, and I know you have a place in your heart for me. Now take me to the air, Draakar, let me feel the wind on my face."

CHAPTER TWO

"*W*hat was that? Did you see that?"

"See what?" his wife asked from her aisle seat on the plane. She craned her neck to look past her husband, sitting by the window. "A bunch of clouds?"

"I'm not sure. It looked like something...something big, just blocked out the sun."

"Well, I don't see anything. Probably just a bird."

"Not this high up, and it was bigger than any bird I've ever seen."

The passenger in the window seat in section 14A on flight forty-seven bound for the United States from Heathrow Airport in the United Kingdom hit the call button for a flight attendant. When she got there, he didn't know quite what to say to her. 'I think I just saw a UFO' didn't sound right. So instead, he just asked for a straight gin and pulled the window shade down over his window. It was going to be a long flight.

MAYA PAUSED on the narrow trail to glance up at the clear blue sky and breathe in the crisp tang of the cool mountain air. She didn't know why earlier in the day she had pulled up her itinerary on her laptop and changed her flight arrangements—yet again. Instead of leaving Ireland this afternoon, as she had originally planned, she rebooked to leave tomorrow night. What possessed her to make those changes and to spend the rest of the day hiking the Sperrin Mountains again, she hadn't a clue. Something drove her to get a look at those stones one more time. She hovered on the verge of a discovery, though of what she didn't know.

She found the beginning of the trail they'd used a few days ago easily enough, even without a map. Their guide, James, had given her specific instructions before she'd set out on her own, which she reviewed in her head. Besides, she remembered the way to the stones, just one winding path. The first time, the entire hike from point to point took about five hours, and only because they went at the pace of the slowest person. Maya figured she should make better time. Even though she'd left late morning, she still had plenty of time to make it to the stones and back well before the sun set. But somehow she had gotten turned around. No one warned her about the sudden fog rolling in today, or how it would hinder her sight of the almost non-existent trail.

"Come on, Maya. Does that tree look familiar? Or is it familiar because you've walked past it three times already?" she asked herself again. Out here in the middle of nowhere, no one would care.

Maya stopped to take a drink of water from the hose attached to her backpack and finish eating half of a power bar. When she looked up again, she couldn't believe the sight in front of her. The thick fog still hindered her vision, but she could just make out the outline of what appeared to be part of the perimeter of the circle of stones.

"Yeah!" she cried, exhilarated, punching a fist in the air. "I've found it again! The stones!"

No sooner had the words left Maya's mouth when the fog cleared. Enough for her to notice, between the gaps of the stones, an odd, rather large shape on the ground in the center of the circle.

She cautiously moved past an opening, entered the circle, and walked toward the form on the ground. The pile didn't move. The closer she got, the shape took on the contours of a body. Someone lay curled into a fetal position on the dirt with his or her back turned to her. She couldn't tell the sex of the person. The thick fog impeded her vision; she could barely make out features of a dark shirt and jean-clad legs. She moved closer until she could kneel over the body. As soon as she touched what she identified as an arm, she knew a male rested on the ground. Hard muscle made up his bicep. His skin felt warm. Maybe he hadn't been out in the cool air for long.

She rolled him over onto his back. Maya gazed into the face of a sleeping, golden angel just before the fog rolled forward and swirled before her eyes, temporarily obscuring her view.

My God, he's just a boy, a teenager. She shook him gently. "Are you all right? Can you hear me? Are you hurt?"

She stopped speaking when she heard a soft moan.

"Oh, my head," a disembodied voice whimpered. "What... what happened?" He tried to sit up but slumped back down to the hard packed dirt.

"Here, take it easy," Maya said, touching his shoulder. "Don't try to get up yet. Don't you know what happened?"

Maya sat back on her hunches. She couldn't see his face clearly anymore, but she could tell his head turned at the sound of her voice.

"I...I don't know. I...I'm not sure," he said.

"Just relax. Give it a minute."

"Oh...my head hurts." The young man groaned again and held his hands to his temples.

Before Maya could ask any more questions, he fell sideways and passed out. She couldn't get him to wake up again. Pulling her backpack off, she placed it near the young man and took out her cell phone. The red glow over the bar on the phone showed her she had no service. She frowned in frustration. "Just great. I spend all this money on a state-of-the-art smart phone and cell service that's supposed to provide international service so I can be connected from anywhere in the world. Anywhere, of course, but wherever I need it most. This sucks!"

The mist lifted. Maya glanced down. The young man's features looked clearer, but the night grew darker. She shivered and zipped up her vest. The temperature in the mountains dropped quickly. Looking around, she saw nothing but shadows. She didn't want to leave him; it would take her at least a two-hour walk to the nearest house and help. Maybe she wouldn't have to go so far. Maybe if she moved around a little, she'd be able to pick up a signal so she could call for help.

Leaving his side, she walked around a couple of feet away from the young man, but still no signal. Maya kept going until she went beyond the standing stones. Once she did, she got a signal, and the call went through.

The emergency people would be there as soon as they could. She put her phone in her cargo pants' side pocket and returned to the boy's side. They could send a chopper in, but the low-laying fog presented a visibility problem. They'd fly in as close as possible to her coordinates, then walk their way up to them. She'd described the area to the operator and had been a little taken aback when the woman claimed she'd never heard of the standing stones. Shouldn't they have maps of the various hiking areas on the mountain? She even checked to make sure she'd dialed the emergency number for Sperrin County. After all, she had programmed the number into her phone while on the first hike out here.

Maya gave the operator the name of her inn and the name of her hiking guide. She tried to describe how to get there, the way her guide had done, but she didn't seem to be very helpful. Hopefully, they'd get a hold of her guide who could bring them to the right spot or they could call her cell and try to track her location from the signal.

Nothing had changed with the young man's condition. She tried to wake him up again by gently shaking his arm, but he wouldn't stir. Pressing her fingers between his jaw and the side of his neck, she checked his pulse. It beat strongly against her fingers, at least confirming signs of life. Next, she checked his pockets for a wallet or any type of identification, but they were all empty. Maya searched near his body for signs of a backpack or any kind of clue as to who he might be or what happened to him, but she could find nothing. The fog continuously rolling around the stones didn't help visibility much.

She got up, extended her search, and walked within the circle of stones to see if she could find anything. Her hand reached out to touch one of the stones. "Ouch! What the..." Maya couldn't believe what she saw. The stone glowed, and she'd definitely got an electric shock, just like before. Only this time, no dirt marred the stone. The glow helped high-light a discernable pattern etched into the rock. "My God! What...what is that? A dragon? So I did see a dragon before. But...but this is impossible. First it's there, then it's not."

A moan from behind her caused her to turn around in time to see the young man trying to sit up. She ran over to him. "Hey, it's okay. Stay still. Don't try to move. Help is on the way."

He ignored her. He sat up and drew his legs to his chest. "Oh, my head." His head fell forward until it almost touched his knees, and he brought his hands up to cradle his temples.

His motions drew Maya's attention to his hair. It was so long that when he leaned forward, it cascaded past his shoulders until it completely covered his elbows.

"What…what happened?" he stammered.

Momentarily lost for words, Maya kneeled down beside the young man. "I don't know." She almost lifted her hand to touch the waterfall of hair. "I found you unconscious here in the middle of the stones."

"S-stones?" He lowered his arms and raised his head to look around him.

The fog had rolled off a little more and Maya sucked in a breath. Oh wow, handsome, and breathtakingly so. He must drive the young girls crazy. The face of an angel stared back at her, a sixteen or seventeen-year-old golden angel with long blond hair. And those eyes. They were eerily familiar. A lot like the eyes from her dream, like emeralds, and they even glowed.

Wait. A. Minute.

They glowed! Light shone from them, like the stone. Maya's head whipped around to look at the stone she had touched, and sure enough, it continued to glow. The emerald eyes of the dragon shone, just like the eyes of the young man. Like the eyes of the dragon in her dream.

"Wh-what the hell is going on?" Maya looked back and forth between the teenager and the stone. She stood up abruptly and moved away from both the young man and the shining stone.

The young man looked at her, then at the stone. "I-I don't know. I don't know. Is it supposed to do that?"

"Hell no! Stones don't just start glowing." At least she didn't think these kinds of stones did. "Who are you? What happened here?"

"I told you. I don't know." The young man's frame trembled. "I-I don't remember." He looked at her, seemingly pleading with his eyes for her to help him, to help him understand.

She took a deep breath. Some instinct told her he would not harm her, and he appeared to be genuinely confused. "Okay, okay calm down," she said to him, but she spoke to herself too. "What's your name?"

"I-I don't know. Why don't I know? I don't remember anything." He dropped his head down and placed his hands over his face. "What's wrong with me?" His head snapped up as he looked at her. "Do you know what happened to me? Do you know who I am?"

Maya could read the turmoil in his weird gaze and felt sorry for him. She slowly returned to kneel beside him, still a little wary of those glowing eyes of his. Maybe they were some kind of bizarre colored contacts.

"No. I'm sorry. I found you lying here. My name's Maya Trent. I'm just a tourist. Maybe you were in some sort of accident and you have temporary memory loss or something." She shrugged.

It seemed to be the most likely scenario. In such a small community, surely someone would know the young man— she hoped—even as a visitor to the area. Which he could be. He had an American accent for sure.

"Help should be here soon. Why don't you just try to relax?" The young man reached out and grabbed her arm. When Maya tried to pull away, he immediately released her. He barely held her, but his touch startled her. His warm hand a contrast against the chilly night air.

"I'm sorry. I meant no harm."

Maya raised her hand and waved his apology away. "It's okay."

"Please, I'm just trying to understand. I don't know why I can't remember anything. I don't know who I am. I don't even know where I am." He looked around at the stones and his gaze paused, focusing on the glowing dragon. "What's that? It looks like some sort of dragon. Dragon. That seems familiar to me. Aargh!" The young man slumped forward again and grabbed his head. "The pain…"

Maya reached out and wrapped her arms around him. "Shhh, it'll be all right. It'll be all right. We'll find out who you are." At least she prayed they would. This went way beyond strange.

"Will you stay with me please, Maya? Will you stay with me until I remember?"

She looked into those eyes, eyes so like the dragon in her dream, and nodded. She would stay with the young man until he returned to where he belonged. For some reason, her instincts warned that he didn't belong here.

The stone continued to glow as she held the boy, but a whirling noise in the distance broke the silence on the mountain. Only now did she realize how quiet the mountain had become while she sat in the circle of stones and darkness descended upon them. Not even the sound of the wind passed through the trees. She tried to see between the stones and beyond the trees, but the fog remained thick there.

"I think help has arrived," she told him. "I think I hear a chopper, but they may not be able to land near us. The fog's still thick around the stones. They'll probably have to find a clearing in order to set down. Then they'll walk up and hopefully be here soon. I'm going to walk beyond the standing stones and see if I can reach them on my cell. I'll be right back."

"Al…all right." He glanced away and then back at her.

"I won't go far. You'll still be able to see me." Maya got up and walked toward the stones, but stopped. The stone no longer shone. She rubbed her eyes and continued moving forward. The nearer she got, the more the etching of the dragon faded away, until it disappeared entirely. "What the…!" she exclaimed.

"What? What's wrong?" the boy asked. "Is something wrong?"

"Th…the stone. The stone is no longer glowing." She stepped back so he could see for himself. As she looked over at him, she made another discovery. His eyes weren't shining anymore, either. "Your eyes…they…they aren't glowing either."

"What?"

"Your eyes. Your eyes were giving off a light like the stone. Who are you?" she finished in a whisper. *What are you?* She silently questioned.

"I don't understand. I…"

Maya shook her head. "It's okay. We'll get to the bottom of this. There must be some sort of explanation." Or she was losing her mind.

"Why would light shine from my eyes? Why don't I remember anything? Aaaargh!" The boy shook his head, sending hair flying in every direction. "This makes no sense. Why can't I remember? I should be able to remember. What's happening to me?" He tried to rise and got as far as all fours.

Maya rushed over to help him.

"Hey, hey, hey, take it easy," she said, helping him to straighten. "Do you think you should stand up?" She placed an arm around his waist and he looped his across her shoulder.

He turned to look at her and had to look down. She was no slouch at five eight, but this boy, this young man, stood over six feet and was probably still growing. "I think I can stand. It's only when I try to remember anything my head hurts."

"Well, just take it easy. I still think you should sit back down."

"No, please. I want to see that stone. Can you help me over there?"

"I…"

"Please. I feel like I need to see the stone."

"Okay, but if you feel dizzy, we stop."

"Agreed."

Maya helped him walk over to the stone, aware he tried not to put any weight on her. She simply guided him. Once they faced the previously lighted stone, they stopped. It looked dark now, just an ordinary looking piece of rock.

The boy raised the arm at his side and laid his palm against the stone. When his hand touched it, both he and all of the stones glowed. They found themselves surrounded by light in a rainbow of colors. Maya could have sworn she heard a low hum coming from all directions just as the boy's body trembled beside her. He threw his head back and roared. Not a scream but a guttural primal cry. The vibration of which burrowed into her soul. The sound of a wounded animal.

Scared, Maya dropped her arm from around his waist and stepped away from the boy, forcing him to release his hold on her. Without her support, he fell to the ground, unconscious again, and the light coming from the stones winked out, as if it had never existed.

Looking down on the boy who lay at her feet, Maya gasped. She *was* indeed losing her mind.

CHAPTER THREE

*T*he good news, despite running into some bad weather, flight forty-seven arrived right on schedule. Best of all, the passenger in seat 14A slept through most of it. He didn't see anything else blocking out the sun. The bad news, he dreamt. He dreamed of a circle of emerald stones, dragons with hides of gold, and a dragon so dark no light reflected off it.

The voice of the pilot came on, announcing they were in their final descent over Dulles International Airport in Virginia. The passenger woke up abruptly, dazed at first, then glad when he realized they'd reached their destination. Well, the first part of it. His wife pulled her seat upright, and he did the same, then put on his jacket. Already he lost the gist of his dreams until they were all but forgotten. He didn't remember anything odd happening during the long flight. He just looked forward to spending time with his daughter.

He'd divorced her mother two years ago and then moved to London. A long time in the life of a child. He hadn't seen his daughter since, but he'd kept in touch with her. Recently remarried, he very much wanted to be a part of his kid's life. She would be ten tomorrow, and he wanted to surprise her.

WHEN THE EMERGENCY and rescue people finally found them, Maya didn't know how long she'd sat on the cold, unforgiving ground with the young man's head in her lap. At least long enough for her butt to go numb. She'd dragged herself and the boy to the outer perimeter of the stones so her phone would work and for the rescue team to be able to locate them. Oddly, beyond the stones, the noises of the mountain came alive, startling her for a moment. This entire day and evening went under the heading of bizarre. She should have run back down the mountain at the first sign of weirdness, but she didn't. The young man, regardless of all the strange things going on, needed help. Needed her. She could not abandon him.

"Here lass," the first man said to reach her, dressed in a padded red jumpsuit with a yellow vest and a patch proclaiming him part of the Irish Mountain Rescue. "What happened?" he asked. "Are you all right?"

"Yes. I'm fine. But he's hurt," she said, indicating the still unconscious boy.

Another paramedic stood right behind the first. The other man checked the young man's pulse, then shone a light into his eyes. Thankfully, the only glow this time came from the penlight in the medic's hand.

The second man had a radio attached to the helmet he wore, and she heard him tell the person on the other end to call off the other teams; they had found the lost hikers. "Let's get him on the stretcher," the first man said. "Can you tell us what happened, Miss? Is this your hiking companion?"

Maya watched as they efficiently and safely strapped the boy onto a stretcher. The second medic helped to lift him to begin the walk back to the helicopter. Both men were past middle age, but even in the padded suits, they appeared built like linebackers. They had no trouble lifting the boy.

"Ah…no. I don't know who he is. I-I found him unconscious in the middle of the stones. He came to a little while ago and spoke a bit. He didn't remember what happened or who he was." She'd decided not to mention anything about his glowing eyes or the glowing stones. Other than sounding demented, something else compelled her to hold her tongue.

"Stones? What stones?" The first medic asked, pausing in stride to turn his head to look around, then continuing forward.

She shifted her body to gesture the way they'd come. "They're right…" But the area now lay in heavy fog, revealing no sign of the stones. "There are about ten of them, right over there." Puzzled, she looked back and forth between the two men who had kept walking and she hurried to catch up to them. "Come on, you had to have seen them when you found us." She raised her hand up to her waist. "The stones are about this high!"

"No." The first man glanced at his partner, a look of confusion on his face. "You see anything?"

His partner wore a similar confused express on his face. Maya could clearly see him because of the LED light flaring from the helmet he wore. He shook his head in the negative. "We barely spotted the two of you," he said. "Maybe the fog blocked our view. Anyway, the important thing is we found you thanks to the GPS signal from your phone."

Maya couldn't understand why they hadn't seen the stones. Granted, the thick fog might obscure their vision, but they should have at least seen the stone they found them near. It had only been a hand span away. Another unexplainable thing she decided not to pursue for now. She looked down at the teenager on the stretcher.

"Will he be all right?" she asked, worried.

"I didn't see any evidence that he took a blow to the head," the first medic said. "But don't worry. We'll get the lad to hospital in no time and the doctors there will have a look at him."

"May I come with him to the hospital?"

"Of course you can."

TALON GLIDED out of the cloud to land in a circle of stones that looked very much like the stones of his home world. He had never been here before, but he knew he'd made it through the portal. Terra called Earth now. The land of the Forgotten Ones.

His golden dragon form shimmered even as he landed on the ground. If human eyes had been present to observe the change, they would have thought they stared at an image coated in fluorescent silk. A male in human form emerged from the center of the shimmer. But in truth, the only human essence existed in the center of the stones in the body of a young man who appeared to be about seventeen earth summers.

Too late, Talon realized, time moved differently for dragons on Akgon. Then again, maybe not. At home, even at four hundred years, brethren considered him barely past hatchling, still young. As a human, he would appear a mere teenager. Those thoughts were of no consequence. He heard whispers. Ones he couldn't ignore.

The Earth and the Stones of Power called to him. They recognized him and welcomed him as the son of one of their own, long gone from this world. Lulling him with their song of the ages. They had a lot to tell him.

The first thing the Stones made him aware of—his nakedness. He enjoyed the feel of air brushing against his skin, but his body temperate warmed the chilled air around him so it felt more like a warm breeze. In this land, his entire body needed covering in some form of cloth, and not the loin covering he usually wore. Mother Earth guided him in what he needed to do.

Magick, to his surprise, ran very strong on Earth, especially at the heart of the Stones. It ignited his blood and his veins flowed with power. He looked down. He found himself clad in what the knowledge in his mind told him were blue jeans, a dark green long sleeve t-shirt and covering for his feet, hiking boots. Suitable clothing for the place and time.

The song changed, coaxing him to sleep, to rest. There was too much to learn, and it would take some time. He was young. His eyes drifted close and his muscles relaxed. Talon lay down on his back in the center of the Stones. He would be perfectly safe. No harm could come to him in the circle of power. So much he needed to know. So much still to do. The knowledge the Stones and Mother Earth had to impart to him numbed his mind. He slept...deeply.

Then knew no more.

MAYA DIDN'T KNOW what to tell the night nurse. It had shocked her when she checked the time, a little after nine. It had taken the rescue squad a lot longer to find them than it should have. During the short ride in the helicopter to the hospital, both medics and the pilot kept insisting they didn't see the stones. They had never heard of anything like she described in the area. They had spoken to the guide, James, to locate her, but he never mentioned anything about a circle of standing stones. He'd given them a rough description of where he had taken her hiking and the GPS signal in her phone did the rest.

The medics had already left. Maya returned her attention to the admittance nurse. "As I've said before, I don't know who he is. I found him in the center of these standing stones, somewhere on Sperrin Mountain. I'll take responsibility for him until we can find out who he is."

The nurse raised her penciled eyebrows and replied, "Peter, one of the guys you came in with, said they found you off the hiking trail. He never said anything about any standing stones. I've lived in these parts all my life and I've never heard of such stones."

Maya sighed. They'd been going round and round about this.

"Look, the doctor will be out in a minute," the nurse continued. "I'll just write him up as an unidentified male. When he wakes, we'll get the rest of the information. Go ahead and have a seat over there." She pointed to a row of seats against a wall. "I'll send the doctor round to you as soon as he's done."

"Thank you." Maya removed her backpack and sat down. She found herself alone and tired in the waiting area. Taking out a package of trail mix, she polished it off along with the bottle of water one of the rescue workers had given her. The entire evening held a surreal feeling, and she still didn't understand what had happened, other than being inexplicably drawn to the boy. He wasn't her responsibility, yet she had found him and promised him she wouldn't leave. She had a lot of questions she needed answers to; answers she hoped he could provide.

She pulled her cell phone out of her pocket and made a call to change her flight reservations and to keep her room at the Inn. It cost her a small fortune. At this point, she'd stay in Ireland for the remainder of her trip. With luck, which seemed overdue, she wouldn't have to make any further changes. Surely the boy would awaken, regain his memory, and be able to put her mind to rest about what happened on the mountain. What she had seen seemed real. A dragon etched into a glowing stone, just like the boy's eyes. How did you explain that?

Maya let her head fall back until it touched the wall, and then she closed her eyes. She wasn't sure how long she slept, but the odd angle of her head caused her neck to ache, jerking her awake. Rubbing her neck, she glanced at the nurses' station in time to see the night nurse speaking to a balding man, then point in her direction. She got up and walked toward him.

"Ms. Trent?" he asked as he held his hand out to shake hers. His white starched doctor's coat brightened up the dreary colored hallway. "I'm Doctor Donovan. I understand you came in with the unconscious young man."

"Yes, Doctor. Can you tell me how he's doing?"

"Unfortunately, he's still unconscious. We've run a few tests and I'm still waiting on the results of some imaging and blood work. There's no evidence of any external trauma to the head to indicate why he's unconscious, so we'll see if there's anything going on internally. If there's no change by morning, we'll run further tests."

"He came to at least twice when he was with me, but he didn't remember what happened to him or who he is. So maybe he'll wake up again."

"Maybe." He paused to check his chart. "I see he's listed as an unidentified male, so I'm assuming you're not a relative?"

"No, I'm sorry. I was out hiking and found him in the middle of a circle of stones, which I know no one around here seems to have ever heard of. Both times I questioned him, he seemed confused and kept saying his head hurt."

"You sound like you might be an American?" Doctor

Donovan said. After Maya nodded, he continued. "When he spoke, did he sound like he might be a local?"

She paused thoughtfully. "Actually, he sounded like an American too, although he could be Canadian."

"Well, if he hasn't awakened by morning, I'll call the constable and see if there's been any missing persons report on anyone fitting his description. They might want to talk to you and hopefully see to it his description is sent to all the agencies handling missing persons."

"Great," Maya replied, relieved. This boy obviously belonged somewhere. "Someone should be looking for him or if he's got a passport, his information would be in some database. Most likely, you can find out who he is."

"I hope so too," the doctor agreed.

"May I see him now? I'd like to stay with him for a little while."

"Well, it's a mite irregular, but under the circumstances, I'll allow you a few minutes with him."

"Thank you, Doctor."

"If there's any change, we have your hotel information and number here in the paperwork and will give you a call."

Doctor Donovan escorted her to the teenager's room and left her. The boy appeared to be sleeping peacefully. Someone had pulled his hair back and tied it with a rubber band. It lay as a long, thick ponytail draped down the right side of his chest. Attached to his forehead were little white disks, what looked like electrodes, and an IV stuck in the back of his hand. A flicker of light drew Maya's gaze up above the bed to intricate-looking machines appearing to monitor his heart and brain activities. Maya prayed the green lights and funny looking graph meant everything was fine.

The doctor said she could only stay for a few minutes, but he had left and she didn't think he'd be back, so hopefully no one would bother her for a while. Since her nana died in a hospital, she hated the place, but she didn't want to leave the young man alone. She pulled the single chair in the room closer to the bed, put her backpack on the floor and sat down, staring at the boy for a long time. Aside from the slight rise and fall of his chest, he didn't move.

"Who are you?" she whispered, though she didn't really expect an answer. She raised her arms above her head to stretch her shoulders. Bringing her hands down, she folded them on the bed and laid her head on her hand. Her eyes closed without thought and immediately she fell into an exhausted sleep.

TALON CAME TO. Awake and aware. He remembered it all. His mother...dead.

The sudden loss of the emotional, psychic link to his mother was the final pain, driving him to total unconsciousness. All brethren are linked in some fashion. The love he shared with his parents provided an almost physical link for him to both of them, and they were likewise linked to him. Now one connection simply snuffed out, like a light turned off, leaving only darkness. Such a thing could only happen with her death. The knowledge of which, on top of what the Stones taught him, had been too much for his brain and emotions to process.

For a while, he hadn't been able to remember his own name. Simply too much knowledge stored into his consciousness at an alarming rate. Part of his mind went blank while he tried to process it all. It might still take years before he could fully access the information the Stones imparted. Some of it he might never be able to use because they were of magicks only a Dark Lord could wield.

Talon turned his head slightly and looked at the woman whose head rested near his hand.

Maya.

Beautiful.

His newfound knowledge told him she had skin the color of leaves on earth when they turned an autumn brown. And her hair, a riot of long curls, rested across her shoulders and captured the many russet and golden colors of fall. While her eyes, if he remembered correctly, were the color of bronze with a touch of gold around the iris. He gently touched the hand lying near his—marveling for a moment at how much paler his appeared next to hers. He did not really have to touch her to know. His need had called her to him. Valour was right. Blood called to blood. She was brethren. One of the Forgotten Ones.

If she could change form, she would be a gold or bronze dragon, or maybe even a very unique combination of both. Dragons came in a variety of colors, and the color of a dragon determined the strength of its magicks. If she could harness the powers of both, it would make her one of the strongest female dragons for as long as there had been dragons. The Earth magicks had indeed changed the blood as the Stones warned him. Even more interesting, Maya was a Dam, a Dragon Queen. But not his, and meant for a Dark Dragon Lord. His father's truemate had found him.

Talon's own mate lived on Terra or earth, but her life essence seemed weak. No, not weak exactly, just not matured yet. Perhaps still very young, a mere hatchling. By human standards, he was young, too. He would have to wait for her essence to grow stronger and bide his time to find her. The Stones would not help him with this. They deemed it his destiny to find her or not. But he would. At the right time she would call to him, and he would be there to answer.

Meanwhile, he needed to try to understand this lost world his truemate belonged to before he could ask her to be a part of his own. The Stones and Mother Earth had explained much to him, but he still needed to experience things firsthand for himself. They also warned him his father would be here soon. Even as he slept, he felt the blood bond linking them grow stronger the moment his father crossed into earth's realm.

Talon would need Maya's help. His father would try to send him back. He would not go. Could not. His dragon sensed loose magick in the world with the scent of a dragon on it, where there should be no such creature. But all wrong in some way he didn't understand. Instinct warned the wrongness was both powerful and dangerous.

The earth magick, far from weak as he'd been told, held immense power for those who could tap into it. His father would know what to do, but he would want Talon on Akgon until the danger passed, and the girl-child of an age to be taken. Talon needed to be here in case of any threat to her. At least if he were here, he would know and be able to do something. On Akgon, he could do nothing to protect her. However, he must not be here when his father arrived. His sire and Dark Lord must not find him. If he could not find him, he could not send him home.

A SLIGHT PRESSURE on her hand caused Maya to open her eyes, only to find herself staring into emerald fire. She blinked. Was she even awake? The last few days seemed like a dream. It all started with dreams of a dragon, then finding the young man in the center of stones. Stones no one seemed to know anything about. Glowing stones and a black dragon with green eyes.

Ha, ha, ha. Don't be afraid.

"Who's there?"

Maya raised her head and looked at the closed door behind her, but no one stood there. She turned to look at the young man on the bed. His open, glowing green eyes stared right back at her.

Don't be afraid, Maya. I won't hurt you. I could never harm you. Thank you for helping me. I remember now.

Maya blinked. She could hear him just fine. Only one problem, his mouth didn't move. Hers did. "What the hell!"

She jumped up, overturning her chair as she backed away from him.

CHAPTER FOUR

*N*o insect, animal or bird sounds were ever heard in the center of the stones because all knew better than to venture into the circle of power. Even the wind only danced around its edge. Just before dawn, something changed. For miles around the stones, not a creature stirred. They sensed something coming and were careful to give the area an even wider berth than usual. Only heavy fog moved across the mountains as a dragon lord from a time long gone glided slowly through the gateway and landed squarely in the center of the Stones.

Black talons dug into the rich soil and the humming sound emanating from the Stones changed to a fevered pitch, far beyond human hearing.

At long last! The Stones sang. *A son of earth has returned!* Rejoiced Mother Earth. *Welcome back!*

The great black dragon reared his mighty head, releasing a sound earth had not heard for over a thousand years.

The roar of a Dragon Lord.

A Dark Dragon Lord, one born to power, stood on Terra once more. The Stones glowed like never before, bathing their Lord in their elemental, earthly light. Power flowed through his veins, the likes of which he had never felt before. The air hissed and crackled with it. A master of earthly elements: fire, wind, rain, thunder and lightning, he harnessed them all.

The sun had not yet risen when, for the second time in as many days, a fast moving heavy fog developed over clear skies and coated the land. Over Sperrin Mountain, sporadic flashes of lightning were seen through the fog, causing more than one hand to raise and make the sign of the cross. When the sound of a roar echoed across the county, people would swear it wasn't like any thunder they'd ever heard before. The ones who didn't cross themselves the first time did so then. Rain and hail the size of small pebbles fell as the sky overhead turned blacker. Against the darkened sky, over one spot on Sperrin Mountain, residents in the area could see a light show composed of a myriad of colors. No one thought to investigate the area where the lights seemed to concentrate, and those who tried to take a picture of it found their digital screens blank.

Draakar released his dragon form, knowing he could call it back at will and maintain it for a while. His dark image shimmered; any human watching would have thought they stared into a black fluid void because it kept changing shape. But no human eyes bore witness to this. Finally, from the center of the void, the image of a pale, naked six-foot-four man solidified and emerged.

Bare feet planted firmly on the earth, shoulder width apart, mimicking a battle stance of old. He raised muscular arms away from his sides, turned his palms upward, and tilted his head back as if paying homage to the sky.

Emerald fire burst forth from his eyes toward the heavens. In response, two bolts of lightning struck each upturned palm. While gusting winds blew his pitch-black hair wildly back and forth across the tops of his well defined gluts. Torrid rain fell and pummeled him with their steady rhythm, driving the memories of a past he did not share with earth into his being.

The wild storm lasted for over an hour while, simultaneously, a dozen people awoke at dawn because of strange dreams. From these strange dreams developed their new reality.

Several inexplicable things happened. First, an account opened in a Swiss bank, which suddenly found its coffers increased by several billion dollars. The young bank president himself took care of this special account. He also opened several other accounts in various countries. All of the accounts were under the name Draakar Akgon, owner and President of Akgon Enterprises, a privately held company.

Among other events, the helicopter pilot who had flown Maya and Talon to the hospital found himself gainfully employed by Akgon Enterprises. He got up at dawn to make several phone calls on behalf of his new employer before leaving his house.

While all of these things were happening, fifty feet around the perimeter of the Stones, the earth began to rumble. The wind and rain stopped as quickly as they started, leaving the Dragon Lord and the surrounding earth bone dry. Not a trace of water appeared on either. The rumble increased in volume. Trees got sucked downward, as though giant vacuums were under them, and dirt flew up everywhere when fissures appeared in the ground. The entire circle of stones sunk into the holes, Draakar with them. A different stone structure of gigantic proportions rose, enclosing both man and stones.

Once the dust cleared, a castle made of stone appeared in the area as part of the mountainside. If asked, people in Sperrin County would say Akgon Castle had stood there for a thousand years. They would tell you about a very old, very private family: the Akgons, whose roots could be traced back to the first Norse invaders.

Draakar lowered his head and hands to his sides. Blood had called to blood, and many had answered. It pleased him to find so many human brethren on Terra still. The dragon's blood had weakened in most, but stayed strong in some, and he would make use of the strongest. More than a handful of those were the ones he used to set events in motion for his presence. He would need their help in the days to come.

Mother Earth and the Stones guided his powers and told him much, but he still had a lot to learn for himself. It had been a long, long time since he walked upon Terra, or rather earth. Much had changed. Dragons were relegated to the role of creatures from fairytales, and magic deemed a thing of science and technology. He would laugh at the absurdity of it all, but in truth, if he did, he'd end up crying for all they had lost.

He didn't understand it, the existence of so much power here and unlike what he had known before. Mother Earth had told him the power lay unused and had simply accumulated through the ages. Something that should not have happened. In the wrong hands, such power could be dangerous. And danger existed on earth, though long gone. He had been right to hesitate in sending Talon here alone.

The power from the borrowed magicks of the Stones he now held would not last. He didn't know how long he could hold on to it, but he hoped it would be long enough to find his son. Only with a truemate could he hope to access and keep this much magicks. Well, he would find his son first, get him to safety, and then he would search for his mate.

He looked down at his nakedness. No sooner had the thought entered his head, with his new knowledge, he covered his body with dark colored clothing befitting a Dark

Lord. In a blink, all black material covered him. From the silk shirt molding itself to his large frame, the slacks hugging thighs built for strength, to the calfskin ankle boots enclosing his size fourteen feet.

Draakar glanced around the dimly lit, unfurnished area surrounding him. It resembled a huge cavern holding muted light. The light source was not immediately obvious, but it emanated from the Stones now a part of the walls.

Each stone made up a portion of the walls, which rose some twenty feet high. Most of the stones depicted scenes of dragons in all of their varied, vibrant colors and glowed with life. One part of the wall, however, appeared pitch black. Unlike the rest of the room, no light reflected off it. Instead, it looked as if it absorbed light.

Draakar walked through this wall. He found what he expected on the other side, a long wide hallway made of rock, and rose steadily at an incline. In pitch darkness, Draakar had no trouble finding his way. He could see perfectly with his dragon's sight. After some time, the hallway came to an abrupt end in front of another wall. Without pause, he walked straight through it.

Beyond it, awaiting him, were the rooms of his castle. He entered his personal library first. The bright light in the room provided by modern electricity didn't even cause him to blink. The entire castle was wired. Modern magic. Nor did he pause to savor the museum quality works of art filling just about every room. Some of the objects d' art were so rare museums would kill for just a glimpse. These things had been hidden from mankind, but all were his by right. Mother Earth had collected and protected them until a child of power could return and claim them. He had. Draakar didn't stop to examine his claim; he had too much to do. He opened the library doors and followed the hallway to the front of the castle.

By tomorrow night, Draakar would have his home on earth full of human brethren. Already one traveled the newly created private road now leading to his castle standing above the Stones.

None would be able to find this road who did not carry brethren blood or who Draakar did not want on it. Potent wards surrounded the place of power. Draakar opened the heavy double oak doors, the entrance to his castle, and stepped into a misty morning. The heavy fog of yesterday and earlier had gone. A light mist now lay over the mountains, giving them an ethereal look. Draakar did not feel the chill in the air, but this weather required outerwear of some kind. Immediately, a supple black leather coat draped his body from shoulders to ankles.

Before Draakar's foot reached the last step, a man stepped out of the black Rolls Royce 101EX, which awaited him in the driveway. Ian McNeil stood beside the passenger door. He would be Draakar's First among the first awakened brethren, his right hand in this realm. Also his driver until others came.

The blood ran strongly in Ian. He had immediately answered Draakar's call. If the man were on Akgon, he would be able to release his dragon form—a red, judging by the color of his hair—but the earth magicks here suppressed the change and were stronger than Ian's ability to control them. Too strong, in fact, for most brethren to wield, except the Dragon Lord.

"Welcome home, Lord," Ian said. "At last we meet."

Ian opened the car door and tried to move out of the way, but Draakar would not let him step aside. He clasped him by the upper arm and Ian returned the salute. An old greeting amongst warrior equals. Ian understood and smiled.

"No, not Lord," Draakar said before he released him. "Not here. Just call me Draakar."

Ian's smile widened. "That's kind of a mouthful. How about Draak?"

"Draak...mmm..." He smiled. He hadn't smiled for a long time. He relaxed a little. "I think I like it. Thank you for coming. I'm ready." His smile changed to a frown. "Now let us go collect my son."

Draakar climbed into the car, not once allowing the disturbing knowledge the Stones had revealed to him to show in his expression, but he worried. A hint of dragon's blood salted the air where there should not have been. And not his son's. Just as there should not have been this much power still on Terra, the scent should not be here. Dragons had been gone, dead or turned human for over a thousand years on Terra. Fully awakened dragons should be impossible. The Stones had provided no answers. Some things even they did not know or refused to share. Some things they left to Fate. But no mistake here. The Dark Lord's senses picked up the stench of twisted and corrupted magicks.

A silver dragon.

While a dark dragon provided balance, a silver dragon thrived on chaos and destruction. Draakar shuddered to think of a silver dragon alive and harnessing this much earth magicks.

"Lor...I mean, Draak. Are you okay?"

He realized Ian spoke to him and met the concerned look of his First in the rearview mirror. Apparently, Ian had noticed his tension after all. "I'm fine, Ian."

Ian glanced at him for a moment more before returning his attention to the road. "Everything has been arranged," Ian continued. "By the time we get back to the castle, the other four people who were within easy distance should be there; the others should arrive in a day or two."

"Good. For now, I will keep the numbers small and start training some of the strongest first." Draakar did a mental count of the human brethren he'd called to him. "That should be a total of six, not including you." If destructive loose magicks were being used by a silver dragon, he would need them all to counter what could result. He had no doubt a dragon roamed earth. It could only be the betrayer whose name the brethren did not speak. Only his crime, the ultimate insult.

It seemed he had not died after all. His mother had not killed him, as they had all believed. The betrayer presented a danger to both brethren and human alike. As Dark Lord, he had a duty to protect and carry out judgment against the betrayer, and as his father's and mother's son, a legacy to see the betrayer dead.

As the Rolls passed smoothly down the mountain, his thoughts turned to his son. The sooner Talon returned to Akgon, the better. It would be years before his mate reached an age to join him there. Draakar understood the time conundrum and realized their mistake. By earth standards, Talon was a mere boy and his mate even younger.

Mates.

Something else Draakar didn't want to think about yet. He did love Sierran, though not his truemate, and mourned her passing. Talon remained all he had now.

No. Not quite true. Another existed. The Stones told him his mate was here, but why hadn't she felt his presence or called to him? The moment he returned to Terra, she should have been drawn to him. As a fully matured female, her dragon's blood would run strong.

So why couldn't he fully sense her? He had only brief,

vague hints of her. Maybe he didn't really want to find her, at least not yet. Sierran's passing still rested fresh in his memories.

Ian's voice snapped Draakar out of his thoughts.

"We're almost there, Draak."

TALON SAT up in bed and pulled the electrodes off his forehead, but the machines continued to function as though he were still attached. Next, he pulled the IV out of his arm, all the while never taking his eyes off Maya.

"I'm sorry. That was clumsy of me. Verbalizing is not something I do very often, but I better get used to it. Please, don't be afraid. You know I won't hurt you."

Maya still hadn't moved any closer. She stayed with her back pressed against the wall and her hand on the doorknob. "How...how did you do that? Who are you?"

"My name is Talon Akgon. Again, I'm sorry. We don't have much time. My father is already here and will find me soon if you don't help me."

"Help you? What's going on here? I repeat, and I'm tired of repeating myself. Who and what are you?"

"I told you who I am and I-I think you already know what I am. What you are."

Maya felt less scared and more than a little angry at his response. "What am I?" she said, pointing to her chest. "What kind of crap is this?"

"Maya, please. I'm begging you. I need your help. I cannot be here when my father gets here or else he'll send me home."

She frowned. "Are...are you afraid of your father? Are you in some kind of trouble?"

"No, I'm not afraid of my father, and no, I'm not in any kind of trouble. He sent me here, but he didn't realize about the time difference or that she would be even younger than I."

"Whoa, hold on. You're not making any sense. What time difference and who are you talking about?"

"I…."

Maya held up her hand. "Wait, let's start over. Your name's Talon Akgon. Are you from around here?"

"Yes, and no."

"What kind of answer is that?"

"The only one I have time to give right now. Listen, my father is on his way. I want you to take my hand." Her eyes opened wide, and she felt her eyebrows stretch toward her forehead. Talon smiled and watched her intently. "Just hold my hand, and ask yourself if you trust me," he continued, while lifting his hand off the bed.

"Trust you! I don't even know you."

"Please, Maya. You're my only hope."

Some primal instinct, or stupidity, caused Maya to pick up the overturned chair and walk over to stand beside the bed. Gingerly, she took Talon's outstretched hand. She did trust him.

"I'm going to link to you. Between the two of us, we will be able to block my father from finding me."

"What'd you mean link?" Maya asked. Too late, Talon had already grasped her hand, and a golden glow immediately surrounded where their skin touched. She felt no pain, was only a little startled by the heat radiating from his skin. When she tried to jerk her hand away, he released her.

"It's all right, Maya. It's done."

"Done!" Maya shook her head. "What's done? I didn't know when it began."

"A connection between us. It's kind of difficult for me to

51

explain, but with this connection to you, I'm able to tap into some of your earthbound essence to mask my own. You now have a link to me and will always be able to have a sense of my well-being and me of you. You'll be able to let my father know I'm fine."

"What have you done?"

"I'm sorry. The link itself is painless, but..." His forehead crinkled, he looked like he didn't want to tell her the rest of it but continued talking. "If I'm harmed, you'll know. This was the only thing I could think of to block my father from finding me. We are now linked. When my father searches for me, he will only sense you."

Maya could only stare at him wild-eyed. She should have been running for her life, but her legs wouldn't move. Maybe because of a major breakdown in the command centers between her brain and her feet.

Talon had no such immobility and got off the bed. One minute he had on a hospital gown and the next he wore the same clothes Maya had found him in up on the mountain. She gasped and her brain unlocked from its frozen state, prompting her feet to take a step back.

"How...how'd you do that?" she cried. "What are you?"

Talon shook his head at her and looked a little sad. "You know what I am. Your blood knows. I have to go now, but we will meet again. Thank you for all that you have done for me, and know my mother did not mean you any harm. She did what she did for the brethren, our race; they both did. I know that now."

Maya could only gape at him, too stunned to say anything. Every word out of his mouth sounded like gibberish. Yet some part of her, a small part, paid attention to his words. He stepped closer to her and gently kissed her cheek. "Do not be afraid, Maya. Welcome to the family. Forgive him...he's here."

With those both joyous and ominous words left hanging in the air, he shimmered and disappeared, leaving Maya with her mouth wide open. *Yep, I am losing it!* She sat on the bed because her knees would no longer support her body.

THE AUTOMATIC DOORS at the hospital entrance slid smoothly open. The man who stepped through them glanced neither left nor right. All eyes swung in his direction and remained fixated on him. He didn't walk, but glided smoothly across the tiled floor with sensuous grace. The compelling aura surrounding the man made him the center of attention. The air around him seemed to vibrate with electrical currents. His presence screamed wealth, power, danger and for anyone with duel X-chromosomes, raw, primal, unadulterated sex. Even for some without.

He never stopped at the information desk, already knowing his destination. He didn't even break stride when the elevator doors opened before him and he stepped on. Without pressing a button, the elevator started and stopped on the necessary floor.

Draakar stepped off the elevator, and for the first time, halted his stride. Actually, too stunned to move. All of his senses registered the presence he'd yearned for, for well over a thousand years. Something he had all but given up hope of ever being able to have. Then another's thoughts slammed into his head. With such force, his eyes blinked twice from the impact.

At last—it's about damn time!

My Queen!

Don't my Queen me! Queens die! I am so pissed at you I could rip out your heart and fry it! Literally!

"WHAT THE HELL!" Maya shouted aloud. She sat on the bed with her head in her hands. "Oh, my God! I am losing my mind! Who or what the hell was that? Get the hell outta my head."

Maya sensed the presence closer to her now, the same presence in her head. She felt rather than heard the door open. Her world narrowing down to small increments of motion, she lowered her arms to her sides and raised her head.

The creature she beheld standing framed in the doorway commanded a mixture of awe, anger, and fascination. No doubt in her mind, a human did not stand before her. Like father, like son. Besides, no mere man could have such an impact on all five senses and then some. She felt saturated in the pheromones rolling off him in waves.

About six-four and wearing a long leather coat covering what she knew would be solidly packed muscle, with a structure of unbelievable beauty for a face. Yet holding not a hint of femininity, stared back at her. His thick straight midnight-black hair hung over his shoulder and past his waist, but his entire demeanor screamed prime male. He assessed her as silently and deeply as she assessed and appreciated him.

Dark eyebrows like wings graced a perfect forehead, while long dark lashes framed eyes flashing emerald fire within their depths. A nose no surgeon could ever duplicate, made for looking imperially at others, followed by a slightly squared jaw in no way weak. His lips—Maya refused to even think about. No, nothing feminine about this man.

No human man entered the room, a dark angel maybe. *Or a dragon.*

The certainty popped into her head and would not leave.

While the son's beauty would make an artist long to paint, he was still a boy. Here before her stood something entirely different. On some level Maya acknowledged all of this. However, the emotion of an inexplicable rage took the strongest precedent, and buried under the rage, hurt from the pain of his betrayal.

Betrayal? It made no sense. She did not know this man, this creature. And yet, some part of her recognized him. Recognized what they could mean to each other, and part of her knew he had betrayed her.

The dragon of her dreams stood before her. A man she should fear, instead anger rose to the surface. A safer better emotion than fear or hurt, and one she could harness.

She blinked, then frowned. Now why exactly was she angry?

CHAPTER FIVE

*A*rthur Ferguson held his wife's hand in a near death grip as he walked with her up to the front door of the rowhouse in the upper northwest section of Washington, D.C. The front yards on this street were well maintained and expensive cars lined the road. Like his ex-wife, the neighborhood appeared classy and pricey. Arthur only observed this in passing, his excitement at this visit uppermost in his thoughts. He and his wife only stayed in their hotel room long enough to change clothes. Arthur couldn't wait to see the daughter he hadn't seen in two years. Living in another country kept them apart.

Distance didn't stop him from keeping in touch though. He'd kept in regular contact with her through e-mails, texting, and even social networks. He even dutifully sent her mother a check each month for her care, but she'd been eight the last time he saw her in person.

Thankfully, despite the way they parted, his ex-wife allowed him to contact their daughter during the entire time he lived abroad. At least he had the chance to maintain a relationship with his child. If his ex hadn't agreed, with him out of the country, it would have been difficult to force the issue. In actuality, their tenacious daughter had insisted upon it rather than any of her mother's doing. In the last few months, things had changed drastically. Tammi, her mother, had cancer and she didn't have much time left. She wanted him to have full custody of their daughter before she died. She did not want her gangster brother anywhere near their child. Neither did Arthur. For once in their lives they were in complete agreement.

Arthur knocked on the front door, and it quickly opened. His eyes traveled downward until they stared into silvery gray eyes, the identical color as his own.

DRAAKAR STEPPED into the hospital room toward his past and his future. Ready or not, it sat in front of him and he would face it, as he had faced everything else in his life, like the Lord of the Brethren.

The door shut silently behind him, closing without him touching it. His woman didn't flinch. The sight of her had his blood humming through his veins. No doubt existed in his mind or heart she was meant for him. She had spoken to him in his mind, or rather her dragon self recognized him and spoke to his. He wondered if she realized what happened.

Draakar noticed something else. He could no longer sense or track his son. The woman before him consumed all of his senses. His link to Talon led him straight to her.

She stared at him with large almond-shaped eyes, shining with an intelligence to match his own. He returned her stare, imprinting every nuance of her into his memory. A warm brown color coated her skin, in stark contrast to his paleness. Funny, though his dragon hide was deep black, his human skin was white. But this mate of his, while very beautiful as a human, would be magnificent as a dragon. The power flowed true and strong in her blood. He could hear it coursing through her body. The magicks lay dormant no more as they rose to consciousness beneath her skin.

His truemate.

He watched her inhale, taking air deep into her lungs as her chest expanded. He did not need to read her mind to know she wrestled in an attempt to bank the unreasonable and puzzling anger she felt toward him—a stranger.

"You...you must be Talon's father. He's not here."

Ah, Talon. What have you done?

"Stop that."

Draakar stepped farther into the room and blocked his thoughts from her. Without taking his gaze off her, he removed his jacket and tossed it onto the chair beside him.

Maya's gasp and reaction to him almost had him grinning. She guessed he could read her thoughts, but she hadn't managed to block him before he pulled her attraction to him from her mind. He reminded her of one of those Olympic ice speed skaters she'd seen on television, all broad-shouldered with a narrow waist. His clothing both covered and showcased lean sleek muscle. She wanted to touch him and imagined his body would feel like steel beneath her fingers. She had to forcibly wrench her thoughts away from his looks and back to her many questions. He could no longer suppress his smile at the things filtering through her mind and his pleasure in her.

"Talon told me to let you know he's fine, but he won't be returning home with you." The words came out in a rush, then she paused and took a deep breath before continuing. He sensed she wanted answers and facing him, a being she was unsure of, seemed the only way to get them.

Draakar patiently studied the woman before him, reading the thoughts she verbalized as well as those she didn't. He found it interesting how easily she could read his dragon mind. He had to concentrate to block his thoughts from her. Some mated brethren claimed there were no secrets between truemates. Perhaps they spoke the truth. Once they were mated, he would never be able to hold anything back from her. He would not want to.

As Dragon Lord, he wanted to claim his queen immediately, but, as human brethren, she would not understand—not yet. He needed to wait a little while, and he still grieved for his first mate. Sierran may not have been his truemate but he owed her a time of mourning. He would also require time to get past Maya's anger. All very real and justified.

"Can you tell me what's going on? Who are you—people?" She left unspoken in the air but very much on her mind the last part of her question: *Were they even human?*

The heat of her anger lay banked in her eyes, and he could hear and feel the confusion in the tone of her voice. She did not understand how she could harbor such anger toward a stranger. Although he and she weren't strangers, not really. They were just a long time in coming. The blame rested entirely with him. He had a lot to answer for, but he would try to make it up to her, he'd spend a lifetime doing it. Gentleness existed within her heart, and he would need it. She would forgive him. She must.

But her anger toward him would have to be addressed. Nor would it be easy for him to get past it and get her to accept him, to accept herself and her true nature. Her brethren blood ran very strong. He couldn't even sense her until he had gotten close because she unconsciously blocked him. She hadn't responded to his call, to him, as her Dragon Lord; or maybe she had and it explained the reason why

Talon had found her first. His call had awakened her. But then, why could he not locate his son?

"I am Draakar Akgon," he finally responded, "and yes, I am Talon's father."

He continued staring at her with unblinking eyes, waiting for her to say something.

"Ah…your eyes." She gestured with her right hand in his direction. "They glow just like Talon's."

"Yes, we share that trait. What is your name?"

"I'm sorry. I should have introduced myself. My name is Maya Trent. Did anyone tell you what happened?"

Ah, a fitting name. It meant *'power,'* the power to create phenomena. The Fates had chosen for him a rare creature indeed.

Unlike other brethren, Dams or Queens only had one mate, could only have one mate. The male must be stronger than they to be able to handle the magicks of a Dam. Only one brethren mate existed for a Dam— a Dragon Lord.

Although not uncommon among their kind, truemate bindings almost consistently held true for Dragon Lords. Even though a male could mate with any strong female, they usually waited for their truemate. He being the exception. He had not, could not. If his powers had not been released through a mating, their race faced extinction.

Dams are rare, and do not have such a choice. They cannot mate with just any male. They die and are reborn over and over until they find their truemate, and they suffer through each rebirth. He had not been on earth to sustain her, just as she had not been there to sustain him when he needed her. Her dragon had been reborn many times in this world and died many times over. She'd come into being too late for him, for the brethren.

Unlike her, he'd survived with Sierran's help. Her powers sustained him so he could give the brethren a chance to survive. Only the internal powers Sierran helped him release through their bond wasn't enough. It didn't last.

His Queen, however, had no chance when he left Earth and he knew it. She had not been born yet. She may not have been born for hundreds of years and the brethren could not wait. The imminent extinction of their kind did not afford him the luxury of waiting.

He'd condemned his unborn mate to continuous rebirths and lonely deaths when he left, sacrificing them both. No longer. He had come for her and he intended to claim her. It would just take a little longer than expected. He would have to give her time, give them both time. He hoped they had it.

He finally answered. "No, I have spoken to no one at the hospital." He didn't add he already knew what had happened to Talon. The Stones told him. Draakar began to suspect how Talon hid from him. He had to swallow his smile at his son's cleverness.

"He was found…I found him, unconscious in the middle of a circle of stones in the mountains. But he's fine now. Look can you just tell me what's going on?"

"I will answer all of your questions…in time, if you answer three for me now." He paused as she tentatively nodded. "Did Talon link with you?"

"Yes."

Draakar heard the hesitation in her voice.

"But he's fine," she hurriedly added. "He said I would be able to let you know he's doing all right and I can sense he is. He just seemed to be a little worried about someone."

Draakar sighed. "Yes, I know." This complicated matters, but Draakar had faith in his son. Talon didn't realize, however, as soon as Draakar mated to Maya, he would be able to find him through their link.

"You said three questions." Maya's voice drew him out of his reverie. "What are the others?"

"First, I want to thank you for helping Talon, and I will tell you all you need to know, but not here. Are you visiting the area?"

"Yes. I'm an American. I'm staying at the Sperrin Inn. Are you from around here? I can't quite place your accent."

"Ah, an American—I would like to visit your country soon. My family has claimed these lands for a long, long time, but my accent is not one you would have ever heard." He paused as he grabbed his coat. "I'll have my driver take us to the inn to get your things."

"*What*! Wait a minute! What are you talking about?"

"I would like you to come and stay with me at Akgon Castle for the remainder of your stay."

She frowned. "Castle! Where is this castle? I-I can't possibly stay with you. You're a stranger! I thought you were going to answer my questions."

"Only if you come with me now. Don't be afraid of me, Maya. Never be afraid of me."

Huffing, Maya crossed her arms over her chest. "Afraid! No. I'm just being prudent."

Draakar raised one skeptical eyebrow and watched in fascination as Maya raised her hand and ran long, slender fingers through the loose curls in her auburn hair. He wanted to reach out and grab one of her locks. He wanted to know if it felt as silky as it looked; he wanted to feel her. Taking a deep breath, he inhaled her scent. She smelled like no scent he had ever encountered before, a mixture of sunshine, earth, rain and woman. The erotic aroma ignited his blood, and he would never be able to forget it.

"Look," Maya huffed again, distracting him from his perusal of her scent. "I don't know you. Yes, I helped your son, but that doesn't mean I'm going to go off with some stranger. Especially one that can do..." She waved one hand in the air. "The things you do. So just tell me what's going on and then we can go our separate ways."

A knock sounded on the door and Dr. Donovan walked in. He took one look at Draakar Akgon and froze for a full minute. He shook his head and extended his hand with a bemused expression on his face before it was quickly replaced with a smile, lighting up his eyes in recognition.

"Mr. Akgon," Dr. Donovan said. "I see you've heard. Sorry about that, but Talon's already gone. I…I released him this morning. He's fine. Everything is fine."

CHAPTER SIX

*M*aya's mouth stood wide open as she watched the interaction between the doctor and Draakar. "What?" she finally got around to blurting out. "I-I thought you didn't know Talon?"

Dr. Donovan finally turned to look at her. "Oh, Ms. Trent, I see you're here. Sorry for the confusion. The nurse called the inn and left a message for you, too. I'm sorry you came down here for nothing."

"What are you talking about? I've...."

Draakar spoke up, not giving her a chance to say more. "Thank you, Doctor. I'm glad to know everything's fine. Talon's already on his way back to school. Please say hello to your wife for me."

"I will."

The doctor turned around and left. Maya couldn't believe her eyes and ears. She shouldn't have been at all surprised. The mere sound of his voice caused Maya's brain synapses to fire off neurons in all of her pleasure centers. She couldn't place his accent, but it wasn't Irish or American like Talon's. It didn't matter. Regardless of his accent,

64

his mere presence caused havoc to her equilibrium. In the last twenty-four hours she'd seen the improbable and the impossible. Compared to everything else, this looked like just a drop in the bucket. She could be a character in a story but instead of landing in Oz, her original destination, she'd fallen down a rabbit hole with neither Queen nor Wizard in sight. And forget about following any yellow brick road or even flying off to Witch Mountain. According to the populace, none of these places existed. Except in fairytales.

Maya sighed. "Just take me back to the inn, please."

"All right. My car should be right outside." Before she could reach for it, he picked up her jacket and held it for her to put on before grabbing her backpack. "Are you ready?" he asked.

Not like he'd given her much of a choice other than to leave without him, without answers. Not happening, besides she didn't think he'd let her leave, anyway.

"Yes." Silently, she followed him from the hospital room. At the elevator she stepped on first and plastered her back against the rear wall. Draakar leaned back beside her. Even with a couple of feet separating them she could still feel the heat of attraction between them. They rode down to the lobby in charged silence, neither willing to break it as they stepped outside to the waiting Rolls and the man standing beside the opened rear passenger door.

"You!" Maya exclaimed upon seeing the tall, handsome man with red hair. "But…didn't you fly us here in the helicopter? I thought you didn't know Talon? Yet, you work for his father?"

Ian glanced sheepishly at Draakar.

"Ian works for me," Draakar answered. He didn't bother to elaborate. "Maya, this is Ian McNeil, my right hand. Ian, this is Maya Trent." *My Queen.* Two pairs of eyes, one a bronze set, the other set blue, snapped around to look at him. Ian gave a low bow as Draakar guided Maya into the car.

Queen? What queen? Maya knew Draakar hadn't spoken, yet she had heard him. She heard him in her head. Just like Talon. Draakar had called her his queen. It hurt her heart to hear him call her that. Why could she hear him in her head, and why did she feel so much anger and hurt toward him?

Ian got in and started the car.

"Ian, please stop at the Sperrin Inn. Maya has to pick up her things. She will be staying with us at the castle," Draakar instructed.

She swung her head around to stare at Draakar. "I didn't agree to that."

"Ah, but you'll still come." The dividing glass panel between the driver and the passenger section of the car slid soundlessly closed.

But Maya heard it click softly into place. "Look. I am not going with you, and another thing, stop calling me your 'Queen' in my mind. I'm not your anything. In fact, stay out of my head." She blew out a breath. "I need answers and with Talon gone, you seem to be the only one capable of giving them to me. So why don't you just tell me now what's going on? Start by explaining what you are, and why am I so angry with you? Then we can each go our own way."

"It's not that simple, and I think you know it."

"I don't know anything!" she exclaimed angrily. "I wish both you and your son would stop telling me I already know the answers to my questions. If I did, I sure as hell wouldn't be sitting here asking them! All I know is what I've already told you." She sighed in frustration. "I found your son unconscious in the middle of these stones that no one else, other than a guide, seems to know about. Stones with dragons etched into them one minute and smooth the next, and which, by the way, glowed just like your son's eyes. Just like yours do."

She took a deep breath. "Still, a lot of this could have been explained away. Not easily but I'm sure there was some sort of 'reasonable explanation.' Then everything changed when your son did the unexplainable. He up and disappeared. Yep. Poof." She waved a hand in the air. "Not a mirror in sight. Just, now ya see him now ya don't, disappears. That can't be explained away. And I am not on drugs. Now, who are you people? Are you even people? And don't you dare give me any bull about me already knowing the answers to my questions."

DURING HER TIRADE, Draakar watched the rise and fall of her breasts and the way her eyes sparked golden fire the angrier she got. By the claw of the first Dragon Lord, he wanted this magnificent woman. The brethren would not be in the predicament they found themselves in if he had simply waited for her birth. Too late for regrets, and he could not regret his son. He had come for Maya now, and he would make things right between them.

The dragon responded to the anger in his mate. *I've missed you. Every day of my existence, I've missed you.*

He watched as she stopped talking. She heard him. While he could say anything to her, he could never lie to her. The dragon would never lie to her. Somewhere deep inside herself, she felt the truth of his thoughts.

His words echoed through her soul and from the depths of her soul, she responded. *Then why did you leave me to be born time and time again without you?*

Maya grimaced and shook her head from side-to-side. "What's happening to me? Why am I hearing voices in my head, and why is one coming from inside of me?" She gasped leaning right up against the interior door. "What have you done to me? This isn't right."

The car pulled up in front of her inn. Before Ian could get out of the car to open the door, like a bat chased by the fires of hell, Maya opened the door and ran into the building. With Draakar right behind her.

"Maya, wait."

She never even slowed. Instead, she increased her pace as she crossed the foyer, passed the lone desk clerk behind the counter, and headed for the stairs.

Do not run from me. Never run from me.

One foot on the stairs, she stopped dead in her tracks at the command in his voice. Although it was not exactly '*his voice*' she'd heard. Something else had spoken in her mind. Something with the power to make her pause. The same something else inside of her, a part of her, responded to the command.

She didn't turn around. She felt Draakar move up beside her. He took her arm above her elbow. Her already accelerated heart rate cranked up even more at his light touch. Maya glanced down at his hand loosely wrapped around her jacket-covered arm. A faint glow surrounded his hand where he touched her. No wait, the glow appeared to be emanating from them both. She was too stunned to tell him to unhand her.

He moved forward and, having little choice, she moved too. Together they walked up the stairs to her room on the second floor. There were six rooms there, but Draakar stopped at the second door on the left, her room. Maya, keeping her eyes on him, never saw him reach to open the door. In fact, like at the hospital she'd swear he never touched the doorknob, but the door opened anyway. Her mind screamed, *If you cross the threshold with him, your life will be forever changed*.

"You…you never asked me your third question," she said. "What is it?"

"Later. Let's get your things."

Maya faced the truth. She'd lost control, and her life had already changed.

It didn't take her long to gather what she needed. Two suitcases stood beside the bed. She'd already packed most of her things for her trip to Paris, which it seemed was never going to happen now. She didn't bother to reason with herself or explain away why she went with Draakar; this had to be done. He'd awakened something in her back at the hospital; she could feel it. She needed answers and she would not get them if she didn't go with him.

She scoffed at herself. She wanted to go with him. Maya sensed he would not physically harm her, and she could trust him with her life. Anger lay heavily within her mind, clouding her judgment, but she needed to understand where the anger came from, anger and hurt. Why did she feel as though he'd hurt her heart—this man/creature she'd never seen before in her life? Yet, she left the inn and got into the car to endure a silent car ride to his castle.

They hadn't driven far when Maya realized the scenery seemed familiar, yet nothing appeared as it should have.

"Wait a minute," she said, breaking the silence. "I recognize this area, and I know this paved road wasn't here before. I just walked this way yesterday, and I walked through a forest on a barely discernable path."

She watched Draakar's chest raise and fall as he inhaled before he spoke. "Yes, you are correct and yet you are not. This road has existed for well over a thousand years, but it was not visible until much earlier this morning. The paving is new. No one has walked the road since it was carved out of the mountain. It has remained hidden."

"*My God!*" Maya shrieked.

"No, by the will of Mother Earth."

"What!"

"I know there is much you don't understand and there is much you will have to learn in a short period of time. Fortunately, you are very strong so you can learn. Unfortunately, because of your strength, you might also be able to resist."

"Resist what?" She glanced around. "We're going to the stones, aren't we?"

"Yes. All of your answers are there. Trust me, Maya."

She stared at him for a long time before turning away from his glowing eyes and gazed out the window. Maya trusted him not to physically harm her, but she didn't trust him with anything else. She couldn't.

She didn't dare.

CHAPTER SEVEN

A sobbing Arthur dropped to his knees in the entryway and opened his arms wide.

"Daddy!" the little girl cried as she wrapped slender, honey-kissed with sunlight colored arms around his neck and squeezed. "Oh, Daddy! I'm so glad you're here! I've missed you so much!"

"Happy Birthday, angel." Tears shone in Arthur's eyes. "Happy Birthday."

Behind him, his second wife patted his back and cried tears of relief, grief and joy. She looked over the joined heads of father and daughter and mouthed a silent "thank you" to the dark-skinned, rail-thin woman standing a few feet behind the little girl. Tammi nodded her scarf-covered head and smiled sadly in return. She had held on long enough for the child's father to come. Her daughter would be all right now. She'd be loved and taken care of. That's all she could ever hope for.

"Wow!" Maya exclaimed.

The car turned at a bend in the road; heavy iron gates directly in front of them swung wide open at their approach. About a half mile away from the gate, she could see an enormous castle of time-aged mortar and stone standing sentential on the top of the mountain. At the same time it appeared as very much a part of the mountainside. It could have stood there for hundreds of years, something right out of a fairy tale. She just hoped she wouldn't be the damsel in distress in some real life Arthurian play to Draakar's knight errand. Oh wait. That would be dragon.

"This is impossible," she said, shaking her head. "This is where the circle of stones stood. I know it! This was not here yesterday."

She twisted around in the seat to glare at Draakar. "I am not budging until you tell me what the hell is going on," she stated as calmly as she could while trembling inside. It wouldn't do to show this man fear. Never show him fear.

He spoke into her mind. *You are brethren, human brethren, but still brethren.*

Brethren...brethren, I do not understand.

Yes, you do.

I...

"NO!" Maya shouted, heart racing. "Not that way. Talk to *me*!"

He nodded. "Very well. You are like me. You are part of a race long gone from this realm and crossed into another world, but your forebears chose to remain on Earth."

Dragon...

"Dragon…" she said aloud, what whispered inside her soul.

"Yes, Maya. You are part creature of legend. We call ourselves brethren. You know my words are true. That is all I'm going to say for now."

"But…"

"No buts. Let's go inside and get you settled. I have company here already and more on the way. I promise we will talk and I will tell you everything you want to know."

"You promise?"

"You have my word as Dragon Lord."

"As what…?"

Ian opened the car door, interrupting them. Draakar exited first and turned to help Maya out of the car. Both he and Ian went to the trunk to get Maya's suitcases while she stood by silently watching them, clutching her matching steel blue carry on and purse.

The men turned and headed toward the front doors of the castle, doors almost twice the size of an average man. Maya looked up at the turrets and battlement, somewhat surprised to find them empty. No armed bowmen watched down on them from the top.

Are you coming?

She jerked and walked toward Draakar, who stood in front of the opened door waiting for her.

"I promise we will talk," he said.

She followed him inside, but came to an abrupt halt in the foyer. What lay ahead mesmerized her. The well-lit entryway of the castle made some deluxe great rooms she'd seen look like closets. She'd had some absurd idea castles should be dark. That is, until she saw this one. Dozens of sconces that looked like upside down frosted martini glasses were anchored every few feet along the stone walls, lit by modern electricity, and completely incongruous to the exterior of the castle. She would not have been surprised to find fire-lit torches and burning candles used within, but was none-theless pleased to find modern conveniences.

Something inexplicably drew her gaze downward to the polished gray marble beneath her feet. Toward the center of the floor, the marble appeared made up of different colors forming some sort of pattern, running about fifteen by twenty feet across the floor. She didn't have time to study it too closely because Draakar and Ian didn't stop walking. They continued down the long wide foyer, past two closed doors, toward a wide stone staircase on her left. Her gaze followed the staircase to a balcony overlooking the foyer. Presumably, the balcony led to the bedrooms, since the men headed in that direction with her cases.

Draakar paused and turned around, searching for her. "You can see it better from the balcony," he said, knowing exactly what she had been staring at and thinking about. While Ian continued walking, Draakar stopped midway on the balcony to wait for her. Maya slowly climbed the stair-case. When she reached his side, she stopped and turned to look over the scrolled iron railing at the sight below.

"Oh. My. God."

Draakar smiled. "No. Oh, Mother Earth."

"Is that…is that…?"

"Yes Maya, it is."

Her eyes feasted on one of the most beautiful mosaics she had ever seen. Unique, much like the man standing patiently beside her. Before her, a dragon in flight had been captured forever in marble reflecting a spectrum of colors. The wings seemed to shimmer as if they beat against air instead of being trapped in stone. The whole thing looked so real Maya leaned forward and extended her hand like she could reach out and touch it. Scared she would fall, she quickly pulled her hand back to her side.

"Come," Draakar said. "Let's get you settled, and then we will meet the others."

She had to tear her gaze away from the image below her. "What others?"

"The other human brethren who also need to be trained."

His matter of fact statement got her attention. "You mean there are others...like...like me?"

"No. There is no other like you. But yes, these are other human brethren."

She raised her eyebrows and stared at him. "You are so confusing. Why are they not like me, or am I not like them?"

They moved away from the balcony and walked through a wide archway, then turned left through double doors and down a hallway. She didn't notice Ian had disappeared into a room until he walked out of the doorway in front of her without her bags.

"After you," Draakar indicated with his head to Maya. "The others are in the library," he told Ian. "Please join them and make sure they've all settled in. Tell everyone we will be down shortly."

Ian inclined his head slightly. "Yes, Lord." He turned to Maya and inclined his head even more. "My Lady, it is a pleasure to serve you." He turned and walked away before she could question him, but he was not the one who would give her answers.

Subdued, Maya watched Ian go through the doorway and close the door leading to the other hall. She moved past Draakar, ignoring him for the moment and glanced around the enormous area. There were only two doors in this section of the castle. They had crossed the balcony over the foyer and taken the hallway to the left, but another hall ran straight ahead, and they'd passed another hallway at the top of the stairs that ran in another direction. From what she had seen so far the castle had more than one wing, and she'd bet money the second door in the hall they stood in led to Draakar's room. But first things first.

She stepped into a sitting room done in neutral colors of cream and bronze. The feel of the room transported her to another world. Oh, not literally, nor did anything look alien or strange. Everything embodied beauty and refined elegance, but all of the furnishings seemed like pieces from a time long ago. Most of all, it felt familiar, like this room was meant for her. Even the colors were some of her favorites.

Maya didn't say anything as she inspected the first room, about the size of a master bedroom in a normal sized home. It had a small desk with a Tiffany lamp on it and a dark brown suede high-backed chair in front of it. There were no windows in here, but a small unlit fireplace lay niched in one corner, and two large comfortable-looking chairs sat before it with a little table between them. It created a cozy spot to sit and read or have conversation. On the table rested a tray with an assortment of cheeses, fruit and crackers, with a carafe of water, reminding her she needed to eat something.

Grabbing a piece of cheese, she nibbled on it before going through the double doors located on the far side of the room. She stepped into a bedroom, done in the same colors as the sitting room, but with gold trim added to the wallpaper. A room twice the size of the sitting room and about as large as some apartments.

A bed fit for a king, or queen sat prominently in its center. She purposely didn't allow her gaze to linger there, refusing to think about how it appeared large enough to cradle both of them in comfort. She finished eating the cheese as she walked past the bed and peeked into the bathroom, gasping at the elegance of the claw-foot tub wide enough to fit two, and the separate more modern shower with its multiple showerheads. While the exterior of the castle looked as though it had been around for hundreds of years and the interior held accessories both old and new, it most definitely had modern conveniences in the bathroom.

Leaving the bath, she pulled open another set of doors and found a closet about half the size of a studio apartment. She almost had a heart attack as she walked through aisle after aisle of clothing. One entire wall held only shoes. Other walls housed cubbies of various sizes, holding every accessory imaginable to go with the clothes and shoes. She knew everything would fit her perfectly.

When she returned to the bedroom, she spied both of her suitcases at the foot of the kingsize four-poster bed. She rubbed her hand along one of the mahogany posts, which were carved like dragonheads. As she turned to leave the bedroom, she noticed a single door tucked in a corner. Opening it revealed an adjoining bedroom, a mirror image of hers, but done in a more sober, masculine style. Just as she knew her own name, she knew Draakar's room. Quietly, she shut the door, but when she tried to find a lock, none existed. Then again, no lock or door made could bar that man's entrance. She returned to the sitting room.

Draakar stood near the door with his legs braced shoulder width apart and his hands hanging at his sides, but curled into loose fists. He appeared tense to Maya, although his words to her came out calmly enough.

"Are you ready to listen now?"

"That's your third question," she stated.

"I know. I'm still waiting for your answer."

"I…yes, I am." She tensed and remained in the doorway to the bedroom, facing him.

"Eat something first. I know you must be hungry."

She had been, but not anymore. Besides she needed answers. "No, I think I'll wait. Go ahead, talk."

I ask again. Are you ready to listen?

"No! Don't do that. Talk to me like...like normal people do."

"We are not people. We are brethren and this *is* normal for our kind."

"It isn't for me."

Yes, Maya, it is.

The sound of the first few notes of Beethoven's Fifth Symphony could be heard coming from Maya's hip. They both looked down at the phone stuck in a side pocket.

She took it out and looked at the caller ID on the display. She sighed. "Excuse me. I have to take this."

He inclined his head and came farther into the room, sitting down on one of the two chairs near the door, making it clear he planned to stay. She turned around and placed the phone to her ear, then walked back into her temporary bedroom.

"Hi, Mom, is Dad on the line, too?"

"Maya sweetheart." Her mother's voice came across clearly, like she stood in the next room instead of across an ocean. "What's going on? Dad's not here, but we thought you were going on to Paris yesterday?"

"How...how do you know I'm not in Paris?" Damn, with everything going on, she'd forgotten to call them.

"Justin called. He flew over to surprise you. Imagine our surprise when he called to say you weren't there."

"*What!*" The idiot! She'd have to give him a piece of her mind for butting into her affairs. "He had no business doing that. In fact, I told him not to come."

"I don't understand. He didn't tell us you spoke. He seemed to think it would be a wonderful surprise for you. Where are you?"

"I'm sorry, Mom. I changed my plans. It looks like I'll be staying in Ireland for the rest of my trip."

"But where are you, honey? Justin said he tried your inn

and someone told him you had checked out. He got us worried. It's not like you to change your mind like this. Did something happen? What made you change your mind?"

"Nothing's happened, Mom. I'm fine. I just decided to stay in Ireland, that's all. And Justin should not have worried you guys. I planned to call you later to let you know I decided to stay after all."

"Well, where are you staying if you're not at the Sperrin Inn?"

"I'm staying with…a friend." Maya hesitated, not really knowing how to explain Draakar to her mother. She couldn't explain him to herself. "I'll call Justin and let him know everything is all right and he shouldn't have bothered you with this." And to tell him to mind his own business.

"What friend?" her mother asked. "I didn't realize you knew anybody over there."

"Just someone I met while I've been here."

"Who is this person?"

"Just a friend, Mom. I'm perfectly fine." Or so Maya hoped.

Her mother sighed. "Your father and I are just concerned, honey, and Justin cares about you, too."

She wanted to turn around and go back to the sitting room to glare at Draakar. Sure, he could hear every word she said to her mother. Could he hear her mother, too?

Yes. I can. And I'm more than just your friend.

Maya whipped her head around to scowl at him through the open doorway.

"Listen, Mom, I have to go. Tell Dad I said hi and not to worry. I'm fine."

"Well, what do I tell Justin if he calls? Where exactly are you staying now? And what's this friend's name?"

"Don't worry about Justin. Like I said, I'll call him on his cell as soon as I hang up."

"Wait, where are you staying? How will Dad and I be able to reach you?"

"You can always call me on my cell, Mom, or send me an e-mail or text."

"Well, what's with the secrecy? Why can't you tell me where you're staying and with whom?"

Maya hesitated again. How could she tell her mother the truth? What could she tell her? "It's no secret. I'm staying at a castle, Mom."

"A castle!"

"That's right, and I really have to go now."

"All right, Maya. As long as you promise to check in with us again tomorrow, so we know you're all right. I also expect a more detailed explanation as to your whereabouts, and who this friend is you're staying with. I know your father would like to talk to you too, but he had to run down to the department to help monitor the phones this evening. He won't be back until late tonight."

Since her dad retired, he sometimes volunteered to cover the fire department phones if any of the operators needed time off or when they were shorthanded. "Mom, I'm an adult. I know what I'm doing." She hoped. "Tell Dad everything is fine and I'll call you guys tomorrow. I love you. Give Dad a kiss for me."

After disconnecting the call, she checked her phone, which she'd turned off while in the hospital. Sure enough, she had missed calls from both Justin and her folks; she was almost sorry she'd turned the thing back on in the car. She returned to the sitting room and sat down in the matching chair next to Draakar.

"Why didn't you tell her where you were and who I am?" he asked.

"I don't really know where I am since and this," Maya waved her arm in a wide arch to indicate the entire structure, "wasn't here yesterday and may not be here tomorrow. Since I don't really know who or what you are, I can't very well tell her about you either."

A low rumble of laughter sounded in her mind.

"Yes. I can see how that might pose a dilemma for you. Let me assure you the castle will be here as long as there are Akgons here, and I will be here a while."

"That's reassuring," Maya replied sarcastically. Draakar's eyebrows rose teasingly at her remark. She read his pleasure with her as if he'd voiced it and shook her head in an effort to clear his thoughts out of it. "Let's try something easy. Why don't you start by telling me why Ian calls you 'Lord?' Are you an Irish Lord or Laird?"

"That's Scottish, but I am a Lord, and my title is one older than Erin, conferred by right as well as might. No one granted it. I was born to it."

"Okay, so not an easy question. I'm not sure I understand." Maya frowned. "And why would he call me Lady? Ian used it like a title."

"Let me start by telling you about who and what we are. But go ahead and eat." He picked up the platter and handed it to her. After she took it and began eating he poured her a glass of water and placed it near her before relaxing back into the chair. His long fingers rested casually on the material of the chair arm. They weren't overly thick but like the rest of him, lean and strong. What would his touch be like? The thought had her wrenching her mind away from his hands and back to what he said.

"The brethren are creatures that are both dragon and human, one and the same," he explained. "Not separated by one side of the same coin, rather picture a coin where one side is a dragon and human and the other side is human and dragon. We are not separate creatures that co-exist, but are truly one creature with one soul in two forms."

"I think I understand. Is your human form the dominant one?"

"Yes, and no. As a human, my dragon within is my guide. As a dragon, my human within is my guide. Both forms exist at the same time, but you only see the outward appearance of one at a time."

"I get it, and the form you don't see sorta acts like a conscience."

"Something like that."

"Is that…is that the voice I hear in my head?"

"Yes, in a manner of speaking, but the voice is your own."

"How come I've never heard it before? How come nothing like this has ever happened to me before?" She continued eating, waiting for his reply.

"Nothing like this has happened in over a thousand years." Maya opened her mouth to ask another question, but Draakar held up his hand palm up, fingers spread, halting her. "Talon's coming here called to the dragon blood of those nearby. Called to you. When I came back, I further called forth the dragon blood of a few brethren—as Dragon Lord, I have the power to do that—and awaken the dormant dragon within."

She lifted her hand and swatted the air. "Came back? Came back from where? A thousand years? What happened a thousand years ago?"

"It has been more than a thousand years since brethren walked the earth."

"But…" Her brows crinkled in confusion. "But you called me brethren and I've always been here."

"Yes. The ones I called are the descendants of the brethren who stayed behind. Those that stayed had to sacrifice their dragon, their magicks to become fully human. These are the ancestors of the human brethren that exist today. You are human, but dragon blood flows in your veins.

It is strong in a few, but weak in a majority. Most of the human brethren will not be able to change into their dragon forms or even heed my call. The ones I have called to me are amongst the strongest."

Okay, way beyond her realm of comprehension, and yet…. "What happened to the rest of the brethren? Why did they leave? Where'd they go?"

CHAPTER EIGHT

*D*raakar smiled at her questions and curiosity. The fact she hadn't run from him in fear gave him hope, but she needed to know more, much more.

"Understand, it was a difficult time for us. The time of man and the one God had begun. Religion supplanted and usurped magicks, or magic as you call it, and fewer people believed." He paused to run his hand over his hair. "And if you did you were condemned. The Earth magicks sustaining our powers and life energies weakened and we didn't know why exactly. Dragons were once powerful creatures, something to be feared, but when we were at our weakest, humans hunted us. Things got worse when one of our own, the betrayer, divulged secrets of the dragon, making us vulnerable and allowing us to be killed. With our magicks so weak we were easier prey for humans. The brethren were slowly being exterminated. Where once we numbered hundreds of thousands, we were down to mere thousands."

Her hand flew over her chest. "That's horrible. Why would people hunt you? Murder you? Why would one of your own betray you?"

"Fear. People fear what they do not understand or see as different from what they know. We had powers humans didn't, and the betrayer thought with so many powerful dragons destroyed, the magicks left would be his to control. He would rule this realm unchallenged. He was wrong. The amount of magicks he can draw forth from Mother Earth is determined by the amount of internal power he can control. While his powers are great, it would have been beyond his abilities. Besides, Mother Earth would never have allowed him control of that much of her magicks."

"You speak of Mother Earth like she's a real thing," Maya said. "A living entity."

"And so she is. She manifests the powers of the earth, of nature, and can channel this to brethren."

"So this entity, Mother Earth," Maya began, "would have stopped him from taking control?"

"Of accessing her powers, but he would still have powers of his own. Human kind had no idea what would have happened to it had he been successful in destroying the brethren. He fed the fear and drove humans to hunt us. The world was made up of the One God and the old ways were considered the ways of evil. They had to be wiped out. Dragons had to be erased from the face of the planet."

"So what happened? How did any of you survive?" Maya asked.

"Some changed by fully embracing their humanity. They literally cut off part of themselves to do it. They drained their magicks, thereby killing their dragons, living only half a life. Fewer still simply ended their existence. The majority of us traveled to the realm of our beginning, Akgon."

Her eyes narrowed as she stared at him. "Us? You talk as though you were there."

He returned her stare. "I was."

"That's…" She stopped in mid-speak and blinked. "What

am I saying? Of course it's possible. Why not? Your son can disappear. Castles can appear and disappear. Dragons are real. So of course, you can be more than a thousand years old." Maya took a drink of water then looked him up and down. "Though, you don't look a day over three hundred and fifty, if that," she finished flippantly.

He frowned. "Ah...actually..."

"No." She held up one hand and placed the glass back on the table she held in the other. "Don't tell me."

This time, he smiled before he answered. "I'm quite a bit more than a thousand years old."

She shifted restlessly in the chair. "How much more?"

"Maya, I'm almost two thousand years old."

The shocked expression on her face made him smile even more. "I know the world as you know it no longer exists. But there is much to look forward to."

"I'm sorry." She shook her head. "This is a lot. Dragons and magic, legend and myth, are real? So is reality a lie?"

"Not at all. There are just many versions of it."

Her head dropped forward until it rested on her knees.

"Are you all right?" he asked.

"Uh-huh," came a muffled reply. She waved one hand in the air. "Just give me a second."

He leaned forward and turned more toward her. "Breathe, Maya."

"Okay, okay, ah, yeah." She sat up and leaned her head against the back of the chair. "I guess there's no going back to that ignorant reality. So, where were we? Oh yeah, you're two thousand years old, or so. Oh, God! Uh, how old is Talon?"

"He's barely past hatchling. He's only a little over four hundred years old."

"Four...four, huh! Okay."

"It will be okay. I promise. Everything will be all right

now."

"So," Maya took a deep breath, "go on. You were saying you left. And where'd you go again?"

"We went back to the land we came from, Akgon."

"So you're not human? You're not from Earth?"

"Yes, and no."

"Jeez, enough with the yes and no answers."

Draakar smiled again at her reaction. She actually took all of this rather well. "We are human. Part of us is human."

"That's impossible."

"Nothing is impossible."

"Okay, okay. Let's let that one go for now. So you went back to where you guys came from, Akgon. So why are you here now?"

"The magick on Akgon is weakening. Our life energies are linked to the magicks of our world. When the magick weakens, we weaken to the point we eventually die." He did not add the conduit the magick flowed through was him, and his magick had been slowly weakening without his truemate to nourish his life energy.

Without Sierran to help sustain his magic, the brethren would not have survived as long as they had. Now strength and power coursed through his veins. Stronger even than the first time he left Earth or left Akgon because he and his true-mate were finally in the same place, at the same time. What powers would they unleash with a mating!

"Wait a minute," Maya said, "I thought that was your 'realm', so why would you be weak there? For that matter, why'd you leave it to begin with?"

"I did not. None of the brethren that returned with me had ever been on Akgon. We are Earth born, but Talon and others were born on Akgon after we arrived."

"Well, were there other brethren already there?"

"No, and it's not clear why the original brethren left."

"I'm confused. Akgon is your surname and the name of your realm."

"Surnames are a recent human custom. Akgon is the birthplace of the brethren and thus the surname we use today on Earth."

She nodded. "Okay, so why are you here now?"

"Because the brethren are being threatened again. The answers to our survival are here. I also believe Earth is in danger. I need your help, Maya."

She shrugged. "I don't know. What can I do? With all the magicks you seem to possess, I don't see how I can help you. Until yesterday, I didn't know creatures, beings...like you, existed. You were something to be found in a book. No strike that. I've never found the likes of you in any book."

Draakar smiled, and his eyes got brighter.

SHUDDERS RIPPLED THROUGH HER BODY, but not in fear. "Please don't do that glowie thing with your eyes."

"Why?"

"It's just kinda creepy." She lied, and they both knew it.

"They merely mirror your own."

"My own? What are you talking about? My eyes don't..." Maya stopped and got up to look at herself in the small antique mirror on the wall beside the mantle. The face staring back at her was one she'd seen every day of her adult life, but the eyes, the eyes, belonged to someone—*something* else. They glowed. In shock, she continued to stare at her reflection. The glow got stronger and brighter, until two tails of golden flames shot out of her eyes toward the mirror. The sound of breaking glass echoed around the room.

CHAPTER NINE

*B*e at ease, my Queen. You do not know your own strength.

But I do, Dark Lord. It is you who has forgotten the strength of a Dam.

Draakar moved to stand directly behind her. He did not touch her, though every cell in his body cried out to him to fuse himself to her. To join with her. To take what he had a right to.

The temptation to finally be able to come into his full power and save his people made him want to rush things, but he could not give into it. It took all of his will not to touch her. He could not let his need rule his actions. He made the error once already; Draakar would not make it again. This time, he would not lose her.

They had to find their way through their separate pasts to each other, to a future together. They were born to be together. Their emotions were already engaged, but the physical side of their joining would have to wait on her trust. Right now, her vulnerability made her a very dangerous

Dam. One who had not learned to control and harness her magicks.

Maya had enough power to change into dragon form on Akgon and here on Earth. The magicks she would unleash during a mating could cause her to change fully to dragon form and sustain it. However, the magicks required for such a change could also be uncontrollable and destructive to her. To gain greater control she had to accept him, but first she had to embrace her brethren half. It would be his pleasure to aid her in all ways.

I feel your need, Dark One, Maya hissed in his mind. *Know the day you touch me without my permission is the day you die.*

Draakar, Dark Lord of all brethren and who bowed to no creature, bowed his head to his queen and stepped back.

My Queen. I am yours to command.

"Why?" Maya asked aloud, spinning around to face him.

"Why what?" Draakar responded, as he willed the mirror to repair itself and it appeared whole again.

But he'd read her mind and knew she would ask the question she found the most troubling and ignore what he had called her. "Why do I hate you?" she asked instead.

He clamped his own thoughts tight and hesitated before he answered. The one question he knew he'd eventually and reluctantly have to face. How did he answer her without driving her away from him? With the truth, just not all of it —not yet.

"You do not hate me."

"No," she whispered, but in a stronger voice stated, "I don't hate you. But, my God, I am angry with you! Why?" Her gaze searched his features, seeking the truth, her lips curved in misery.

"I have wronged you. For that, believe I am truly sorry. I have mourned us in my heart for all of these last thousand years. Know what I did was for the good of the brethren."

"What did you do?" *Why was I sacrificed?*

"My father was killed, betrayed by one of our own kind, and my mother died trying to avenge him. Like my father before me, I became Dragon Lord. My first duty was to the brethren, even at my own expense. We needed every ounce of magicks to open the portal to Akgon. Once connected, someone had to hold the gateway open." He paused, took a hard breath and stared into her eyes, willing her to understand. "I was the only one strong enough to do that, and as the leader, I had to go with them. When we arrived on Akgon, we found it to be a magicks rich realm but wild magicks, in need of balance. I had to stay to provide that balance for the power there, so the brethren could survive."

But you had no right to sacrifice me. You could have come back. Once the magicks were tamed and a balance achieved, you should have returned to Terra. Just as you are back now, but it's too late. I will not forgive that. You did not return for me after you knew my first cycle had come. I existed, but you were nowhere to be found. You condemned me. I know what you want. Now it is my turn. I condemn you now.

She looked away from him.

What of the brethren? You have a duty....

I hold duty to no one.

Maya.

She turned to face him again, and her eyes had stopped glowing. "I'm sorry, Draakar," she answered sadly. "It's a lot to take in right now. I need...I think I need time to process it all."

"I understand."

"I know there's more, but can we continue this later? I think I need to be alone for a few minutes."

He had more to say, much more, but wisely didn't. She definitely wasn't ready to hear about Talon's mother and he needed to find the words to tell her. "Of course," he said instead. "Take your time. Why don't you rest a little? You've been through a lot in a short period of time, and there's still more to take in. I'll go and tend to my guests. Come down in a couple of hours. We'll have an early dinner."

"Fine. Ah, this place is enormous. How do I find the dining room?"

"We will await you in the library. You can find your way to any room in this castle. All you have to do is think about where you want to go. If you need me, it is the same. Just think of me and you will always be able to find me. I cannot hide from you, Maya. I'm here now and I'm not going anywhere." He didn't tack on, *not without you,* but the message lay in the silence between them.

He let the heat he held within for her rise to the surface and knew she wasn't immune to him when he observed the faint flush on her cheeks. "I will wait for you, Maya. It's my turn now." He bowed and closed the sitting room door behind him.

SHE LAY on the bed for a long time, no longer hungry or tired, just staring at the high ceiling. A work of art, in and of itself. In vivid colors, it depicted a golden dragon kneeling before a woman dressed in a green and gold gown with long, flowing black hair. The artist painted the woman turned toward the dragon so you couldn't see her face. One hand rose so she touched the spiked ridge atop the dragon's bowed head. If this picture had sound, the dragon would have been purring. This damsel had tamed the mighty beast. But the art represented a work of fantasy. Right? She wasn't so sure anymore.

Incredible couldn't even begin to describe the last twenty-four hours. She didn't know what to believe. Could all of it be true? She had also guessed at what Draakar didn't say. Talon had a mother and Draakar was the father. At the thought, a sharp emotional pain stabbed at her heart, forcing a cry of despair past her lips.

Maya? Maya, answer me. Are you all right? I feel your distress. His thoughts came again in her head. Thoughts she did not want.

No, Draakar. I'm not all right. Not at all. But I will be. Please, just leave me alone. I will be down shortly.

Maya abruptly shut down the mental connection between them. Though she sensed it there still, like a living thing hovering around her subconscious, ready to return as soon as she dropped her guard. She wouldn't—couldn't—communicate with him that way: dragon-to-dragon and mind-to-mind. Too intimate. He had no right to lay a claim on her. None. She would not think about the other voice in her head, the one speaking thoughts that were…her own.

Okay, she had no choice but to accept she might be brethren and maybe could communicate telepathically. Well, she was human too and Earth her home. What could she possibly do if the brethren race were dying, and Earth might also be in danger from this renegade dragon? Of course, she'd do what she could to help, but she would do it her way. She'd be damned if she became his consort, or whatever, when he had another.

Maya got off the bed and checked her watch. There was just enough time to call Justin before she changed for dinner. She didn't want to talk to him, but if she didn't get the call over with, he would just keep pestering her parents until she spoke to him.

Her feelings for Justin had changed. Maya wasn't sure when. No, that's not exactly true. They had never changed.

She'd always known she could never love him as a woman loves a man. Oh, she cherished his friendship, but nothing more would ever exist between them. Determined to make her feelings clear to him once and for all, she pulled out her cell phone and called Justin.

He answered on the first ring. "Maya. Thank God! Are you okay? Where are you?"

"Hello to you too, Justin. In answer to your questions, I'm fine and since you're in Paris, you know I'm not. The question is, why are you in Paris?"

"I thought I'd surprise you. Imagine my surprise when I arrived at the hotel your parents said you'd made reservations only to find out you'd canceled them."

"Justin, I told you not to come. It's your own fault for not listening to me."

"But…"

"No buts, Justin. Please, do not bother or worry my parents again because I changed my plans without consulting you. You are my friend Justin, not my keeper."

"I care about you, Maya, and I thought I was more to you."

She sighed. "I know you care about me and you tried for it to be more, but you know I've never thought of you as anything more than a friend. It's why I've not been able to sleep with you, and why I never agreed to marry you when you brought the subject up."

Justin's voice came across hoarsely. "I've never pressured you about sex. I was willing to wait until after we were married."

She took another deep breath. She'd hurt him, but she had no choice. "That's not going to happen. Listen, Justin, I'm sorry you went all the way to Paris. You can either go home or enjoy your stay. It's up to you."

A moment of silence sat between them before he responded. "I can't believe this. We need to talk and not over the phone. Are you coming to Paris?" His voice no longer sounded winey, but more authoritative.

"No, I'm not," her voice came out even more so.

"Then where are you? Still in Ireland?"

Maya hesitated. "Yes."

"I see…"

"I'm not sure you do. Like I said, stay or leave Paris." She had to be clear and firm with him. It was the only way he'd heed her once and for all. "Do what's best for you, but don't come here looking for me, and don't worry my parents about my whereabouts again. There's really nothing more for us to talk about. I'm sorry, Justin. We've always been good friends, and I'd like us to continue to be so, but that's all we can ever be to each other."

"You don't mean that."

"Yes, I do. I'll call you when I return home. Have a safe trip." Maya disconnected the call before Justin could reply. She would have disconnected the call even sooner had she known what he did after she hung up on him.

Sonofabitch! Justin screamed at his cell phone. *How dare she hang up on me! How dare she not agree to marry me! After all this time of careful planning, after finding her at last! I swear I'll make the bitch pay for this! She will be my mate!*

Justin placed several calls on his cell phone before he left his hotel room.

Maya had no trouble finding the library. She stood in front of the closed doors, listening to the muted sound of the voices within. Her hand hovered over the brass doorknob, when suddenly the doors swung open on their own. Draakar stood before her, looking every inch the Lord of the Manor born. He gazed into her eyes. The desire burning in his emerald orbs froze her where she stood. It scared the shit out of her and she feared her eyes might have been burning right back at him.

The man defined incarnate perfection. Dressed once again in all black, a long-sleeved silk shirt and pants hugged his powerful frame. His beautiful long hair lay pulled back away from his face so she could savor every inch of his finely chiseled features. Not just his looks drew her, though they were sufficient all their own, but also the man himself. Even with her eyes closed, she'd still know when he was near. This fascination with him had to stop. She did not want this.

I told you if you touch me without my permission, I will kill you where you stand.

He said nothing, merely stepping aside for her to enter, and then she heard him in her mind. *I bow to no other's will but yours—for now.*

She paused beside him, sending a sharp glance his way before he turned to face the room. "Ladies and gentlemen," Draakar said without raising his voice but still getting the attention of the others. "This is Maya." Anyone with at least one working ear could easily detect the clear ring of possessiveness in his tone.

Maya pulled her gaze away from him to look around the room, lined from the floor to about fifteen feet up with books, but several people were also within the room. Drawn to them, she didn't get a chance to examine the books. They all stood, one by one. Almost everyone bowed their heads when she made eye contact. She recognized her sandy-headed guide to the stones as well as one of her fellow hikers; somehow not at all surprised to see them here. Ian grinned at her before he bowed his head. A tall, handsome man she didn't know stood near the end of a long sofa, but he too showed her deference.

The last person in the room, a striking redhead with green eyes, stood near Ian. She barely glanced at Maya; too busy ogling Draakar with such desire written all over her face. Momentarily forgetting her earlier antagonism toward him, Maya wondered why Draakar didn't take her up on her blatant invitation, but the dragon part of Maya would have none of it.

I don't think so!

The woman's head snapped over to meet Maya's blazing gaze. Maya was aware her eyes flashed golden fire. She could feel the heat in them. She had a point to make, and my God, she'd make it.

In fear and awe, the woman dropped to her knees with her chin down, unable to look at the aura of fury and power surrounding Maya. A neat feat because the woman wore a long skirt, making the position look uncomfortable. Maya didn't care.

Your name?

Cassandra, my Lady.

Do you know who I am?

Yes.

Never forget again.

I won't.

I know you won't.

I swear it!

No need. The minute you do, you cease to exist.

"Oh, get up," Maya said, shuddering, still not used to hearing voices in her head and not quite ready to believe one of those voices really belonged to her.

Cassandra got up awkwardly and looked everywhere but at Maya and Draakar. Ian must have taken pity on her, because he placed his arm around Cassandra and whispered something in her ear.

DRAAKAR NEVER TOOK his gaze off Maya. She didn't realize it yet but she had just made the first move. She had placed a claim on him in front of witnesses, in the usual way of the brethren, even if she didn't consciously know it but her dragon did. The females were quick to claim whomever they considered theirs. He smiled. "Come," he said holding out his arm for her to take.

FOR A FULL MINUTE, Maya stared at the black silk shirtsleeve covering his arm before placing her hand on it. She might as well have been holding a band of steel. Immediately a golden glow surrounded her where she touched him. He lost the smile around his mouth and gave a low-throated growl, vibrating through Maya's soul. When she tried to remove her hand he covered it with his own, sending heat from his palm to every nerve ending she had. She glanced at her arm, surprised steam wasn't escaping through her pores.

No, he sent to her only. *By your own free will, you touched me.*

All eyes in the room remained riveted on the couple

standing by the door, who were oblivious to everything and everyone around them.

Do not push me, Dark One.

Lord. I am Dark Lord.

No creature is Lord of me.

Ah, but I'm not just any creature. "Come, let us have dinner." Draakar led Maya to the dining room across the hall and the others fell in behind them.

A huge mahogany table with clawed feet dominated the room, giving it a look of old-world elegance about it. Maya didn't know much about antiques, but it appeared to match the rest of the house, or rather, castle—pricey. The table had eight comfortable cushioned armchairs around it, but still large enough to easily accommodate more. Although she did find it odd there were no place settings on the dark polished wood top.

She looked around the room and saw all the walls but one were painted a dark avocado. There were electric iron wall scones in the shape of medieval torches around the room, as well as an iron chandelier with two tiers of electrical candles hanging over the center of the table. The muted lighting was enough to bathe the room in a soft glow yet keep it free of shadows. One wall depicted a scene of a bronze dragon sitting on top of a rocky mountain ledge, spewing red flame into the sky at a burning purple sun. Maya thought the same artist who painted the scene also painted the one on the ceiling in her room. Maybe even created the mosaic in the foyer.

Draakar escorted Maya to the seat at the right from the head of the table. Ian took the seat on his left across from her. Ian started to place Cassandra beside him but the low growl coming from Maya's throat must've changed his mind. A trembling Cassandra immediately moved herself as far away from Maya as possible and kept her gaze focused on the tabletop. The guide, James, smiled as he took the seat beside Ian.

Maya's fellow hiker took the empty chair beside her. A fellow American, if she remembered correctly, named Paul. He and his wife, Cindy, were both avid hikers and had been on the hike to the stones with her. He looked like a cover model for anything outdoors and his wife looked complete East Coast debutante. They made a gorgeous couple, but she didn't see his wife. Did that mean his wife wasn't brethren? A distinguished-looking stranger, who might be some sort of businessman, sat next to him. He just looked the part, right down to the staid pinstriped vest he wore.

After they were all seated, Draakar sat down at the head of the table then went around the room and introduced them by name. When he got to the guide, Maya spoke. "I already know James. He was my guide on a hike to the standing stones, along with Paul here and his wife. They were also part of my group. We all visited the stones. At this very spot," she said staring pointedly at Draakar.

"That's right," Paul replied, looking at Maya and James. "We were all on that hike." He shook his head. "I just realized Maya's right. The stones were here. They drew us to this place."

"They are still here," Draakar said. "The castle stands over them. This is a place of power and is highly protected. None around here otherwise know of the Stones of Power. The only reason you were guided to them is because they allowed it, and even then, you still didn't know you had been called to them."

"That's true," James said. "All of a sudden I possessed knowledge I didn't have before, and I just knew the way to the stones. But I didn't know their purpose. I only knew I had to take these people there."

"Most of what you need to know, your dragons already

possess. It is the human in you who will take some time to come to terms with these truths and understand this ingrained knowledge." Draakar's gazed briefly touched on each of his lost brethren—*Lost no more*, Maya thought—but his gaze rested longest on her before continuing.

You all were able to hear and answer my call. Your dragons have awakened. That was your first test. You have also passed the second test. You were strong enough to find your way to this place. Being here means you can call magicks and be trained to use your powers. As I said, no one comes here who the Stones do not want.

Draakar paused and looked around the room. He had everyone's full attention. *There will be many more trials for you to overcome, but it will all be worth it. So far your dragons have been acting on instinct and guidance from both myself and the Stones. Now it is time for you to learn to draw from your own powers. To touch Mother Earth directly yourselves. The Stones have judged you worthy. It is time to claim the birthright long denied you.*

How do we do that? Maya asked.

Trust in yourself, both human and dragon. The first conscious use of power for you will be easy because it is triggered by one of the more basic instincts of all creatures—hunger. It is dinnertime. There were no place settings on the table when you sat down. Now there are.

Everyone looked down at the previously empty space in front of them. Only now green satin oval-shaped silken table mats filled the space, on top of which sat spotless black china plates, solid silver cutlery, empty water glasses as well as both red and white wine glasses.

"Oh, my!" Cassandra exclaimed.

"Yes. Exactly that," the businessman, Robert Durham, said. Draakar had introduced him as the Akgon banker.

Now ladies and gentlemen, if you want to eat, Mother Earth will provide. She provides all for us. She is the source of all. Call to her. Tell her of your need, and she will provide.

"I...I don't understand," Maya said. "How? How do we call to her?"

Let your dragon guide you to her. The dragon links us to her. Trust your dragon, Maya. Call to Mother Earth.

Maya closed her eyes and blood flushed to her skin, not unlike when exposed to the heat of the sun but burning from within. She felt...energy. Yes, a good word for what infused her. Pure energy gathered in her core. She gasped. Her mind and body filled, became weighted by it. It came from...the ground. Rose up from the earth and consumed her. *Mother, Mother Earth, provider of us all. I have need.* Maya thought of one of her favorite dishes, a cold bottle of sparkling water, and her white wine glass half way full of her favorite Riesling. She opened her eyes and looked at the feast created before her.

DRAAKAR WATCHED THEM ALL, but his gaze constantly kept returning to Maya. *Mine*, his soul sang, *Mine*.

The brilliant golden glow surrounding her lit up the room. Maya completed the simple task of power he set for them first. Steam rose to the painted ceiling from the plate of hot penne pasta with prawns in a white wine sauce in front of her. She even remembered the garnish. Fresh parsley and grated Parmesan cheese sat on the top. Her white wine glass was halfway full of...his senses indicated a Riesling from the North Western section of America, and a bottle of Perrier stood beside the water glass now full of ice. Excellent! As

Draakar expected, strong in power. The task showed she also paid attention to the details. He looked around at the others.

All had varying degrees of success, Ian's meal being the next most complete. Ian grinned at him. "I created one of my favorite dishes, fish and chips, along with a frosty mug of ale." He raised his mug of dark liquid, blew on the foam before taking a big sip.

"I think you forgot something though," Draakar said.

Ian looked at his plate again, then smacked his palm over his forehead. "Aarrg. I forgot the vinegar for dipping."

Draakar smiled at his first. Ian generated a bright red glow from his use of power, but not anywhere near the strength of Maya's. Interestingly, Cassandra and Paul were both bronze dragons and equally strong. Both had medium rare steaks and baked potatoes without toppings of any kind on their plates, and their water glasses were each half full. James had a cheeseburger on his plate, no condiments, and all of his glasses were empty. He had a green glow, marking him a green dragon.

Robert, his banker, though, would need a little work. His bun-less hotdog lay buried underneath green peppers and mustard with sauerkraut beside all of his empty glasses. Despite this display, of them all, Robert, with the exception of Maya, had the potential to control the greatest power. He accessed the magicks of a golden dragon but not stronger than Talon's power.

These five would be both his and Maya's vanguards. Along with the two coming tomorrow, who should be a blue and a brown dragon, would make up their elite Firsts. They were among the strongest of the Earth brethren. After training, he hoped, they would also be the salvation of both Earth and Akgon.

Everyone looked down at their food and around at their

tablemates. Each face wore varying degrees of smiles, and all were pleased with what they had accomplished.

Excellent. You have all done well. For now, let us enjoy what Mother Earth has provided for us. Just concentrate again for anything else you want or to complete your meal, then eat.

Maya looked at the empty spot in front of Draakar. "What about you?" she asked. "Aren't you going to have anything?"

He looked at her through narrowed eyes. "I like what you are having. Why don't you provide that for me?"

Draakar watched the play of emotions cross her features, should she or shouldn't she, over doing something directly for him versus further testing her powers. Testing her powers won. The energy rush brethren experienced when using their magicks proved a powerful lure. Maya repeated exactly what she created for her own plate on his.

"Oh my! I did it!" She clapped her hands and everyone around her grinned. Even Cassandra smiled at her exuberance.

"Please, everyone, eat," Draakar said, grinning at Maya. "We will continue your lessons after dinner."

Maya took a few bites, then put her fork down. "Draakar, why do I get the feeling you're holding something back from us? I know you need help to save your realm, but what is it exactly you expect us to do?"

"I was wondering when you would ask," Draakar replied with a smile. "Tonight, I will show you how to use more of your powers. How to focus and control them. They are second nature to you, and the more you use them, the easier magicks will come. Tomorrow when the last two have arrived I will tell you all what is going on and what is expected of you."

CHAPTER TEN

*M*aya pushed the door to her bedroom open. She had been the first to turn in. It had been a long night and an even longer day. A lot to absorb in a short amount of time. Already she could feel the changes in her body. An awareness and acceptance of newfound knowledge and memories crowded her mind. Memories imprinted in her blood before her birth and shared by all brethren. Her legacy. So much to learn; too much for her brain to process at once. It had to slowly be revealed but it would be there when she needed it.

The brethren race had an unbelievable past. They had already been driven from their home world once. Now they could lose it again. And what of her own world, Earth? Draakar hadn't said exactly what he needed them to do. Maya had already pledged to help save their world in any way she could, as well as her own. Any way except what instinct warned her Draakar wanted. She would not allow him to use her that way. She would not become some sort of concubine in his harem.

Her body tingled. She raised her hands above her head to

stretch. Her dragon blood hummed with her magicks. She opened her soul to the energy pulsing through her veins all around her, rising up from the Earth surrounding her like a warm blanket. How could she not have felt this before? *She is me and I am her.* Maya smiled. The voice inside belonged to her. *She is the dragon.*

She tested her newfound powers by using her mind to dim the lights in her room, giggling when it worked. Heading for the bathroom, she decided to take a shower before bed. She hadn't had a chance to shower this morning, not with Draakar breathing down her shoulder while at the inn. He always managed to be right beside her. She barely had time to wash up and change her shirt. Still, instead of feeling grimy, now she felt refreshed. Her magicks might be at work there but she would enjoy the feel of water striking against her skin. She found it invigorating.

Mmm, did you know dragons love water? There are many waterfalls on Akgon.

A stunned Maya straightened up. *Do you mind? Get out of my head!*

I can't.

Then let me help you!

Suddenly, blessed silence, but she could feel Draakar's reaction to the mild shock she sent to him through their link. Maya wasn't sure how she did it, only the result. Whether she wanted them to be or not, they were linked, and he had the power to slip into her thoughts. At least, for a while, she had gotten him out of her head. She hadn't hurt him, not really. Just gave him something else to think about. Before she shut him out, she sensed his amusement more than anything else.

DRAAKAR RUBBED the side of his cheek and smiled, not surprised by what Maya had done—sending the physical equivalent of a slap across his face or, in this case a love tap. He wanted to join her in the shower. Then again, he could. Payback time.

Time to show her not only did their telepathic link work both ways, but what else it could do. By the time he stepped into the shower room mirroring Maya's, his clothing had vanished. Naked, he placed his head under one of the multiple showerheads and his hands flat against the warm wet tiles. The water fell hot and steaming against his sensitized skin, but the sensation did not cause blood to pool in one spot within his body between his thighs. One woman did that. He closed glowing eyes reflected off the polished tiles and projected his image to the woman on the other side of the wall.

His mate.

MAYA HAD JUST PUT shampoo in her hair and turned to look around. She could have sworn something or someone stood behind her, but she remained alone in the shower. Nothing but the wet tiled walls. Shrugging slender, bare shoulders, she allowed the dual showerheads to beat a soothing rhythm against her skin. "Must just be this place," she mumbled to herself. Shutting her eyes, she placed her head under the falling water and saw him.

On some shared psychic plane, he stood right in front of her, live, up close and personal. Behind closed eyes, she worshipped a body sculpted like a painting of Thor, the Norse god of thunder, she'd once seen. Except where Thor flashed golden lightning, Draakar raged all dark storms. "Oh, Mama!" she whispered reverently, frozen in place. Did the sound of thunder rumble from the vicinity of her heart?

He stood in his shower, facing away from her. His wet hair glistened, covering his back like an onyx-colored curtain. It ended at the top of the most perfectly defined ass that ever walked on this realm or any other. The man might have long, thick, beautiful hair, but absolutely nothing feminine existed about it or the rest of him. Male strength and power radiated off him in waves. His long legs were spread apart and flawlessly shaped, and his thighs...Lord have mercy, they were formed for riding.

Maya felt torn between wanting him to turn around and mortified he would and find her standing there, gawking at him. No, not gawking; outright drooling with her mouth wide open, tongue hanging out, and saliva dripping from her chin to mix with the other moisture running between her legs.

His biceps flexed and his hands pushed against the wall as he lifted to rotate his head. Her eyes snapped open and the vision, no, not a vision, disappeared, but Maya could swear she heard the echo of rich male laughter mixed with thunder, or a playful roar. She quickly finished her shower, not once closing her eyes again.

She put on the robe she'd left on the vanity bench, then towel dried her wet hair. Normally, she slept only in boxer panties, but as long as she stayed in this house, she'd wear pajamas to bed. Her suitcase lay on the quilt and she opened it, not quite ready to wear any of the gorgeous clothes in the closet, and pulled out her own t-shirt and clean underwear. It might seem stupid, but she felt better knowing something stood between her skin and his, no matter how flimsy the something. His physical presence in the room with her appeared to be irrelevant. The laws of physics did not apply to him.

A lot had happened to her in a day. Maya lay in bed thinking about everything she had learned tonight and unconsciously sent her mind reaching outward through the castle. She touched each of her fellow brethren just briefly. They were all as wide-awake as she, thinking about everything they too had learned. Both excited and in awe of Draakar and—of her. She immediately pulled back from their thoughts, refusing to think about why they would feel that way.

Why should they not be in awe of you? Draakar sent, once again stealing into her thoughts. *You are very powerful. Your power is second only to my own.*

You are so full of yourself, Dark One. I promised to help, but I will not be their queen. I will not be your queen.

We shall see.

She sensed again he'd been blocking something from her all night, even stronger now. *What else have you not told us?*

Changing the subject?

Not at all. There is nothing to see, but there is something more you are not telling us...something that may not be clear in our shared memories. I know you said the brethren on Akgon are in danger, but you also alluded to a threat here on Earth.

There is a threat here on Earth, but it is not the same threat. At least, I do not believe they are related. Tomorrow, after the last two I have summoned arrive, I will explain everything.

She rolled onto her side and stared at the heavy beige curtains over the window. *Everything?*

Everything you all should know. When you, Maya, are ready to hear the rest of what I have to say to you alone, then I will tell you everything.

You owe me no explanation, Dark One. There is nothing you can say I don't already know.

You only think you do.

You have a son. He has a mother. That is all I need to know.

Maya didn't bother giving Draakar a chance to respond. Oh, he tried, but she wouldn't let him back in. Finally, Maya fell into sleep, albeit a restless one. She dreamed. Dreamed of a dragon so dark, no light reflected off its hide. She watched as it attacked another dragon. A silver dragon which seemed to absorb all light around it until it remained the only source of light, and the dark dragon got lost in the brilliance of the light. Maya came awake abruptly, breathing heavily, and automatically reached out through their link for Draakar.

Maya, what is it?

Nothing. It...just nothing. A bad dream.

What did you dream about?

Dragons...not surprising, considering.

She could hear his low chuckle as though his head lay right next to hers on the pillow. *Not at all shocking.*

What color dragons did you dream about?

Why?

I merely wondered if you dreamt of me.

Conceited, aren't you? She smiled, even though he couldn't see her.

But of course, now stop stalling. You said you dreamed of dragons...plural. Were they the same color or different colors?

There were just two, a dragon so dark it was devoid of all color, and one of such pure light it appeared silver.

And what happened?

The silver dragon sucked up all the light until the dark dragon simply disappeared into the remaining darkness. What does this mean?

It was just a dream, Maya.

Do not lie to me, Dark One! I am no fool. You are the dark dragon. I do not know the silver one, but it was a male, and he hates you. It is a portent of things to come.

The problem with the future is that until it comes to pass, we do not know what it is.

You play with words?

No. I merely speak the truth.

If it comes to power, I will fight by your side. If you are to be destroyed, it will be by my hand. Now let me rest, Dark One. I still have much to learn.

She felt Draakar's grin into the silence of the night. *Goodnight, Maya, be at peace.*

Not quite yet.

By the Claw, she had such strength and had blocked him easily. Either that or she was extremely pissed, probably a combination of both. He sighed. He had his work cut out for him. Another long day awaited him tomorrow. At least the balance on Akgon would hold for a while, even without him there, but eventually he would have to return with Maya. He meant what he'd said. He would never leave her again.

Mother Earth fueled the powers he now drew on, but they were temporary. *She* could not sustain him alone, but being near Maya also helped draw forth some of his own powers. Hopefully, his borrowed powers would last long enough for him to do what he must to protect Earth. Still, he had to mate with Maya in order to have full access to his own magicks. She held the key to open up all of his powers, and only if she came to him willingly. Their joining must be based on one all-powerful factor—love. He snorted. Fat chance of anything happening between them anytime soon, even if he was already halfway in love with her. How could he not be? His truemate, created for him alone. He needed her. All brethren needed her.

Draakar rolled onto his back. His thoughts were not only of her. He also needed to find his son, and see his son's mate protected until she came of age. The Stones were still conveniently silent as to the exact whereabouts of either.

The weight of his responsibilities lay heavily on his shoulders this night, but at least he had found Maya. Hope existed for them where there had been none before. Together, he and Maya would be able to restore the balance on Akgon until Talon could cede him. First, they had to save Earth from this old threat, and the sooner he found his son, the better. Draakar already had a private investigator, who possessed a little brethren blood, out looking for him. He had the man searching for Talon in the States because his young mate lived there. Draakar had been able to glean at least that much from Mother Earth.

CHAPTER ELEVEN

*M*aya thought she wouldn't be able to sleep after their exchange. When she rolled over, the next thing she knew, a sliver of sunlight had slipped through a break in the closed curtains. She must have slept after all. Morning had come.

Good morning, golden-bronzed one. Hurry up. I am waiting for you.

Good grief, already! Could that designation be any longer? At least let me get up and have a cup of coffee before you begin to harass me!

Ha, ha, ha...I'll wait for you. Will you take a shower again this morning?

Maya let loose another surge of energy along their link, a little stronger than the first instance. This time he must have expected it because he sent it right back at her, albeit toned down. He'd changed her original energy to a more feather-like caress against the right side of her face.

Oh, don't do that. I warned you not to touch me.

I didn't. I merely returned what you sent to me.

Laughing outright this time, Draakar closed their connection.

"Oh, that man! That...dragon!" Maya wailed to no one in particular. "I am so going to make him sorry he did that!" Throwing off her covers, she stomped to the bathroom to get ready to do battle with her nemesis for the rest of the day.

A surprise awaited her when she opened her sitting room door. Ian stood with his hand raised to knock. Maya greeted him with a smile. "Good morning, Ian. Did you need something?"

"Yes, Maya," he said. "Ah, may I come in for a minute? I just needed to talk to you before you go down to breakfast."

"Sure." She stepped aside for Ian to enter, just as Draakar opened his door. A low growl sounded from his throat. He stepped out of his room toward her. She smiled and closed her door in his face.

What is this? Draakar sent to them both.

Not any of your damn business.

Ian! Draakar roared in his First's head.

Forgive me, Dark Lord, but I must speak to Maya about Cass... uh, Cassandra. I want to make sure there are no bad feelings between my Lady and one of her chosen. Cassandra was wrong to do what she did yesterday and is truly sorry for upsetting her.

Cassandra has nothing to fear from me. However, Maya is her queen and she must answer to her. She should not have upset her, Ian.

I know, Lord, and she didn't mean to. She is still much grounded in human ways of ah...attraction.

Yes, she is, but that is no excuse. Truemate bonds are life bonds and she knows she is not mine. It is Cassandra who must face Maya, Ian. But don't worry. All will be well. Maya has nothing to worry about and she knows this. Do not tarry long in her room.

No, Lord...I mean yes, Draakar, I will not.

Whatever happened to Draak?

Maya could picture a smiling Draakar as he cut off his thoughts from Ian and headed to the kitchen. But he stayed in her mind. *It has been a long time since I have been able to smile so much. Leadership is a burden I have gladly worn, but thank you for bringing a lightness to it. Whether you want to admit it or not, you give me hope.*

Maya did not respond to his thoughts. What could she say? Instead, she chose to continue her conversation with Ian.

"Well, what did you want to talk to me about, Ian?"

Ian shifted his attention back to Maya. "I'm sorry, Maya. I just wanted to ask you to try to befriend Cassandra or Cass, as she prefers. Please don't hold her initial attraction to Draakar against her. It was no her intention to insult you."

The more nervous or emotional he became, Ian's brogue grew more pronounced. She immediately put him at ease. "Well, of course I wasn't insulted. I'm the one who should apologize for acting the way I did yesterday. I was just a little tired and out of sorts. Please tell her she has nothing to fear from me. Draakar is a grown man, eh, dragon. His personal affairs are none of my business. He certainly means nothing to me."

I heard that outrageous lie.

It is no lie. Maya savagely blocked the link, though each time it got harder and harder to keep him out of her head. The more they communicated mind-to-mind, the easier it became to do so. She turned her attention back to Ian, who watched her with one eyebrow raised as if he too didn't believe his own hearing.

"He is the leader of the brethren," she felt compelled to add, "and I'm here to try to help his people, race. As part brethren, we all must do what we can to help him. I'm sure he'll tell us what needs to be done after the other two people, ah brethren, arrive."

"Whatever you say, my Lady. By the way, the last two are already here. I put them in their rooms before I came to see you. Thank you, my Lady. Cass really is a verra bonnie lass and wants to be friends."

"Please, just call me Maya, and I'm sure Cass and I will get along just fine." *As long as she stays away from Draakar.*

By your command. Ian bowed.

"Stop that! Come on," Maya said, opening the door, "I'm hungry. Let's go have breakfast. I'm sure we'll have to conjure it up. What are you going to have?"

"You're right. I hadn't thought about that. Mmm, I think I have a taste for some of me mum's white hog's pudding with tomatoes, and brown soda bread, or maybe baked beans."

"Hogs what? Baked beans for breakfast!" Maya exclaimed incredulously.

"There're other things you can have for breakfast besides bacon and eggs, ya know." Ian laughed, probably at the look of revulsion on her face. "And the white pudding's best for breakfast because there's no blood in it," he further explained.

"Okay, so I admit I was going to go for a western omelet," Maya said, "but still hog's pudding and baked beans...maybe I'll try the beans for dinner. You can keep the pudding bloodied or not."

"Trust me, you'll love it."

She raised both eyebrows and stared at him. "I don't think so."

By the time Maya and Ian entered the dining room together, they found everyone already seated and two more people at the table, a man and a woman. Both appeared in their mid-twenties and were people of color, but she didn't know their nationalities. She did know they were brethren, perhaps because of the rush of blood through her body alerting her to the presence of her own kind. They faced Maya and quickly stood, bowing their heads.

"Ah, hello," Maya murmured a bit self-consciously, unwilling to acknowledge the bow or the reason behind it. "Sit down, please. Sorry to have kept everyone waiting." After they sat, she approached the newcomers, and they looked up. She shook the woman's hand first. "Hi, I'm Maya."

"Good morning, my Lady. My name is Sherri Besnard." The woman spoke with a French accent. Maya liked the sound of her voice, low and smooth. It made a person want to smile and have her talk some more. She returned Maya's stare with beautiful large slanted eyes, giving her an exotic look. Her almond complexion suggested a racially mixed background. Come to think of it, they all had mixed racial backgrounds.

"I'm Darryl Jenkins, my Lady," the man said, interrupting her thought and shaking her hand. She stared at his upturned face, the color of dark chocolate, with an infectious grin on his handsome features. She smiled back.

"Are you American?" she asked, hearing a little of urban in his accent.

He nodded his shaved head. "Washington, D.C., born and bred, Lady."

"We're practically neighbors. I live in Maryland. Please sit down. And call me Maya." She walked around to take her seat near Draakar, but did not look in his direction. She didn't want to see satisfaction or desire in his stare. If she looked, she'd find both there. His emotions beat at her own, or maybe they were all hers. She clamped her mind down tight.

Ian laughed. "I guess we have to come up with breakfast, too," he said. "Maya and I have been discussing what we want."

THE GROUP FOUND it easier to wield magicks today. The newcomers were a little behind, but the others gave pointers and Draakar presided over them all, confident they would soon catch up. He waited until they finished breakfast before he gained their attention.

Now that we are all here, I can tell you everything. It is time for you to understand who you really are, and to help all brethren. It is the reason you have been called.

One minute everyone sat at the dining room table, the next they all stood in a circle in an enormous cavernous chamber. Everyone seemed shocked and glanced around. An area aglow in a rainbow of colors illuminated etchings of dragons with various colored gems for eyes around the walls. The sweet smell of clean, crisp mountain air tickled their noses. They could see the rough ground of baked dirt and stone beneath their feet.

Draakar stood in the center of the group. "You all have been imparted with most of the knowledge of what you are and how you came to be here," Draakar began, turning slowing to make eye contact with them all. "What you do not know is I have come to understand why the brethren left the world of our beginning in the first place. I believe the Dragon Lord who led them could no longer sustain the balance of powers on Akgon, and so came here to a world where they would be able to adapt and survive."

"Because of the magicks here?" Maya asked.

He swung his gaze to her. "Yes. Earth held magicks dragons could wield and a habitable environment to our kind, at least initially. Now that your dragon blood has awakened, you will come to understand for dragons to survive our life energy must feed off the energy created by magicks. Earth has it in abundance. Only a handful of dragons survived to make the first crossing. They were the last of the brethren and the strongest. The memories are sketchy here, so bear with me." He shifted, clasping his hands together behind him and glancing around the chamber again until he'd met each of their curious gazes.

"Even though we retain our history through imbedded memory in our blood, we do not retain much of the first brethren's memories."

"Why is that?" James asked.

"Neither myself nor my advisors, the oldest of the brethren, are sure. We don't even have a memory of the exact numbers of the brethren who survived the crossing or exactly who they were. We believe the survivors would have been a Dark Dragon Lord and his elite Firsts, as you are mine. So because my memories of this period are not complete, I also know your memories of brethren history are even less so. Even after you come into all of your powers, they may never be fully intact. But I digress. In dragon form, these first brethren were both revered and feared. Many humans came to worship them and for a time, dragon and man lived in peace."

"Well, what happened to change that?" Paul asked.

"The brethren were always curious about humans and wanted to walk amongst them. They were also probably lonely for companionship. We are not sure if there were any mated pairs among those first brethren. We do not believe there were because we also think they were primarily males. Dragons do not mate with their own gender. That doesn't mean they won't have same sex relationships, just not a mating.and they would have wanted to find truemates. The one soul placed in the world to complete theirs has always been of the opposite gender in order to call forth all of their magicks and preserve the strongest of the brethren bloodline through procreation. "

Draakar paused and looked pointedly at Maya, who stared unblinkingly right back at him as if his words had nothing to do with her. But he sensed the slight increase in her heartbeat. His words affected her.

"I think the first Dark Lord," he continued, "used Earth magicks to shape-shift into human form and showed the other brethren how to speak to Mother Earth and gain access to the magicks."

"But you're not sure?" Maya asked.

"No, but it makes the most sense. The magicks of Mother Earth would have been easy for a Dark Lord to access. Also, I am of his line. Only a Dark Lord or a son of one can beget a Dark Lord, and only between truemates. Using Earth magicks we believe they were able to change so they could live amongst humans. Some obviously did find their true-mates. The leader being one of the few who did. The first offspring of the mixed matings could also explain the lapse in our ancestral memories. Before we got to Akgon, my memories and those of the other brethren were strongest after the first matings."

"What about the ones who couldn't find truemates?" Sherri asked. "What did they do?"

"They merely found suitable human mates. Eventually, they took their mates and families and began to live apart from humans. All of the first brethren offspring were able to change. We became both dragon and human, brethren of Earth and Akgon."

"But why did they live apart from everybody else?" Ian asked.

"Because they were feared," Maya answered.

"That is correct. Man began to fear dragons. Humans thought dragons were stealing the females. The ancestors thought in order to maintain the peace it would be best to live separately, and for a long time this worked. There was this new race, and while they looked human, they could do things no human could do. And the villagers knew it."

Draakar opened his arms and gestured around. "They came here, to this remote mountain, and created a small village around the Circle of Stones. This circle is a circle of power as well as a gateway for those with the power and skill to open it, though none ever did. There was nowhere they wanted to go."

Everyone looked around and he knew as they all peered harder at the walls, it became clear the Stones of Power were indeed a part of the chamber walls.

"Wow!" Darryl exclaimed. "*They did build a town...a village here*. I can see it in my mind."

"Very good, Darryl." Draakar smiled as he watched the confusion on some of their faces. "Darryl is correct and in time, the memories of that village will come to all of you. The first brethren chose to die when or soon after their human mates died, but they left many progeny who were long-lived. Eventually, some moved to the foot of the mountains and beyond, and the brethren grew and lived longer.

"As ages passed, man began to hold dragons and magicks less in awe and more in envy and fear. Christianity replaced the old ways and magick was seen as evil. Dragons became associated with the devil and blamed for everything bad happening to poor villagers. A renegade among the brethren helped fuel fear among the humans. The brethren, for some reason, were able to access less and less of earth magicks to help protect themselves. As a result, they stayed in dragon form to better harness magick, which did not help alleviate the fear."

"Is what I'm remembering true?" Ian asked. "My memories show brethren were hunted and literally cut down. The magicks no longer protected us."

"Yes," Draakar replied. "Humans had found a way through our protective shields. Later, we discovered they had help. The renegade betrayed us. He lived amongst us, but helped the humans hunt and destroy dragons. One night, when only a few were present, they attacked the village we created at the foot of this mountain. All within were slain. No human could have destroyed all those brethren on his or her own. There were powerful brethren in the founding village. My father tracked the betrayer, and they fought, but humans fought with the betrayer and they helped him slay my father. My mother died avenging him; we thought she had killed the betrayer."

"What do you mean, 'thought?'" Maya asked. "Didn't you have a body?"

"When we found her, we also found a body near hers engulfed in dragon flame. We assumed it belonged to the betrayer because we could find no trace of him. I think we were wrong. When I first arrived here, I felt a recent vibration on the wind and caught a whiff of something in the currents. The vibration and scent are distinctive marks of a silver dragon. There has only ever been one silver dragon, and that is the betrayer."

"You mean this dragon is still alive?" Ian asked incredulously.

"Yes, and if he is, then there must be a reason why he is active now. He was here before I crossed over. I believe he never left, never drained his magicks, and never died."

"How come we didn't know about him before now?" Maya asked, shaking her head. "If there was a dragon flying around, believe me, he would have shown up on the evening news."

"At the very least YouTube," Darryl joked.

Draakar frowned. "He may have just been biding his time. I do not know. What I do know is the silver dragon will bring nothing but death and destruction to Earth. Like nothing you have even seen before. His is the way of chaos. He must be stopped. This is a selfish creature who wanted to control all the magicks here on Earth and to have humans serve him a thousand years ago. He thought it his right. None of that has probably changed."

"You sound like you knew him," Robert said.

"I did. He was my father's brother."

Gasps ricocheted off the stonewalls.

"Never in the memory of brethren have there been a silver and a dark dragon born from the same line. As rare as dark dragons are, silver dragons are rarer. Purer brethren usually have one birth. Those with lesser blood are no different from most other humans when it came to procreation. However, only the strongest amongst us ever have multiple births and then never more than two. I was an only birth and the third new generation of dark dragon lords, and that also had never happened in brethren memory."

"But I don't understand," Ian said. "I thought only dark dragons could have dark dragons?"

"Yes, but even with the holes in our memories, we know it is rare to have such consecutive births. There should have been generations separating such births. Only one generation had passed before my grandsire's birth."

"How far back do your memories go?" Maya asked. "Is it just to the time here on Earth or do they extend back to Akgon?"

"At first it was just to the time here on Earth, but after we returned to Akgon, some of us picked up memories from there too. Not everything but enough for us to more fully understand the significance of the dragon colors as well as maybe the importance of finding truemates."

"I can see we all have different auras of colors surrounding us," Maya began, "and I know that has something to do with the color dragon we would become if we could change. Does color also indicate the level of magicks we can use?"

"Very good, yes," Draakar replied. He noticed she didn't ask about truemates, and what that meant to brethren. He read the question she wanted to ask as it formed in her mind, but she'd asked a different question, so he answered what she had. "While you can all access the magicks of Earth, you can only hold so much of it, and this affects what you can do. For instance, very few of you will be able to control enough magicks to change into your dragon form here on Earth. On Akgon, it would be different; you would all be able to change. The magicks there are different. It is the home world of the brethren; therefore, it is easier to take our dragon form. Our powers are greatest there."

I will answer your other question later.

CHAPTER TWELVE

*M*aya started to respond to Draakar, then she realized he had only mind-spoken to her. No one else had heard, so she continued to stare blankly at him, refusing to acknowledge him. She didn't want to know the answer to the question she hadn't verbalized. Or did she?

"How many colors are there?" James asked, interrupting her train of thought.

"There are eight. Black is the strongest because black is a conduit and contains every color. Black also controls the greatest amount of magicks on any realm," Draakar answered. "Silver absorbs color and reflects them all, but to a lesser degree. Next strongest is gold, then bronze, red, brown, green, and blue. There are times when there is a limited combination of colors. These brethren tend to be stronger than some of the purer colors, with the exclusion of black and silver. Usually a red is involved in any combination, a red and gold or a brown and red. This, however, is the first time in memory when there is a brethren of gold and bronze."

All eyes turned toward Maya.

"If I had to guess," Draakar continued, "I'd say because the brethren drained their powers back into Mother Earth, this may have changed the magicks in some way. So we may see combinations we have not seen before. Maya is the strongest female brethren in memory. There is none other like her. She is also a Dam."

"No," Maya whispered. Spoken so quietly, her 'no' carried more weight. It became a desperate plea. Her body took on a rigid stance. She knew what he meant to say next and did not want him to do so.

You bastard, don't you dare!

They already know, Maya. They sense the power in you. And already sense what is between us.

They sense nothing! There is nothing between us.

She turned to walk away from him, but his next words spoken verbally stopped her.

"A Dam is the rarest of all females. She is one born at a time the brethren have great need, and our needs here on Earth and Akgon are great indeed. The betrayer is alive, and we must try to determine where he is and what he's up to. Above all, he must be stopped. For what he did to my parents and for the destruction he brought down on the brethren, and what he will still bring. After brethren and human alike are safe on Earth, then I must return to our home realm. Time is of the greatest importance. My world, our home world, is also in trouble and running out of time. I may need your help to reopen the portal to return. The balance of powers there is weakening and must be restored or the brethren will die."

Yes, return, Maya thought bitterly as she turned around to face him. His precious brethren still needed him. He would not remain on earth. This was not his home, and he had someone waiting for him. She would do well to remember that.

"If you know who the betrayer is, can you tell us his name and show us in our minds what he looks like?" Robert asked.

"His name has been stricken from memory because he deserves no such respect. He is merely referred to as the betrayer. I know what he looks like in dragon form, but I do not know his human form. He may have some resemblance to my father." Draakar sent an image of his father's human form to all of them.

"He looks a lot like you and Talon," Maya said.

"Who's Talon?" James asked.

"His son," Maya replied before Draakar could.

"Yes," Draakar said. "He is here somewhere, looking for his truemate. By human standards, he is a mere teenager, about seventeen of your earth years, and the woman destined to be his mate is still a mere child."

"Where is he?" James asked.

"I do not know—yet. But I will and soon." Draakar gazed at Maya like she held the solution to a puzzle. Maya's heart rate sped up, freaking her out because she guessed her connection to Talon related to the solution in some way.

"Wait a minute," Cass said. "I thought Maya was your tru—"

Before Cass could finish her sentence, Maya's gaze swung to her, instinctively closing off her vocal cords. The other woman found her voice silenced.

Maya focused her mind solely on Cass. *Careful there. Have a care in what you say.* Maya abruptly released Cass' voice.

Cass coughed a few times before she could continue. "Ah, never mind."

Draakar never took his eyes off Maya's. *Enough! You should not fear her question.* He sent to Maya but said aloud, "Talon's mother was not my truemate."

A confused Robert looked back and forth between

127

Draakar and Maya and said, "I thought dragons only bonded with their truemates?"

"A time existed before the brethren left Akgon, when that was true. Once the brethren settled on earth, not all were able to find truemates amongst the humans. As time passed, there were fewer truemate bondings. Even on Akgon, a true-mate bonding is not common."

"That's because you left them behind when you returned," Maya stated calmly. Inside, a storm raged. She wanted to yell and rant and rave. Probably why his realm lay dying. The same way she died time after time because he hadn't been there for her. He took someone else as mate for life.

"THAT IS TRUE," Draakar spoke slowly. "Some were left behind, some died. Understand, truemate or not, dragons mate for life, which is a very long time and is also why so many brethren are unmated. Females can also only mate with a male stronger than themselves. They wait as long as they can, but eventually, the needs of the brethren demand a bonding. We weaken otherwise." Draakar wanted Maya to understand what he had faced. His heart clenched because he didn't believe he succeeded or that she'd forgive him anytime soon. At the time, he could not have made any other choice.

His heart heavy in his chest for a past he could not change, he continued. "Talon's truemate is here, and he came back for her." *As did I*, Draakar sent mind-to-mind to Maya. "Talon is also among a growing number on Akgon who have decided not to mate at all unless it is with their truemates. If Talon can find his lost brethren mate, then there is hope others can, too."

"Well, what happens if you're already bonded and your truemate shows up after the fact?" Sherri asked.

"Somebody dies," Maya interjected.

Draakar sighed. "It has never happened in my time or our memories, so I do not know." Looking directly at Maya again, Draakar stated emphatically, "But the bond between truemates is like nothing else. The pull is irrevocable. It is not something you can turn away from, ignore, or be broken."

"Does this have something to do with the problems on Akgon?" Darryl asked, frowning.

"My advisors and I aren't sure," Draakar replied. "But I believe it does. I have come to believe only with a bonding of truemates are brethren able to access their full powers. Only with all of my powers will I be able to maintain the balance on Akgon, and only with the majority of the brethren with truemates can we hope to continue on Akgon."

"Well, looks like you figured out how much you needed your truemates too late."

Draakar's eyes glowed, illuminating the area a pale green, letting Maya know her words had found its mark.

"It is never too late. Not time, distance, or death hath dominion over the bond between truemates."

Not this time, Dark One, not this time. You should have remembered that before you bonded with another.

HE WATCHED Maya walk to the darkest wall in the room and step right through it, even though no doorway stood there, and nothing indicated the wall wasn't solid. Still, Maya never paused. Her mind screamed at him she wanted out—now. Draakar could only hope she didn't walk out of the castle and walk away from the brethren, from him as her thoughts told him she wanted to.

CHAPTER THIRTEEN

*D*raakar escorted Paul to the front door. He had to return to his wife.

"I'm sorry your wife twisted her ankle yesterday, but to be honest, it could have also been the magicks at work. Especially, as you say, a root seemly sprung up from nowhere. Sometimes Mother Earth engineers things because you needed to come here alone."

"Yeah, it sure stopped her from coming on the overnight hike we were supposed to take together with James. But she insisted I still go." Paul shook his head. "And when I called to check on her last night, she seemed fine and had plenty of company around at the inn."

Draakar stopped at the door and turned to face Paul. He would return to America in a couple of days to start his part of the search for Draakar's son and the betrayer.

"I honestly don't know what to tell my wife," Paul said, looking down on the tiled floor, then raising his face to look at Draakar. "We've always been honest with each other. We've only been married for two years, but we've known each other since we were teenagers. She's my best friend, and I've always loved her. How do I hide this from her? Do I even tell her what I am? What the children we've been talking about having someday could be?"

"Only you can answer those questions, Paul. If she loves you, she will accept you. Humans have loved and accepted brethren as mates. Some were even truemates. You have not changed." When Paul gave Draakar an incredulous expression, he smiled. "No, you haven't, not really. What you are now, you have always been; whoever you were before, you still are. It is just that you are so much more than you thought you were."

Paul shook his head. "I understand what you're saying. The question is, though, will she? Will she be able to accept all of this?" He ran his hand through his hair in nervous frustration.

"If you want, you may bring her here for dinner later tonight. Tell her I am a friend of James whom you met while camping on my land. I can read her mind when I meet her and tell you if she can be trusted with our secrets. I would go with you now, but I must remain here." Draakar sighed. "If my powers were at their peak, I could have just tuned into her through your mind and read her, but alas, my powers aren't there yet."

"I don't know. That seems wrong somehow."

"It's your call. Bring her to dinner anyway. In fact, why don't you both spend the last two days of your stay here? There is a pool out back and tennis courts." As soon as the words left his mouth, the Earth rumbled. Anyone watching from the windows of the castle would have seen a section of forested land ripple into the ground and vanish. In place of trees, a tennis court and a thirty-foot long infinity edge pool rose from the ground.

Without pause, Draakar continued his conversation. He placed his hand on Paul's shoulder and gave him an encouraging squeeze. "We all need to spend a couple more days together working on your skills. This will also give you an opportunity to see how she deals with it all. If you decide to tell her and she can't accept it, I can also take those memories from her. Just let me know what you would like to do."

"Thank you, my Lord."

"No, Paul, just Draakar while we are here."

"Okay, Draakar, or is that Draak?" Paul grinned for a moment. Draakar could feel Paul's anxiety relaxing a little at the thought of telling his wife about his dual heritage. "I'll bring her back with me later tonight, at least for dinner. Thank you for thinking of it. I'll talk to her about staying here and see what she says. Maybe after dinner I'll have a better handle on what to do."

"You don't have much time."

"What…what if you discover she's not my truemate?"

"I may or may not be able to tell. I will be able to tell you if her answers are true, as she believes, but I cannot read her heart, only her thoughts. When it comes to human emotions, the head doesn't always speak for the heart. Frankly, as your own powers increase, *you* will be able to tell. In your heart, you will know. Your powers will only increase to their fullest potential if yours is a true bonding."

Draakar did not tell Paul what he now understood. If his wife were not his truemate, Paul would not be much use to the brethren on Akgon or Earth. His powers might not ever grow beyond what they were now, and as time progressed, they could weaken. In fact, they would begin to lessen as soon as Draakar returned to Akgon. The brethren were weak already because not enough truemates had paired, and he needed them strong.

But the decision belonged to Paul, and Draakar would honor Paul's decision. Draakar, like Valour, believed one of the reasons for their diminished powers stemmed from fewer true bondings amongst the brethren. Yet he could not force them to wait for their truemates when he had not. However, he'd told everyone the truth at the Circle of Stones. Hope existed because a growing number of the young on Akgon were not bonding, and hope for them dwelled here with the Earth brethren.

"I understand." Paul took a deep breath. "Truemate or not, I do love her. What if I don't want to know? It makes no difference to me."

Draakar just stared at Paul. How should he answer his question? It had taken him a thousand years to fully understand it did make a difference. Each brethren must make the decision on his or her own. Just because mates chosen from necessity were not truemates didn't mean love could not grow. It could and it did. He had loved Sierran. Not at first. He had been fond of her, and eventually, fondness had grown into love.

How could he not fall in love with her, after all she had done for him and the brethren? She had been a caring, compassionate, and beautiful woman who had given him a son he loved. Yet, sometimes, the depths of his soul ached because it knew a different kind of love waited out there, and from time to time he felt its pull.

Only one could forever calm the fire raging within his dragon. A truemate, and Draakar knew she existed. Had known for a long time because his soul suffered with her each time she entered the world alone. He had just found Maya and already he understood the difference between love for a good woman and love of his woman. He tried to find the words to share some of his thoughts with Paul.

"I did not love Talon's mother when we were first mated because she was not my truemate, and we both knew it. But she loved me and I grew to love her, and Talon was the result of our union. That was all I had or could have and I knew contentment."

"Was it enough?"

"That is a question only you can answer, but I am here now."

Paul glanced away, then returned his gaze to Draakar's. "I think I understand. You're right; it's a question only I can answer. I'll see you later. Thank you, Draakar."

Draakar clasped his shoulder again, and they shook hands. He wished Paul luck. Standing at the open door, he watched as Ian drove the Benz back down the driveway to return Paul to the inn. He'd sensed the presence behind him for some time and finally turned around. His gaze immediately sought out the one who stood at the top of the balcony.

MAYA LOOKED at this man who drew her like no other. Today he wore all black again, a favored color of choice for him: jeans, a long-sleeved silk shirt, untucked of course, with a Naru collar and black cowboy snakeskin boots with silver tips. He'd pulled his hair back and tied it at his nape with a leather thong. His features appeared sharper, more defined. If the man looked like a dark angel before, he looked like a dark god now. If he could get any more handsome, Maya didn't want to see it. Green eyes glowed, daring her to deny him. She forced herself to ignore his looks and her strong attraction to him.

You never answered his question, Dark One. Was it enough?

No.

Maya maintained eye contact with Draakar, trying to decide his sincerity from a single word answer, seemingly carrying so much. Finally, admitting to herself the truth behind the word, she inclined her head slightly in acknowledgement. *Good.* Maya turned and walked away.

Stop running away.

Don't flatter yourself.

Forgive me, Maya.

Not today, maybe another.

I will not ask again. But it is time for you to hear it all.

You do not need to ask for that which will not be given, and I already know all I need to know. You did not love her at first, but you love her now, your mate. Maya continued walking down the hallway toward her bedroom. Draakar materialized before her. His bulk and six-foot-four frame blocked her room's closed doorway. She halted an arm's length before him, clenching her hands in frustration. His nostrils flared, anger and hurt simmered within the depths of his flashing eyes. Raising her chin, Maya refused to let him intimidate her.

Loved her, Maya loved her. She's dead. Just before I arrived, she died giving the last of her life energy to Talon and to me so I could return here and try to right so many wrongs.

Wh-What?

Do not hate her, Maya. She was not trying to hurt you. I was not trying to hurt you, but we did not know if or when you would be born. The brethren needed me. They needed my strength, and they still do. As their leader, I had no choice. Our survival left me with no other option.

Maya wrapped her arms around her waist and shook her head, either in denial of his words or because she didn't want to hear it, or maybe both.

Sierran was the strongest amongst the females. We grew up

135

together. We were friends. She knew eventually our mating would destroy her. I did not know how much our bond weakened her until it was much too late. She hid it from me. I didn't know until recently. Over time, I drained her powers, taking the life energy she freely gave to help sustain me so I could sustain the brethren. This kind of draining does not happen between truemates because the bond sustains both; it works both ways. Truemates strengthen each other.

Maya inhaled sharply, unshed tears bright in her eyes. She held her hands up and covered her face. *Oh, God! I...I didn't know! I didn't know!* She lowered her hands, but wrapped them back around her waist. "I'm sorry, Draakar. Sorry for her, sorry for you, sorry for us. I understand now, but that understanding doesn't change the pain I've had to endure because of your choices. Because I too had no choice then and I have none now. Please let me pass. I want to be alone. Both of your choices condemned me to that, so let me be alone."

Emerald fire sparked from Draakar's narrowed eyes; frustrated anger radiated off him in waves. He shook his head sharply. "No, Maya. You are not alone. Not anymore. I am here. Do not shut me out now. Give me a chance. Give us a chance to be what we always should have been."

She hung her head, unable to look at him. She refused to accept his words and what they could mean to her.

Ask me how she died.

You just told me.

Draakar stood unyielding before her. She could feel his gaze boring into her. His pain became hers.

Ask!

NO.

She died helping me open the portal that would send me back to you. Knowing it meant her death.

NO... NO...! Maya threw back her head and roared. All within the castle felt her pain, anger, and remorse.

MAYA'S EYES flamed and her form shimmered and grew until it rose above him. For a moment, Draakar caught a glimpse of a bronze dragon with golden scales. As quickly as it started, the shimmering stopped. The form receded and a heavily breathing Maya bowed her head, this time in reluctant acceptance.

He understood how she felt like her very being was rent asunder. The hurt and betrayal surrounding her heart and soul cracked like a solid block of ice. The sound could be heard in the silence engulfing them both. They seemed to be poised on a precipice and only one way to freedom lay before them, a leap right over the edge.

A leap he also understood Maya might never be ready to take.

Draakar closed the distance between them, slowly raising his hand until it touched the side of her face. She didn't kill him or even burn his hand as she lifted her head to stare at him with a fiery gaze. He took that as a good sign.

As he lowered his head toward her, she broke from his hold and disappeared, transporting herself behind the closed door of her room.

THE LATE ARRIVAL at the Sperrin Inn stepped out of the hired car he had just arrived in and looked toward the north-eastern end of the mountain. A brush of power carried on the wind came from that direction. Hazel eyes set in a handsome face widened in surprise. Silver lightning flashed within their depths.

CHAPTER FOURTEEN

hocked, Maya glanced around, unsure how she had done it other than having an overwhelming desire to escape and being not at all afraid of using her magicks. Her blood still hummed with the residue of power.

I'm sorry, Dark One. Truly sorry, I am, but I...I need more time. I can't do this. Not now. Maybe not ever. Perhaps when the threat to Earth is over, you and I can have a conversation and come up with another option for the brethren.

Conversation is not what we both need. There are no other options for us. Somehow, I will give you more time. It cannot be much. We may not be able to wait until after the betrayer is stopped.

Feeling on somewhat surer ground, Maya opened her closed door to find Draakar leaning against the doorframe. It probably seemed cowardly for her to 'talk' to him from behind the door. It appeared cowardly to run, but a coward she wasn't. "I won't need much time," she said. "Let's focus on what has to be done right now. I'll be back down in a little while. Will we meet in the library?"

"I think poolside. The others have discovered the tennis courts and pool and are on their way down there."

"Shouldn't we be concentrating on finding this betrayer?"

Draakar raised his hand as though to touch her, but then seemed to think better of doing that and instead crossed his arms over his chest. "We are. As I said, time is of importance. I must find him. The longer he's loose, the more of a danger he becomes, especially if he finds any awakened brethren. They will be the first he goes after. I must make sure I trained you few in the use of your powers, so some of you can train others. The pool and the tennis courts are to help with your training."

Maya surprised herself because not only did she not step back, but she wondered what his caress would have felt like. She mentally shook herself to get back on track, and not allow her emotional confusion when it came to him. "How?"

"You all already know how to create things out of the magicks flowing through Mother Earth. Now you need to harness the power of manipulation."

"Isn't that the same thing?" Maya asked.

"Not at all. One is the creation of something out of what is apparently nothing. The other is the use of matter already there, bent to your will. As with all things, some will be better at it than others. A few, no matter how much they practice, will never go much further than what they will accomplish in a couple of days. You will not be among that number. Go ahead and change, then come down."

Maya didn't think she would be in the latter group either. She was tired of having her guard up against the man before her all the time. She needed to act normal around him, as normal as they could be. "Too bad I didn't bring a swimsuit," she said, staying away from further confrontation about their relationship. "Oh, well, I'll play tennis then."

"You don't need a suit," Draakar said with a grin. His

breathing softened, and she could feel him relaxing. He made an effort to put her more at ease. He didn't try to kiss her again. On the one hand, she was thankful, but another part of her…well, it wasn't so sure.

"I'm not skinny dip—Oh, yeah, I can create one."

"No need. There is one waiting for you on the bed. It should fit. When you are ready, come down." His eyes drifted to her lips and his voice lowered an octave. He leaned in close enough for her to feel his warm breath against her face, but didn't touch her. Then he whispered, "I'll be waiting for you."

A promise. At least she took it as one. Silently, she thanked him for not pushing her further. If he had kissed her like, she knew he wanted to, any choice she might have had about accepting him completely into her life or not would be gone. She hadn't been lying to him; she needed time to think about it all. Time to come to terms with the fact he had loved another woman…dragon…whatever!

Yet he was right. She could not hate the other woman. Besides, why should what he did matter to her? He didn't love her, and she didn't love him. Oh, he wanted her. The attraction between them had pulsed with energy from the first time they laid eyes on each other, but she could be nothing more than a necessity to him. A way to save his race. Somewhere inside, she knew this last thought to be a lie based on self-preservation.

Draakar had loved another and had placed his needs and the needs of the brethren before her own. Even though it seemed selfish, Maya needed to be the one who meant more to him than anything or anyone else. *I too, have paid a price with the pain of each of my rebirths, with the agony of coming into this world time after time, only to be alone, always alone. I have more than earned the right not to settle for anything less from my Dark Dragon Lord.*

The thought came after he turned aside to move down the hallway. Maya quickly closed the door of her sitting room, knowing he probably heard it. She sensed him briefly pause, but then he continued away from her suite. Maya breathed a sigh of relief.

In the bedroom, on the bed, rested the most beautiful gold-colored two-piece bikini Maya had ever seen. The embroidered tiny golden sequins around the edges, while beautiful, made it completely impractical to swim in. She walked over to the bed and picked it up. The front portion of the bottom barely covered her hand.

"I don't think so," she said to the empty room.

Why not? Draakar asked in her head.

Maya didn't bother replying. She just focused on the material until it expanded enough to her satisfaction. She also added a long sarong and slipped her feet into the matching sequined slippers she spied at the foot of the bed.

Glancing beyond the bay window, she noticed the trees swaying in the distance. The weather for the week had been in the mid to high 50 degrees, but she'd bet a month's salary the area around the pool would feel like they were in the Caribbean. If it didn't, she could make it feel that way around her body. Her dragon gift. Exhilaration and sadness competed inside her body as she embraced her brethren heritage, knowing she'd never be simply human again.

AT THE FAR end of one of the tennis courts, Maya stood with her hands hanging loosely at her sides and her sandaled-feet planted firmly on the ground. No breeze ruffled the curly hair framing her face. The slit on the side of her bronze sarong allowed for the showcasing of one long, sleek, beautiful leg. Her eyes concentrated on the ball on the ground in front of her.

Without a racket in sight and without moving a muscle, she raised the ball off the ground and sent it flying across the net at a speed tennis stars would envy. Since Maya began playing an hour earlier, no one had been able to return her serves…until now.

The ball travelled right back over the net directly at her head, with the velocity of a heat-seeking missile. She had just enough time to duck. "No fair!" she yelled.

"Concentrate," Draakar said. "Why did you duck?"

"Oh, I don't know," Maya replied sarcastically. "Just the natural reaction to anything that could either maim or bury me!"

The onlookers standing on the side of the tennis court laughed. Draakar faced Maya on the other side of the net, grinning. While some people were dressed appropriately for the pool or to play tennis, not Draakar. With his hair hanging loosely down his back, he still wore his signature look: black silk shirt, jeans and snakeskin cowboy boots. Not surprisingly, he did not look at all out of place. Then again, neither did Maya, wrapped in her sarong. Draakar looked comfortable, no matter where he was or what he wore.

With a predatory smile showing all teeth, he said, "Again, and this time, don't duck. This is about manipulating matter. Concentrate."

"All right already."

Again, Maya slowly levitated the ball, stopping it once it reached the front of her face. With a mental push, she served it even faster than before, back across the net to Draakar. This time she mentally prepared for his return serve. When he sent the ball at rocket pace across the net, she sent it right back at him, and the game was on. The entire game played out without the opponents moving. There were no tennis rackets, and no one physically touched the ball. Yet the ball remained the only thing in motion. No one had ever seen a weirder game of tennis.

Unfortunately, the back and forth only lasted for a few minutes before Draakar upped the ante. "Good, Maya," he said. "Very good. It is a start. What would you do if I did this, I wonder?"

The ball came toward Maya, traveling so fast it became engulfed in flame before it crossed the net. Maya couldn't wrap her energy around it fast enough to send it back across the net. She had less than a micron to react, and react she did.

Going purely on instinct, she constructed a wall—a glowing, translucent, golden, paper-thin shield. It stood as tall as she and was wide enough to protect her. It appeared in front of her just in time. The inflamed ball hit, barely creating a ripple in her golden shield. On impact, the ball made a popping sound and, turning to ashes, fell to the ground.

Bravo!

"Wow!" came from the lips of more than one of the brethren bystanders.

"Bloody hell!" Richard exclaimed. "Can we do that, too?"

"At that speed?" Draakar raised one eyebrow. "Eventually, but you can create shields now." He walked over to the sidelines to talk to those who had gathered to watch. "Our shields are what protect all brethren from harm. It is a natural form of protection for us. Maya reacted by instinct and raised hers. She used it as a wall, but it can also be raised to encompass our entire bodies." He demonstrated by encasing himself within a translucent emerald shield. It shimmered a few inches around and away from his body. "In a time gone by, brethren entered battle thus encased and nothing created by humans could penetrate the shield, or so we thought."

"How did the betrayer breach the shield?" Maya asked, coming over to stand beside him. Drawing the information from her ancestral memories, she knew the betrayer had found a way for humans to breach the shield.

"At one point, the magicks of Earth were weakened, as well as the inner magicks of the brethren. We became vulnerable; the shields were no longer effective against all weapons. The betrayer discovered silver-tipped spears could penetrate our shields."

"Just spears?" James asked.

"That's all that was used. Arrows weren't large enough to hold the weight of the silver required to down us in dragon form. No human could ever get close enough to us to use a sword or a knife. We were still faster and stronger. Normally, there would be no contest. However, a spear could be thrown from a distance. While we could fight off a few men with silver spears, we could not fight off many spears, or even one spear in the back. If even one breached the shield and pierced our skin, it meant instant death."

"Is this the secret the betrayer passed along to help mankind destroy the brethren?" Ian asked.

"Yes. And he led many raids against the more powerful of us. While he held off anyone who could help or acted as a distraction, his men were able to surround the more powerful brethren and take them down. Then they went after the lesser brethren."

"Does silver still have this same effect on brethren?" Maya inquired.

Draakar frowned. "I don't know."

"Well, let's see." Maya walked over to Cass, who wore a shiny bracelet with ends shaped like arrowheads. "Cass, is that bracelet made of silver?"

Cass looked down at the bracelet on her arm, then back up at Maya. "Yes, my Lady, sterling silver."

"I wear silver too. How come we can wear silver if it's dangerous to us?"

"I never said it couldn't be worn. Only that in the past, it was used to penetrate our shields. But what we used in the past would have been a purer form of silver."

"Well, sterling silver is still mostly silver, so let's see if it's still a weakness." Maya enwrapped herself in her shield. "Cass, take the bracelet off and straighten it. See if your bracelet can get past my shield."

"Wait," Draakar said, walking over to Cass. "Give the bracelet to Maya. She can see if it would penetrate my shield."

"No, Draakar," Maya argued. "I think we will have to test it on all of us. I don't think we can take any chances with this. Just because silver may or may not have any effect on you doesn't mean it would have the same lack of effect on the rest of us. We should all be tested."

Draakar stared at Maya for a moment. *Very well, My Lady, but I will go first.*

Maya dropped her shield and took the bracelet away from Cass, who couldn't hand it over fast enough, and stepped back.

"I will change the composition to a purer silver," Draakar said.

Are you sure about this, Dark One? Maya asked as the bracelet in her hand glowed and changed to a more brilliant silver sheen.

Why? Is that the sound of worry in your voice? Concern, perhaps, for me?

Maya didn't bother to respond. She stepped nearer to him. She thrust the bracelet slowly toward Draakar and encountered a barrier pressing against it until it bent the tip of the bracelet.

"I guess that means your shield works," Maya said.

"Your turn," Draakar said, dropping his shield and enclosing both the bracelet and Maya's hand in his own.

She couldn't have moved if she wanted to. The heat generating between them consumed her. Six pairs of eyes watched as a soft golden glow emanated from around their joined hands before gradually expanding. Until it completely encompassed their Lord and Lady. The separate male-female forms within expanded and elongated. They seemed to shine and shimmer before flaming into a very real Dark Dragon Lord and his golden bronze companion. His great wings unfurled from his sides, expanded, then folded to enclose the smaller bright form standing before him. A uniform gasp echoed across the court.

A stunned Maya raised golden eyes to stare into blazing emeralds. *What are you doing?*

You know.

What have you done? I asked for more time!

I am giving it to you, but this bond between us has been formed before time began and it will not be denied. I called to you and you came. You need to see for yourself all of what I am, what you are, and what we can be together. I do not require your pledge now, but before all and Mother Earth on this world of both our births, I give these pledges to you now. My life is yours. My soul is yours. Ever they are intertwined with yours. These pledges I made to no other because my soul has always belonged to you. I eagerly and gladly await the time I can complete the rest of the bonding ritual.

The others listened as their lord made his pledge to his lady. They watched in awe the powerful and beautiful creatures of legend standing before them. A moment framed in time they would never forget. Though none who observed the two consciously realized it, each watcher decided they too would bond only with their own truemates.

However, one amongst them carried a heavy heart. She suspected what they shared would be forever out of her reach.

The magicks surrounding the pair caused the hair on the bodies of the other brethren to rise as it reached out and included them. They actually saw the links their Lord and Lady forged, binding one to the other. The bonds formed very visible tendrils of power. It looked like thin black, gold, and bronze intertwined threads pulsing as if alive. These tendrils reached out to connect each of their chosen protectors to them. One by one, each human brethren pledged his or her life to the Dark Dragon Lord and his lady of golden bronze.

Maya and Draakar returned to their human forms and the glow surrounding them dimmed, then disappeared. He released Maya's hand, retaining the bracelet in his. From the first time she'd laid eyes on Draakar, she'd been very aware of him. In the grand scheme of things, that meant nothing. She had no idea of just how much more aware she could be. Each time his heartbeat, she could feel the contraction of the muscle as if it were her own. For every breath he took, the air might as well have entered her lungs.

The bond created a new awareness of Draakar on a level she had no experience with and little control over. Most of all, she could feel his intense pleasure with her. If she probed a little more, she could feel...no, she wouldn't go there. For her, his thoughts were only covered by a sheer curtain. One she could move aside at will to venture within. He had no secrets from her should she choose to look. Neither did she, but he would never touch the curtain in her mind without her permission. Not yet. Nor could she bring herself to accept his invitation to bare his.

She raised her shield. Draakar barely touched it with the bracelet before he could move the bracelet no more. Neither said a word. Maya merely stepped back as he turned to his brethren. One at a time, he had them attempt to raise their shields. They were all able to do so. Some needed a little push, but it could be done. Though none of them could change into dragon form, the silver bracelet could not breach any of their shields.

After the last one tested his shield, the brethren moved off; some went back to practicing control on the tennis courts, while others wandered over to the pool. Maya and Draakar continued to stand apart from their Firsts, staring at each other, caught in a warp of emotions. Suddenly, they turned sharply to look in the direction of the village, even though they couldn't see it from the mountain.

What is...? What is that I sense, Dark One?

Paul.

He's in danger.

The others must have sensed something too, because they all stopped what they were doing and looked toward the village.

"Something's very wrong," Draakar stated. "I'm going to the inn."

"I'll come with you," Maya said.

Draakar returned his gaze to her. *Together we are stronger than you alone,* she said to him. He nodded his head in acknowledgment of her truth. He held his hand out to her.

Ian, you and James follow in the car. Everyone else, stay here.

Maya placed her hand in his. *Together then.*

Draakar enclosed her smaller hand within his larger one and drew on the power of their bond. He used her nearness to charge his own magicks. An electric surge bounced off each and every one of her nerve endings. *Remember how you willed yourself to your room?*

Yes.

Think of Paul and the inn.

One minute, Maya stood on the side of the tennis court, the next she and Draakar stood in one of the rooms at the inn. The sitting area in Paul's room.

Draakar didn't look around as though he already knew what they'd find. *Do you smell it, Maya? The metallic scent of death, and even stronger, the stench of the silver dragon. The betrayer has been there. The chaos has begun.*

Maya faced the closed bedroom door. Before she could take another step toward it, Draakar stopped her with a thought.

Don't, Maya. Wait here.

He moved past her and, turning the doorknob, stepped into the room.

CHAPTER FIFTEEN

*M*aya couldn't just stand there and let him deal with whatever resided in the bedroom alone. Paul was brethren; one of theirs. She got as far as the doorway before Draakar turned and used his larger frame to block her view. The solid immovable wall of his silk clad chest stood in her way.

"It's his wife," he said tonelessly. "She's dead. Paul's not here."

"Dead! My God! The betrayer…he did this. But…where's Paul? I don't get a sense of him. I thought he was the one dead in the room."

"No, he's not dead, at least not yet. He has been taken. The betrayer knows he is awakened brethren. It is as I have feared. He will try to use Paul to enter the circle of power."

"Why would he need Paul to do that?"

"Because the wards surrounding the Stones bar the betrayer."

"I don't understand."

"No time to explain. We must get back to the castle. I

already turned Ian and James back. They'll meet us at the castle."

"What do we do about Paul's wife? And Paul? Don't we have to notify the authorities?"

"I will take care of her before we leave. I'll clean things up too, and have someone find her who can summon the authorities. Then we have to get back. I will need to be within the circle of power to try to locate Paul. I can barely feel my link to him, just enough to know he's alive, but not enough to find him. The energy signature of his life force is being blocked."

Maya squeezed Draakar's hands, and he closed his eyes. The surrounding air crackled as power surfaced within him. He stepped away from the door for Maya to look into the room. Cindy lay in bed, seemingly asleep, but Maya's enhanced senses screamed otherwise.

"How...What?" she stuttered, unsure what she expected but not this serene scene before her. Given the violence she'd first sensed, Draakar must have made some changes.

"I had to clean things up so there will be fewer questions. It will appear as if she died of natural causes."

"Twenty-something year olds do not die of natural causes."

"No one will question this."

This time Draakar didn't offer Maya his hand. He took hers and returned them to the castle. The brethren already waited for them in the center of the Circle of Stones.

WE DON'T HAVE much time. Please join hands and form a circle around Maya and me.

Draakar watched as each of his brethren unconsciously stood with their backs to the etchings of dragons on the Stones, matching their color.

Maya, take both of my hands.

She did and placed her forehead on his chest. The Stones around them hummed and glowed. The light in the cavern grew so bright everyone had to close their eyes, but all could still see with their dragon's inner eye what happened in the cavern. A wide spectrum of colored lights emitted from the Stones throughout the cavern. At least one of the lights pierced all the brethren within the circle, crisscrossing through the two at the center, Maya and Draakar, sending all of the light through them. Then abruptly, the lights withdrew, and the Stones went silent and dark.

For a moment, the only sounds were inhaling or exhaling of air, and then both human and dragon sight were gone. The Stones began to glow softly, once again bathing the cavern in light, and their sight returned. Everyone released their joined hands, but he didn't let Maya go.

He's dead, Maya said, raising her head and looking at Draakar.

No, was Sherri's mental cry. *I...I can still sense him.*

Draakar inclined his head to Sherri. *You are correct, he is not dead yet, but his life energy is very weak. When the betrayer could not breach the barrier using Paul, he tried to kill him. If we don't find him soon, he will die.*

Why? Sherri asked. *I don't understand why try to kill him? Why kill his wife?* "It served no purpose," she finished out loud.

"That is what the betrayer does," Draakar said. "He causes fear and confusion. The only thing he cares for is power and control. The Stones are a conduit for immense power. If he were able to control the Stones, he would be unstoppable. My father used the circle's power to create the wards surrounding the Stones. He wanted to prevent the silver dragon's entry. However, the betrayer will not stop trying to find a way past the wards."

Then he must be stopped, Dark One. We must stop him.

I couldn't agree with you more, Maya. First, we find Paul, and then we will find the betrayer. The Stones, unfortunately, are not being helpful in locating either, so we are on our own.

"If he tried to breach the wards, he must have left Paul somewhere on the mountain," Maya said. "Maybe he's also near."

"That's true. Paul isn't far, but his life energy is weak and I can't get a specific location on him from here," Draakar said. "The energy emitting from the wards interferes with Paul's."

"Well, if Paul is somewhere nearby, I can help find him," James spoke up. "I grew up in these mountains."

"Okay," Draakar said. "Since the Stones won't reveal his exact location to us, let's track him the old-fashioned way. James, you and I will go back to the inn and we'll see if I can pick up a trace of Paul or the silver dragon from there."

"What about his wife?" Sherri inquired. "Shouldn't we call the police?"

"It has been taken care of," Draakar stated.

"While you all are trying to track him from the inn," Maya said, "the rest of us can search the area around here."

"Don't go beyond the wards. The betrayer would not have been able to come any farther than the outer edge of the wards, so stay within its perimeter. Go in groups of three. Even together, you still do not have enough experience and don't control enough magicks to confront a silver dragon. If you see anything, call to me."

By your command, Dark Lord, Ian said.

"Maya will lead one group; Sherri and Robert go with her. Ian will lead the second group; Cass and Darryl go with him. You all have a balance of power sufficient to hold off the betrayer, at least long enough for me to get to you."

"What should we do if we find Paul?" Maya asked.

"Call me and I will come to you. Do not touch him or approach him. It could be a trap."

"What about if we find the betrayer?" Ian asked.

"Join hands and form a protective circle with your shields and call to me. I will come. Do not attempt to confront him."

Be safe, Draakar sent to his brethren. *One last thing: protect Maya first.*

No one has to protect me, Dark One. I protect myself.

DRAAKAR NEVER BOTHERED TO RESPOND. He and James were gone. Maya sighed and turned to the other brethren. "Let's go."

She led the way out of the castle, and they walked together to the wrought iron gate at the end of the driveway. Once away from the castle, the air grew cooler. The sun, at least, shone. Suddenly, clouds moved in to cover the sunlight, and the day became overcast and colder. Everyone changed earlier, but they all stopped a moment to add jackets to their bodies. Even though they could regulate their body temperature and air around them to some degree, old habits died hard. Maya grinned when she noticed the colors they favored were also their dragons' colors.

"Let's go about a half mile from here," Maya began. "That should be the very edge of the wards, but still within its protection. From there, we might be able to see or sense something along the perimeter."

"How do you know we'll still be within the perimeter?" Cass asked.

Maya turned to her. "I can sense it."

"She's right," Ian added. "So can I. We'll go this way." Ian gestured toward the left. "And you guys can take the other direction."

"How will we know if either group finds anything?" Sherri asked.

"We call Draakar and send to each other," Maya responded.

The groups separated and after they had been walking for a while, Maya's senses became more attuned to the surrounding environment. The unnatural lack of sound caught her attention first. There were no animals or insects anywhere near them; not even a bird flew overhead. Even the trees made no sound or motion as the wind passed through their leaves. Yet she could feel a slight breeze against her face and could sense a current in the air. No doubt the ward surrounding and protecting the Circle of Stones.

Without warning, she felt a break in the currents up ahead. It signaled the end of the wards, but not the enchantment barring the mountain from the innocent, causing those wandering too close to turn away. Though something lay at the edge of the wards. Something the enchantment did not work on. Something seemingly familiar to her, yet it was not Paul.

"I think I sense something just up ahead," Sherri said, voicing Maya's thoughts first.

"I feel it, too," Maya said.

"Do you think we should call Lord Draakar?" Robert asked.

"Not quite yet," Maya replied. "As long as we stay within the perimeter of the wards... Let's try to get a little closer to see what we've got."

They made their way through a cluster of trees to arrive in a small rocky clearing. Sitting on the ground with his blond head bowed to his chest and his back resting against a large boulder, appeared to be a sleeping Paul. Remembering Draakar's instructions, the group didn't try to approach him.

"Paul." Sherri called to him from their vantage point several feet away, then sent, *Are you all right?*

He gave no indication he heard her. "I think we should call to Draakar, now," Maya stated and opened up her link to him. The moment Maya stepped into the clearing, she knew not only had she been sensing Paul earlier, but she had picked up an echo of something else. Some kind of energy source with a familiar feel to it.

Someone she knew? How could she know the betrayer? Maya shook her head. Impossible. She had not been alive when the brethren were betrayed. *Ah, but I didn't have to be*, she thought. *It's probably just an ancestral memory.*

CHAPTER SIXTEEN

*L*ocal law enforcement and emergency personal swarmed around the inn. Draakar and James stood in the lobby and saw an investigator approach the owners. Draakar made his way to the investigator and spoke to him. He wanted to make sure Paul would not be a suspect or subjected to questioning. He placed memories in the investigators minds. They had already notified Paul, and he suffered a nervous breakdown upon hearing of his wife's death. He would remain at Akgon castle, a guest of Lord Draakar and available if needed. There would be no need.

Head bowed in respect, Draakar watched Paul's wife's body taken out on a gurney. The body would remain at the morgue until Paul contacted the coroner. Her death would be attributed to natural causes.

Unobserved by anyone, Draakar and James went up the stairs and entered Paul's room. A residue remained of both the betrayer's and Paul's essence. They followed it as far as the road, but couldn't track them once outside.

"I don't get a sense of either one of them," James said.

Draakar called on the Stones to reinforce his powers.

With their assistance, he had no trouble following the tracks of chaotic magicks left by the betrayer.

"I don't sense Paul but I have the betrayer's scent now," Draakar said as he and James, moving swiftly, followed the trail up the mountain. *It almost certainly never occurred to him to hide his passing more,* Draakar sent to James. *He had every reason to believe he was the last aware brethren left until he found Paul, an awakened dragon. He's probably trying to use Paul's magicks to enhance his own and break through the wards around the Stones.*

Ah, James sent back, *the Stones barred him from the circle. Unworthy.*

Yes, if the Stones did not want him in the circle, no power on earth could get him in. My father bound the wards with the will of the Stones. But the betrayer, whether he knows that or not, would still ignore the ban against him and continue to try.

They arrived at the clearing just as Maya sent out her call.
I am here, my Lady.

Three heads swung around. Behind them, at the edge of the forest, stood Draakar and James. Draakar approached the body on the ground. "Stay back." He crouched down beside him, stretching his arms over Paul, but did not touch him. Fingers spread wide, he passed his hands back and forth over Paul's body. His audience watched green light shine from his palms over Paul. Draakar felt the presence of Ian and the other brethren as they approached the area. After a brief time, Draakar lowered his arms and gathered Paul into them. With a slight flexing of his jean clad thighs, he stood in one fluid movement, cradling Paul's only slightly smaller frame as though he were a child.

"Will he be all right?" Sherri asked, coming nearer.

"Yes. He needs rest now. Go back to the castle. I will take him to his room and join you soon."

"What happened to him?" Sherri asked.

"The betrayer tried to steal his energy."

As the last syllable left his mouth, Draakar disappeared from the clearing with his burden.

THE REMAINING brethren turned to make their way back toward the castle, but Maya, coming up the rear, felt a tingle crawling up her spine—not a pleasant sensation. They were being watched. She whipped around and glared at the very edge of the wards, expanding her dragon senses. There seemed to be something there, a shadow where there shouldn't be one. Instinctively, she took a step in that direction. Then the sun, as suddenly as it had disappeared behind clouds earlier, burst forth, momentarily blinding her. When Maya again focused her eyes, the shadow had disappeared. She continued to stare at the spot. This time, a chill invaded her bones.

IAN GLANCED BACK. Maya no longer walked with them, so he stopped and turned around. She stood several feet behind them.

What is it, my Lady? Is something wrong?

They all stopped and turned to Maya.

I'm not sure. For a moment I thought I saw a shadow, but it's gone now. Don't worry about it. Come on, let's get back to the castle.

The brethren waited until she walked between them, and they formed a protective circle around her. Ian relayed what Maya sensed to Draakar and his strident command came back to them all, except for Maya, loud and clear.

Protect your queen!

They made their way back to the castle without incident. Completely unaware of the menace following them with shining silver eyes until they were out of his sight.

THE FORM HIDDEN in shadows watched from beyond the wards, silently raging. Everything had gone wrong. He couldn't breach the barrier, and the awakened one had gotten away from him.

The awakened still lived because he had been distracted. The ripple of power coming from the direction of the inn, a power with a signature that should not be there, made him hesitate. A Dark Lord. The knowledge caused the intruder momentarily to release his hold on the one the others called Paul. With a strength this Paul should not have possessed, the fool had lunged through the barrier where Arwan could not follow. Known by many other names over the decades, Arwan remained his true name, and this name suited him best. In the old tongue, it meant God of death. Soon, they would all learn to fear his name.

He'd returned to the inn in search of the power source and followed the trail back here. A Dark Lord on earth? The silver dragon raged. This should not have been yet somehow had come to be. As impossible as it seemed, he'd felt him. Then again, Arwan reconsidered, the Dark Lord would probably think it impossible for him to still exist as well. Yet, he did.

Only this time, they would not deny him what should have been his all along. All of this paled to the fury rolling inside him, knowing the Dragon Lord could do what he could not—call the blood and awaken the dragon within. He had seen more than one awakened with his own eyes. Arwan had tried, but he never could call forth the dragon in others. He could not awaken the dormant magicks. He could only bind some of the weaker minded with a little brethren blood to him, although one mind showed great potential.

Most of all, his fury centered around the fact *this* Dragon Lord awakened Maya. *His Dam!* He'd found her first! With her, he'd be able to call forth the dragon brethren. How dare the bastard get in his way! The Dragon Lord could be only one person, his weak brother's whelp. All use of power carried a signature, part of the essence of the brethren wielding it. A dark dragon's power being the most distinctive of all. It could only be Draakar.

Well, Maya belonged to Arwan. He had searched for her for hundreds of years from the time he first sensed her being, always getting closer to finding her. He had been aware each time she came into the world and each time she left it. But he could never find her at the right moment of her existence. This time, his timing had been perfect. Over the last couple of years, he'd carefully cultivated their relationship, and he'd planned to make her his mate. She was meant for him. He just needed a little more time to convince her to come to him willingly. For with her powers fueling his, no one would be able to stop him. Not even the Dark Dragon Lord.

Unfortunately, as long as she remained within the protection of the wards, he couldn't have her. He had to get Maya away from there. The Circle of Stones did not represent the only conduit of power, and Arwan had spent ages finding and collecting other sources. Though none were as powerful as the Stones. Still, with a little help from the humans, he commanded they should enhance his powers enough to defeat the Dragon Lord. He just needed to lure Maya back to a place he could control. Where he held more power than the whelp. He knew just how to get her away from Draakar.

After Arwan arrived at the airport, he took out his phone to call one of the men who, over the years, had helped him successfully get rid of any obstacle standing in his way. A favorite, because this man appeared different from the others he'd used in the past to do his bidding. Luck had nothing to do with finding this particular man while hunting for Maya. He didn't believe in luck. He made his own.

A few years ago, he'd been drawn into a bar he had never been to before. When he entered the place, psychic energy in the air had the fine hairs on his skin standing at attention. It was not the *Dam* he searched for, but something not unlike the life energy brethren emitted, just different, weaker. Instinct told him the source of the life force emanated from the brown-skinned man who sat by himself at the end of the bar. It took less than a second for Arwan to know before him stood a human of brethren origins. The first Arwan had encountered in hundreds of years who recognized his power and accepted him as master without mind manipulation.

A week after meeting this man, he had found Maya. His Fate, and at long last, his time, his destiny, were at hand, and nothing was going to stop him from taking his rightful place as Dragon Lord of all humankind.

When the person Arwan called picked up, he didn't bother with a greeting. No need. Isaiah Turner knew only one person called on this line. "I want you to do something for me that will require a light touch."

Isaiah's background served Arwan well. After spent years mastering the dark rhythms of the streets and preying on others, the brief time Isaiah spent in prison hadn't changed his talents. Isaiah had proven his cunning to Arwan many times in the past. Isaiah also feared no man, except him. Arwan knew Isaiah wasn't really sure if his employer was human, nor did he care.

"I'm listening."

THE DARK LORD stood over a spot just beyond the wards. Stooping down, he touched the soil. He picked up a little bit of dirt and rolled it between his thumb and forefinger. His pupils dilated and his nostrils flared, emitting a small amount of red smoke. *You stood here, betrayer, and watched us. You masked yourself well, but I have your scent now, and it will only be a matter of time before I find you and finish this once and for all.*

CHAPTER SEVENTEEN

"*H*ow's he doing?" Sherri asked as she stepped into the spacious room decorated in shades of bronze and tans set aside for Paul. Maya understood what she asked, but to her ears it sounded like 'ows e dooeng.' She found Sherri's accent delightful.

"He hasn't moved," Maya replied as she sat on an antique chair at Paul's bedside. He still lay flat on his back, his eyes closed. The same way Draakar left him.

"Why don't you go get something to eat?" Sherri suggested. "Take a break. I'll sit with him."

Maya glanced from Sherri to Paul. She nodded her head. "I've already had something, thank you, but I will take a break. Have you eaten?"

"I'm not very hungry. If I need anything, I can always think it up," Sherri said with a brief smile.

Maya vacated the chair she sat in, and acting on impulse as Sherri passed by, she hugged her. Before she released her, she whispered, *He's alive and with life, there is always hope.*

Sherri turned quickly and stared at her. Saying nothing, she sat in the empty chair. Maya paused at the opened door and glanced back over her shoulder, watching as Sherri pulled the chair closer to the bed and took Paul's hand. A faint glow surrounded their joined hands, and Paul moved. He didn't regain consciousness, but rolled onto his side to face Sherri and curled his knees up to his chest. Maya slowly closed the door on the pair, quietly backing away.

"Is he resting?" a deep voice asked behind her.

Startled, Maya whirled around, her arm making contact with a hard, muscular chest. She didn't give herself time to think. Resting her face against Draakar's chest, she wrapped her arms around his waist, needing to feel the strength, the power, she would find in his arms. Just this once. That's all she would allow herself.

She shivered from the contact. *Hold me. I just need you to hold me right now.*

All you need do is ask. His arms enveloped her, and warmth and comfort flooded her system.

DRAAKAR PLACED his chin on top of her head, knowing contentment with his mate. He breathed a sigh of relief. At last, he held her in his arms. Where she belonged.

Determined not to let this moment pass them by, he transferred them to his sitting room. He had no idea how long they stood there holding on to each other. Whatever she needed, he would provide, even if he had to stand there for an eternity. Much too soon, she pulled away from him, but she didn't go far, just removed her hands from around him. Slowly, reluctantly, he released her and let his hands fall to his sides. Still, she didn't step back. They were making progress.

"Are you all right?" he murmured.

She looked around. He could tell by her expression she'd just noticed they were no longer in the hallway, but in his sitting room. She made no effort to leave. Again, progress.

"I'm not sure," she said, wrapping her arms around her body as though bereft of his touch. "I can maybe understand why the betrayer would hurt Paul, but why kill his wife? She had no power and couldn't help him in any way."

"He thrives off the negative energy of others, Maya. Killing, instilling fear, and destroying others is the way he gains satisfaction and power over others. With him, it's all about control."

"I guess if he'd kill his own people, his own brother, he'd have no problem killing an innocent."

"That's not all that's bothering you though…is it?"

"No. I sensed something earlier. I…I think I even saw something out there on the mountain. It looked like some kind of a shadow, but it seemed to have a tangible presence. The essence of it somehow felt familiar to me." She shook her head. "That doesn't really seem right."

He shrugged. "The betrayer may have cloaked himself from your eyes, but you were able to sense him because of an ancestral memory of his presence. That may be why he seemed familiar to you."

Maya's sigh seemed one of relief. "That's what I thought. It was just a memory. It was just such a strange feeling." She looked around again and stepped away from him. "Ah, Paul's still unconscious, but he seems a little better," she continued, and he read her nervousness. "I…left Sherri with him and he had rolled to his side by the time I left."

The way she moved away from him and her eyes wondered the room to anywhere but on him, told him she was aware of his nearness as he of hers. "If he's got movement back, that's good. He should be waking soon."

"What did the betrayer do to him?"

"He tried to steal his powers, possibly by trying to drain his magicks and taking it into himself."

"My God! Can he do that?"

"He has tried before, but I have no memory of it working. While he can drain magick, as far as I know, he has not been able to absorb what he's drained, at least not for any length of time. If enough of our magicks is drained, the brethren is most likely to die. Paul, somehow, must have been able to get away from him long enough to cross over the wards. The power there the only thing capable of saving him. I had to draw a little of earth's magicks into Paul to restore his energy balance until he can heal himself. To do that, both his body as well as his mind need to rest. He's suffered twice fold. He had to watch his wife killed, helpless to stop it."

"Oh no, poor Paul! His wife seemed like a nice person. She didn't deserve this, neither does Paul."

"No one does. I'll check on Paul soon."

"Ah, you don't need to actually go and see him to do that, do you?"

"No, but I was. Is there some reason why I shouldn't?"

"Sherri's with him, and I don't think they should be disturbed. Give them a little while."

"Why?"

"Well, for one thing, Paul moved for the first time after Sherri touched him, and when she did, her hand on his glowed."

"I see. Do you have any idea what that could mean?"

"I'm not sure, but watching her with him, I just get the feeling there may be some feelings involved; at least on her part. Could they be a pair?"

"Maybe, or Sherri could be a healer. If so, the glow you saw may have just been the use of her healing power. She does radiate an aura of natural empathy. It has been a long time since the brethren had a healer other than myself, and my abilities would be nowhere near a natural empath. They were the first ones destroyed during the purges. We don't know why. We'll just have to wait and see how strong Sherri is."

"Okay."

"But for both their sakes," he continued, "I hope they are not a pair. Paul's suffered a shock, and it will be some time before he will be able to look beyond his grief. As a result, his powers will be greatly lessened, and if he rejects Sherri, hers will be as well."

Draakar did not tell Maya he could read Paul's emotions. Even unconscious, Paul suffered with guilt because he'd been unable to save his wife. Draakar could hear the echo of her screams in Paul's mind, and they gave him chills. He could only imagine what Paul must have felt to watch his wife tortured and murdered before his eyes.

"If they are a pair, I hope he turns to her," Maya said. "Why would he reject her?"

"Sometimes loss can affect people in destructive ways," Draakar responded. "He will blame himself for what happened. We'll keep an eye on him. He just needs time to heal physically and mentally. While his body will be fine in a day or two, I'm afraid his emotional health may take longer to recover."

I know what it's like to lose someone you love.

He picked up her surface thought, and for a moment, the echo of her pain sliced through his own heart. "Yes, your grandmother. She died recently. I'm sorry I never had a chance to meet her, but if you'd let me, I can get to know her through you. I know how much you loved and miss her."

"She would have liked you," she said while smiling, and cocked her head to examine him. "She always had a thing for handsome men."

Draakar grinned, standing straighter. "So you think I'm handsome?"

Maya snorted. "You've got a mirror. Just don't let it go to your head. I'm not." She took a step toward him and the tips of her fingers gently touched his arm. "Wait...something just occurred to me. If I'm brethren, then one or both of my parents are brethren. Does that mean my grandmother could have been brethren?"

It took Draakar a moment to answer her question, mesmerized by her unconscious touch of his arm. Unconscious or not, the gesture still sent a charge up his arm, raising the fine hairs all over his body. She must have sensed his response to her, probably because he could feel a soft glow emanating from his eyes. She quickly removed her hand. He took a deep breath to calm his racing blood and forced his mind to slow down and answer her query.

"That's more than likely true. For you to have the powers you do, my guess is both of your parents are brethren, possibly even truemates. I cannot say for certain if your grandmother was brethren, though." Draakar moved farther into the room and sat down in one of the two matching chairs, inviting Maya with a casual flick of his wrist to sit in the other. "Tell me about your grandmother. Nana, right? Let me get to know her through your eyes. Let me get to know you."

CHAPTER EIGHTEEN

A fair request and Maya read sincerity in his words. Yet, even sitting, Draakar dominated the room, enveloping her within his spell. "I don't think that would be such a good idea," Maya decided.

"What? Getting to know you better? I don't want to read your memories. I want you to tell me of them."

Maya allowed her body to relax. That was the last thing she wanted, him in her head anymore than he already resided there. "All right." She sat in the chair next to Draakar and curled her feet up against her side. A wine decanter and two glasses half-full of red wine appeared on the table between the chairs. He picked up a glass and offered it to her.

"Thank you," she said, and took a sip of the rich burgundy, then began to talk. She talked about her family and about her grandmother. Then he told her about life on Akgon, and showed her what it looked like by opening his mind to her.

"Oh, wow!" she exclaimed. "Purple and blue sky. Why, this is beautiful! I love it! Except for the twin suns, it's not much different from earth."

"Days are slightly longer there." Draakar smiled as he spoke. "But the nights are filled with colorful shooting stars streaking across the skies." The very vivid picture he placed in her mind took her breath away. The stars, of course, were dragons in flight, surrounded by their auras.

"It does seem a lot like earth. Maybe because the trees and landscapes look very similar to ones here on my planet."

"Some of them are very similar. We have something that's very close to pears. The trees look the same, as does the shape, but instead of a yellowish color they're more of a royal blue color. The taste is the same, though."

"It also looks like your world has an abundance of water-falls." Maya could grow to love it there. Wait, where did that thought come from? She could never go there, not even for a brief visit. Going there would mean leaving her family and friends, everything she knew. Going there would mean accepting Draakar and responsibility for the brethren. No, she couldn't do it.

She leaned forward and placed her empty glass on the table next to the empty bottle. Had they really just drunk an entire bottle of wine? Not something she did often. Then again, since she'd met Draakar, she had ventured way past her comfort zone. Beyond any known zone.

"I think I'll turn in now." She got up and stretched, raising her hand to her mouth to cover a yawn. "What will we do about the betrayer?"

"Tomorrow I will try to find his trail again, but for tonight...are you sure you want to leave?" Draakar looked at Maya over the rim of his wineglass with hooded eyes.

He seemed relaxed and poised, but hooded eyes or not, she felt his constant desire for her. It vibrated off her own. "I think I better," she said, turning away from him.

She made it as far as the door.

Just before her hand touched the doorknob, two cloth-covered arms appeared over her shoulders and large, long-fingered hands pressed flat against the door. If she leaned back a hair, she would touch him. Hell, she could already feel him. He didn't have to physically touch her. Her body vibrated with awareness of his. Every pore opened wide, infusing his scent into her body; every hair reached, straining to brush against his flesh. He bent his head forward and his ebony tresses cascaded over her shoulders and onto her chest, forming a shroud around them. Every cell in her body came to full attention in anticipation of his caress.

She raised her head to rub the side of her face against his smooth skin. The friction caused both their bodies to give off a soft glow. He withdrew his hands from the door and gently clasped her shoulders. His mouth hovered near her ear, and she turned her head to bring him nearer so she could feel his lips against her skin. The pressure of his hands on her increased, silently encouraging her on. She needed to touch him like this, to know his taste, his kiss and assuage this burning curiosity.

Just once.

Her words came out as a harsh breath against his lips. "Once is all I need, just this once."

I am always yours to command.

Nothing about their kiss seemed slow, gentle, or innocent. Their mouths didn't touch, they fused, and the glow surrounding them grew brighter. Hotter. Catching both in an inferno of need.

Draakar brought one hand up to cup her face. The other he wrapped around her waist and pulled her against his body until she had knowledge of every hard ridge of him. She shifted closer, wanting more as her heart raced to catch up with the demand of the blood, pumping through her veins because of his touch.

He moved his mouth to her cheek, neck, anywhere, and

everywhere he could touch. He couldn't seem to devour enough of her. One of the fingers he splayed on her face ended up in her mouth. Maya swirled her tongue around it as she began to rub her body against the hard planes of his. The entire room looked as though bathed in a bright golden bronze light.

I will die where I stand if I cannot get inside you now.

His thought mirrored her own. The shrill ring of an old-fashioned phone eventually permeated the sounds of their labored breathing. Suddenly, infecting the fantasy he'd woven between them.

"What in all the hells is that?" Draakar snarled.

Gasping for breath, Maya struggled out, "Ah, my...my cell phone. I've got to answer it." Shaking her head, her brain began to function again. "That's my special ring for calls from home. My parents only use it if...if it's important."

"What could be...?" Draakar began.

Maya let him see the memory of the last time she'd heard this particular ring. Her mother used it to tell her about her grandmother. He kept quiet, but kept his arms loosely wrapped around her waist. Enclosing her in a different kind of warmth, letting her know whether good or bad happening in her life, he remained here for her. *You are not alone.*

Maya shifted so she could take her phone out of her back pocket and taking a deep breath before she answered it. Still, she stammered. "He-Hello." She paused. "Dad, Dad, I can barely hear you. What's wrong? What's going on? Ohmygodohmygod! No! I'm coming. I'm coming home." Another pause then, "Yes, yes. I'll call back with the details. I love you, Dad. Tell Mom...tell Mom, I love her and I'm coming. I'll be there as soon as I can."

The phone fell from her nerveless hand, but Draakar caught it with a look. He returned it to her belt clip. Holding her in his arms the entire time, Maya knew he listened in on the conversation from both sides. Grateful she didn't have to explain a thing, Maya looked at him. This time tracks of tears covered her face and more pooled in her eyes. She buried her face in his shoulder.

"Mom…Mom. Please God, not my mom!" Her body trembled with the force of her emotions.

"Shhh. All will be well. I have already sent Ian to get the jet ready. He will fly us to the States. I've alerted the other brethren. They will meet us at the car where your packed bags are already waiting. All we have to do is go."

She fought to stop the tears and accepted his help. *One less thing to worry about.* She raised her head and wiped her face, trying to pull herself together. "Just like my nana, Draakar," she spoke in a voice roughened by grief. "My mother was involved in a hit and run just like Nana. What is wrong with this world?"

"She is alive, Maya, and she will remain that way until I can get there to make sure of it. I had Ian call in a skilled human doctor with a little brethren blood to oversee your mother's care. I also asked Mother Earth to help maintain her life energy, which she can do. Now, I just need to get us there."

Evening settled on the mountain, and Maya clung to him as they walked down the castle steps. Four of their brethren waited for them beside the limo. Robert opened the door for them and Draakar followed behind her. Darryl and Robert climbed in behind them. James shut the door and got behind the wheel. Cass sat up front to keep him company.

Maya found herself burrowed under Draakar's arm, but she raised her head to look at their companions. *You all don't have to do this. Please, you don't have to come with us. Stay and finish practicing your magicks.*

Cass turned around to face her. *We go where you go, my Lady,* Cass sent, expressing her sympathy and resolve in that one look. Maya nodded in silent acknowledgement. She and Cass had made peace of sorts between them.

We can practice anywhere, James sent, interrupting Maya and Cass' visual communication. *Besides, you might need us.*

"What about Paul?" Maya asked aloud to no one in particular. "He will need looking after for a couple of days."

"Sherri is staying with him," Draakar said. "They will both be safe here. As soon as Paul is able to travel, they will join us."

"Won't they need to remain here?" Maya asked. "What about the betrayer? I can't let what is happening to me stop the rest of you from looking for him."

"He is not an immediate danger," Draakar replied. *Yes, we need to find him, but you are more important.*

Maya turned to give him a sad smile when she caught his thought.

"His scent is no longer in the area," Draakar said aloud. "He knows he can't get past the wards on his own. Right now, your need comes first. Besides, my instincts are telling me he will follow us in the hopes we can somehow provide him with the means of entry to the Stones." Draakar paused before continuing. "I hope he follows us," he growled. "I want this over with, so we will travel to the United States. In any case, I suspect Talon is there."

"We're stronger together anyway," Darryl said. "So we stick together."

"Thank you. All of you," Maya said and looked at Draakar again. She could sense his fear—he thought he would not return to Akgon in time—and also his need to stop the spread of evil on earth. Yet he remained with her. *Thank you.*

We take care of our own. I told you, you will never be alone again. I will always stand by you. My Lady.

Draakar didn't say it as a title, but as something more intimate and personal to him, and Maya accepted it as such.

She laid her head on his shoulder and closed her eyes, trusting him to get her to her mother's side and to keep her alive. More importantly, she began to trust him with herself. The feel of a firefly's kiss on her forehead woke her up from an all too brief dreamless sleep. The moment she opened her eyes, the worry and fear rushed back in.

"We're here."

The words vibrated through her. Maya's head rested on a chest that should not have been comfortable to lie upon, but it was. Reluctantly, she pushed her body off Draakar and looked around the empty car. They were parked on the tarmac near an airplane with a Celtic design of a black dragon painted on its tail. It could only belong to Draakar.

"Our things have already been loaded and everyone has just boarded. They're only waiting for us. Are you ready?"

"Yes, yes," she said, brushing her hair away from her face. "Ah, what about customs?" He gave her a direct stare and raised one dark, empirical eyebrow. "Yeah. Right. Forgot about that mind thing."

He touched her hand, and she froze, turning her gaze back to his. In what seemed like slow motion, he lowered his lips to meet hers as she raised them to his. This kiss, while not as all consuming as their first one, in some ways packed even more heat because of its gentleness, its awareness. A promise. Something shifted inside her. Unsure what, she pulled away from him.

"We'd better go."

I am here, Maya, always.

I know. I am starting to believe it.

He stepped out of the limo first and then helped her out. They did not have far to walk together to get to the stairs of the airplane. Once onboard, they found Ian in the cockpit and, to Maya's surprise, Draakar took the empty seat next to him.

He could read the question as it formed, so answered before she could verbalize it. "Yes, I am going to sit with you, but I need to watch Ian's takeoff. I have the knowledge to fly this thing, but I wanted to see how it's done firsthand. Once we're in the air, I'll relinquish my seat to Darryl. He wants to learn to fly, too. This is the closest he'll come while on earth. After we're stable, I'll come and sit with you. Unless you'd prefer I sit with you during takeoff? I'd let you sit up here, but as you can see, there is only room for two. Next time I'll get a bigger plane."

"No, that's okay. I'm fine." She managed a smile. Such a guy thing learning to fly, but come to think of it, she wouldn't mind learning either, but not today. "You go on and help fly the plane. Just get me home in one piece. That's all I ask."

He smiled and stood. "Come on, I'll walk you to your seat and buckle you in."

Taking her elbow, he guided her to her seat. The plane had all the comforts of a commercial airline. While not as large as the one she crossed the Atlantic on, it was not exactly small either. Twenty spacious leather seats filled the aisle with enough legroom for a seven-foot man to stretch out. From the way Cass laid on hers, they reclined to a comfortable lying position, too. Two people could walk side-by-side down the aisle, and the rear held a bar with a kitchen. Draakar gave her a quick kiss and had turned to leave when she stopped him with a mere touch on his arm.

"I just remembered. I left my purse with my passport back at the castle."

"No, you didn't. Look under the seat."

She leaned over, placing her hand under her seat. She felt a familiar shaped bag. "My purse!" she exclaimed. "I should have known."

He inclined his head. "You are welcome. Now sit back and

try to relax. I will be back to join you once this thing is in the air."

Draakar returned after a while. Even though the take off and rise to the necessary altitude seemed flawless, Maya's nerves stood on edge and she found herself glad for his company. She hadn't realized she wanted company until he sat beside her and took her hand. Even though the others sat a few feet behind her and if she wanted companionship, all she had to do was join them. Really, she wanted *his* company.

"Is this the first time you've flown?" she asked.

Draakar grinned. "No, of course not."

"You know what I mean."

"It is not the first time I've flown. However, it is the first time I have been flown."

Maya smiled, enjoying his sense of humor. "This must be strange for you, having to rely on a machine to fly."

"Yes, it is a little strange, but exciting. I promise, though, it would be even more exciting to be able to show you how to fly, to cut through the wind with you at my side."

For the first time since she got the phone call, Maya allowed herself to relax. "I don't think that would be such a good idea."

"Why not?"

"I won't want to be mistaken for a UFO."

"Ah," Draakar replied straight-faced. "Not a problem. I can cloak us."

"Cloak us?" She frowned. "As in, make us invisible?"

"In a manner of speaking, yes. You might be able to do that as well."

"I would like that."

"I will show you how after your mother is well. Why don't you try to get some rest? Even though we're flying faster than this plane normally can, it will still be some time before we reach Dulles Airport."

"What about fuel? Does this plane hold enough to get us there, or will we have to stop and refuel?"

"That's not a problem either for us."

"Yeah. I guess I have to restructure my entire way of thinking, my expectations of how of things worked before I was aware of magicks, and my expectations with the use of it."

"It is as natural to you as breathing. Your brain merely has to let your instincts take over and you will be fine."

"Promise me something."

Without hesitation, he said, "Anything."

"Be careful what you promise me, Draakar. Promise you can make her well." She read his thoughts; he understood she referred to her mother and what she expected him to be able to do.

I will not disappoint you. "As long as she is alive when I get there, I can keep her well," he spoke aloud. "Now get some rest."

"I don't think I can sleep. I've got so much on my mind."

"I know, but your mind and your body need the rest. These seats go pretty far back." He touched the button, angling both of their seats into recliners, and raised the armrest between them. Removing the barriers, he placed his arm around her and drew her against his side. "Put your head on my shoulder."

For once, Maya did as he asked and promptly fell asleep, wrapped in his arms.

Is she sleeping? James sent to Draakar.

Yes. I think I'll let her sleep until we land.

That's probably a good idea. Um, I've been thinking. I'm a bit of a gambling man, and I'm thinking it would be pretty high odds there would be two hit and run accidents in the same family. Maya told us on the hike her grandmother was killed in a hit and run. Even for Americans, that's a tad much for both grandmother and mother.

Draakar smiled, but a cold one he knew did not reach his eyes. *Yes, the thought had occurred to me, but I think Maya believes it to be just a coincidence. With a silver dragon loose in the world, I am reserving judgment, and until I learn otherwise, I will not say anything to Maya.*

Then neither will I.

Get some rest. I am afraid that we will all need it.

CHAPTER NINETEEN

*E*arly on a cold March morning, the little girl stood dry-eyed beside the open ground. She stopped watching the oak-colored coffin the moment it lowered into the hole. A man's pale, large hand held her small tan one and on the other side, a woman's soft dainty hand enclosed her other. She looked up at them both. She'd already said her goodbyes to her mother the day before. This small ceremony was a mere formality. Her mother died telling her how much she loved her, and how much her father and his wife loved her already. These people would be her parents now, her family. They were the only ones at the graveside.

"Daddy," the child said in her soft little girl voice.

The child watched tears puddle in the corner of his eyes because she'd called him Daddy.

"Yes, angel?"

"I think we should leave now. Mommy's gone to heaven to be with the real angels."

A little over six feet tall and built like a wrestler, Arthur dropped to his hunches and hugged his daughter, who barely reached his waist. "Yes, angel, she's your angel now and will always be watching over you."

The child briefly returned his hug before pulling back. "I know, but can we go now?" the child asked again, a little more anxiously this time.

"Yes, Arthur," his wife said, giving the child's hand a brief squeeze in support. "I think it's time to go. The bags are already in the car; everything is taken care of. We can head straight to the airport from here."

Arthur stood up and gathered his small family to him. He looked into the grave, holding his last ties to America, to his youthful self. Silently, he said goodbye to the woman he had once loved and who had given him their precious child. He turned with one arm around each of the women in his life and said, "Let's go home."

Their rental car had just driven out of sight when a black SUV with tinted windows drove through the gates of the cemetery from the opposite direction. The car drove down a windy trail until it came to the walking path leading to the freshly dug grave. There it stopped, and the driver stepped out, a man about average height with a slender yet muscular built. He wore stonewashed black jeans and a brown leather jacket cut to reach his thighs. The brown leather cap perched at an angle on the side of his head obscured his face.

Standing silently before the hole in the ground, with one red rose held loosely in a dark brown hand. He watched the grounds' people fill it with dirt. The onlooker twirled the flower once, then threw it into the grave. He had arrived a day too late. "You haven't won yet, li'l sis. Sooner or later, I'll find her." After uttering those softly spoken words, the man walked back to his car and drove off.

ALL EYES TRACKED the progress of the two women and five men as they seemed to glide through the terminal in Dulles Airport. They looked like something right out of a science fiction movie. One of them stood out from the group. He wore a black leather coat, the bottom brushing against his ankles. His extremely long hair blended with the dark coat so perfectly you couldn't tell where it ended, and the coat began. If possible, he looked even more disturbing than the others.

A stunningly beautiful woman with a rich almond complexion walked alongside him. Her hair hung in a wild mass of loose curls framing an oval face. It spread downward to nestle around her shoulders on a shape hugging, golden-bronze, floor-length leather coat. The two walked slightly ahead of the others, who seemed to flank them. Those others appeared to be more than a mere entourage. They also wore long leather jackets, but in different, interesting, and striking colors that seemed to flow as they moved through the terminal. Exactly who or what they were remained unclear, but people instinctually stepped out of their way.

Behind the group were three porters with suitcases on carts. It seemed at first the group would continue non-stop until they left the building, moving in synchronicity, headed for some unknown mission. No one would dare to hinder them, but suddenly they stopped. Everyone else went back to whatever they had been doing, pointedly ignoring the group.

A little girl between the age of ten and twelve, with hair in two thick braids hanging down her back, stood in front of a magazine rack about ten feet away from Draakar. *She* had drawn his attention. He knew what she was and suspected her connection to his son. He stood immobile in shock when he felt her probe his mind.

Greetings, Dark Lord!

The voice in his head belonged to a child, but with a lot of raw strength behind the probe. More than most adults had. When fully matured, the young lady would be very powerful. He continued to stare at the back of her head as she thumbed through her magazine, seemingly oblivious to his presence behind her.

Do you know who I am, little one? Even when he responded, she still didn't turn toward him, but continued to look through her magazine.

Yes. I think so. You're the Dark Dragon Lord. I've been dreaming about you. Sometimes it's a little confusing and weird. I think there are also others, another—one of gold.

Do not be afraid of your dreams, little one.

I'm not—sometimes they're kinda cool, even if I don't always understand them.

You will understand everything in time.

I tried explaining them to my mommy, but she said the same thing you just did. My mommy died yesterday and my daddy is taking me to live with him and my new mommy. We're going to fly on a plane. I've never been on a plane before. Will I be able to fly someday?

I am sorry about your mother. And yes, I think one day you will fly.

Is it okay to tell my daddy about my dreams?

If you want. But do not worry if he finds them confusing, too.

Maybe I'll wait until I understand them a little better.

The young girl put the magazine she read back on the rack and turned her head in the opposite direction, as if she were watching someone.

I've got to go now. That's my daddy. See ya later, Dark Lord.

Till we meet again, little one. If you ever have need of me, just call to me and I will come.

Cool!

Draakar watched as a man stopped before the little girl and took her hand. They walked away from the brethren. As they moved farther off, the child turned around and looked right at him, then turned to face forward again. Leaving Draakar feeling as though he'd taken a punch to his gut.

"What the hell?" Maya exclaimed.

They all watched the little girl skipping happily along beside her father. They had also seen the flash of silver in the child's eyes. "Yes, I know," Draakar said. "Come on, let's get in the limo."

The brethren continued moving as though nothing unusual had happened. But something had. They walked out of the airport. A black limousine sat at the curb near the exit with the rear doors standing open. The driver had already placed their luggage in the trunk. The group had barely settled in their seats before the questions began, for everyone had felt the child's probe and heard her thoughts to Draakar.

"What in both of our worlds was that?" Maya asked.

"Earth magicks at work would be my guess," Draakar responded. "I told you, when the brethren drained their magicks into the earth, both Earth magicks and human brethren were changed somehow. The brethren of Earth are now...different. It's the only thing that explains this."

"Ah, did everyone notice the lass had silver eyes?" James said, shaking his head in confusion. "How could she have silver eyes?"

"Does this mean she's a silver dragon?" Maya asked, confused. "*The* silver dragon we're looking for? But she's just a child."

"This makes no sense," Cass said.

"I believe she is a silver dragon," Draakar said, "but she is not the one we are looking for, and interestingly, she's female. A first in memory, and probably due to the influence of Earth magicks. There has never been a female silver dragon in brethren memory. Nonetheless, the one we are looking for is definitely an adult male. The girl also doesn't have the scent of corruption about her. Nor does she carry the scent the male on the mountain left behind."

"That's true," Maya replied. "I sensed none of the things I sensed about the other presence. But who is she?"

"I believe she's Talon's mate."

"*His what?*" Maya and Cass cried in unison.

"His mate. The one he came to Earth to find."

"Ah," Maya said, nodding her head. "It's making sense now. This is the 'she' Talon kept referring to."

"Wait a minute," Cass said, "she's just a little girl."

"Yes," Draakar replied, "but she's still his mate and besides, by earth standards, Talon is only a teenager."

Maya sent a mental picture of Talon to Cass, who nodded. "Ah," Cass said, "I get it now. They'll make a cute couple…in about twelve years."

"Well, where's Talon?" Maya asked. "He must be here somewhere searching for her."

"Yes, I think you're right. In fact, I'm sure he's on this side of the Atlantic."

"But…she just left," a puzzled Cass said, "and they were headed to the international section, so that means she's leaving the country."

"That's right," Draakar conceded. "No matter, I should be able to find her again now that I've established a link with her."

"Wow! What a coincidence that we'd run into her here," Ian stated.

"I don't believe in coincidence," Draakar responded. "Not for brethren. I am beginning to suspect things have been set in motion, of which I have been unaware, maybe even before Talon's arrival. Our coming here at this time is no fluke." He pushed his hair behind his ear. "Let's focus on one thing at a time. We're headed straight to the hospital. Maya, Ian, and I will stay there and the rest of you can go on to the house I own here and settle in. After I heal Maya's mother, we'll meet you there. I will communicate with the Stones and Mother Earth then and see if they can shed any light on this."

Maya's tone held surprise when she asked, "You can communicate with the Stones from here?"

"Yes, from anywhere on Terra. My power, for now, is linked to them." Most of the powers he now possessed were borrowed from Earth magicks to enhance his own. He needed his mate to be able to call forth all of his own powers. He needed Maya, and they were rapidly running out of time.

CHAPTER TWENTY

*M*aya sat next to him and silently reached over to squeeze his thigh. At least she tried to. Might as well have tried to squeeze a bowling ball. Absolutely no give existed in those muscles beneath her fingers. When she would have withdrawn her hand, Draakar placed his over hers. He kept it there for the short ride from the airport to the hospital. She didn't bother to try removing it; she knew it would be pointless. Besides, she enjoyed the sensation of her hand engulfed by his, like he held something precious to him and he would take care of her.

The early spring scenery passed, but she saw none of it as the car sped down a very quiet Fairfax County Parkway to the hospital. Her mind focused on an internal debate. Her feelings for Draakar were evolving too fast, yet not fast enough. How could that be? They had just met, yet they had always known each other. According to him, Fate decreed they belonged together and had imbedded each with an immediate recognition, if not acceptance, of the other. Because she had recognized *him*.

She didn't want to accept what her senses told her, but

could no longer deny he needed her as she needed him. She knew that in her soul. It called to his. The question remained, could she forgive him? He was here with her now when she needed him. Not a bad beginning.

They arrived at the hospital much too soon for Maya. She looked up at the innocuous-looking structure. Nothing particularly remarkable or memorable about it, yet the building chilled her down to the bone.

Her nana died in this place, and now her mother lay in intensive care. If she never had to set foot in there again, it would be too soon for her. If not for Draakar, she didn't know what she would have done.

He helped her out of the limo. Maya couldn't hide her anxiety and fear from him. He kept his arm around her waist as they entered the hospital. *We're here, Maya, and your mother is still alive.*

I know, but I'm...I'm still worried. It's like déjà vu.

She felt his kiss on the top of her head as they walked past the nurses' station in search of her mother's room. Because of Draakar, no one bothered them. A slight tingling at the base of Maya's spine told her he used some of his powers.

Yes. I am, he said to her, having read her mind. *I'm merely planting the thought that we belong here so we won't be stopped or questioned.*

Maya smiled, grateful for his presence. He found her mother's room and stopped in front of the open door. Maya stepped around him but halted. Maya saw what he did. A man sat beside the hospital bed holding the hand of the woman lying comatose on it. A woman who looked a lot like an older version of Maya. It took a minute for the gray-haired man to realize others stood there. He raised swollen red-rimmed eyes to the doorway.

"Maya, Maya. Thank you, God!" the man cried.

Her father never got the chance to do more than rise

from his chair before Maya caught him in a tight embrace. "I'm here, Daddy, I'm here," she cried in her father's arms.

In the short period of time she had been gone, her father, a big man, who at six feet always stood so straight and tall in her eyes, seemed to have shrunk into himself.

Ian, why don't you wait outside in the hall, Maya heard Draakar send.

Ian quietly backed out of the room and softly closed the door.

After they embraced for a few moments, drawing strength from the presence of each other, Maya's father raised his head. He blinked; she knew he had finally noticed Draakar. "Who's this, baby?" he asked.

She turned within the comfort of her father's arms and stared at Draakar. "I'm sorry. Where are my manners? Daddy, this is Draakar Akgon, and he can save Mom. Draakar, this is my father, Vincent Trent."

Her father looked at her, then back at Draakar. "Is he a doctor?"

It was a reasonable question, but she saw what her father did. Draakar looked like no doctor she'd ever seen, but how should she answer his question?

Tell him the truth, just maybe not all of it...not quite yet.

Grateful, she nodded her head. "Not exactly."

Draakar stepped forward to shake her father's hand. Maya felt him pause before answering. "No, I am not a doctor in the conventional sense, but I am a healer. I can save her."

"How?" her father asked. "The doctors can't seem to do anything more for her. She's slowly bleeding to death. She can't undergo any more surgeries. All they can do is fill her with pain medicine. They don't expect her to last the night," he choked out.

Maya wanted to weep at the sight of more gray in his

short-cropped hair and the additional lines around his eyes which were not there a week ago. Her parents always appeared younger than their age, but today her father looked much older than his fifty-nine years. "Dad, he can help." She looked at Draakar and in that moment she trusted him completely, not just to heal her mother, but also to heal her soul.

Draakar moved around to the other side of the bed and gazed down at her mother. Her father never took his eyes off him, but Maya sensed the moment hope infused her father's heart.

She's brethren, Maya. Draakar sent. *Can you feel it? So is your father, although he merely carries a hint of brethren in his veins. No dragon dwells within. He cannot wield magicks, but he shows great inner strength and determination. I see where you get yours from.*

Maya took her gaze off her mother to look up at Draakar, who glanced at her briefly. *Your mother, however, is dragon but it's still dormant, buried deeply. That just means she may not be able to wield much Earth magicks. She is sensitive to it, as is your father. I will have to call forth her dragon to aid in her healing. Once I awaken it, she should be whole.*

Maya nodded, silently giving him permission to do whatever he thought necessary. He wasted no more time. "Maya, take your father's hand, then place your hand in mine."

"Maya, what's going on?" her father asked.

"It will be all right, Mr. Trent. Please take your daughter's hand."

When her father still hesitated, Maya grasped his hand, then reached across her mother for Draakar with her other. He placed his palm on her mother's forehead, linking them all. A soft golden glow surrounded her mother's face, then spread until it encompassed her entire body. It probably only lasted a few seconds, but when it disappeared, both

Maya and her father blinked at its absence. However, her mother's chest rose and fell, like she had just taken a deep breath, then her head moved to the side. Her breathing no longer labored, nor were her facial features contorted in silent pain. Her entire frame relaxed and appeared more like a natural sleep.

Draakar removed his hand from her mother's forehead and released her hand, then stepped back a little. "She'll be fine now. She just needs rest for a day or two to continue to heal. She should awaken by morning." The beeping monitors seemed a more normal-sounding rhythm, further giving truth to his words.

Maya watched as her father looked over his wife at Draakar, who stood on the other side. Tears slowly rolled down her dad's age-lined face. He stuck his hand out to grasp Draakar's. "Thank you. I'm not sure who you are or what you did just now, but thank you. You saved her. She's the love of my life, and next to Maya, the most important thing in it."

Before anyone could comment, a sharp knock sounded at the door and Ian poked his head in. Draakar glanced over at Maya. *Ian warned me there was a man at the door who wouldn't go away and insists on seeing you and your parents. He claims he's your fiancé.*

What?

Draakar nodded. "Let him in now."

Justin shoved his way past Ian and stopped dead in his tracks when he saw Draakar. A pissed Maya watched as Justin's eyes kept moving anxiously between Draakar, her father, and herself. How dare he tell Ian he was her fiancé! But she couldn't take him down for the lie. She wasn't supposed to know. Still, she glared at him.

Finally, he spoke. "Maya, honey, thank God you're here," he said, stepping closer to Maya. He quickly enfolded her in an embrace, which she returned, but when he tried to kiss her mouth, she angled her head so his lips ended up on her cheek.

Funny, she used to think him a handsome man. Justin didn't look so handsome anymore. She had never really noticed the weakness to his chin and the penchant he had for avoiding prolonged eye contact. She sighed, not surprised to see him here. Ian trying to keep him out might have made him desperate. Anyone close to her parents would have been concerned about her mother. While she appreciated him being there for them, having him in the same room as Draakar make her uneasy. It felt all wrong. Justin felt wrong, and his lie stung.

Turning to her father, Justin said, "Vincent, I'm sorry I was gone so long. I had to go down the street for a decent cup of coffee." He held the coffee toward Vincent.

Maya's father took the still hot cup. "Thank you, Justin."

CHAPTER TWENTY-ONE

*A*ll this time, Draakar never said a word. He just silently watched and assessed Justin.

He saw a lean, good-looking man about thirty, a little shorter than his six-plus frame, with blunt military-style cut blond hair and eerily hazel eyes. He sensed strong emotion from the man, his need to possess Maya, and his wariness at finding another man here with her. Draakar subtly encouraged his unease; the man had every right to feel wary. Nor did Draakar forget the lie the man told to try to gain entrance. He believed it. The man displayed an unhealthy possessiveness toward Maya.

The Dark Lord also sensed something else about this Justin. He carried brethren blood, but like Maya's father, he sensed no dragon within. He blocked Draakar's mental probes so he could not read his mind. A sensitive to magick energies, and one with strong natural barriers.

Interesting.

Draakar would have to touch him to breach the barriers and read his mind, frustrated he had to do so. His powers weren't at full strength, and he had to expel some of his magicks to heal Maya's mother. So far what he could sense on the surface of the man appeared relatively harmless—concern for Maya's mother and jealousy toward Draakar. This Justin had no right to be jealous. Such a privilege, should he choose to exercise it, belonged solely to him.

"Who's this?" Justin asked, indicating Draakar with his chin. "A new doctor? And who's the guy at the door who wouldn't let me in?"

"Mr. Akgon," Vincent began.

"Draakar, please, and if I may, Vincent."

"After everything you've done, of course," Vincent readily replied. "Justin, this is Draakar Akgon, and…yes, he's a special doctor Maya brought with her."

Draakar read the doubt in Vincent's mind. Vincent's confusion, and for reasons he couldn't explain, the importance of letting Justin believe Draakar was just a doctor. Draakar knew Maya's father thought he had saved his wife. His daughter trusted him, so he would too. He would keep the man's secrets. Whatever they were. Draakar smiled to himself at Vincent's thoughts.

"And I believe he's helped her already," Vincent said aloud.

"Well, that's wonderful news," Justin said, smiling at everybody. "Mr. Akgon, how can we ever thank you?"

Maya raised her eyebrows at Justin's proprietary manner and then glanced at Draakar. He smiled at her. But when he turned that smile on Justin, it never reached his eyes.

"I'm sure Maya will find a way," Draakar said, leaving no room for argument in his tone.

Draakar could feel Justin gearing up to respond and so could Maya, because she spoke into the momentarily charged silence. "Dad, I know you've been at Mom's side all night. Why don't you go home and take a little break? She's fine now, and like Draakar said, she'll probably sleep 'til morning."

"Yes," Justin said, nodding in agreement. "He's been here all night."

"You've been here with me most of that time," Maya's father said to Justin. He looked between Maya and Draakar. "As soon as Justin found out about the accident, he rushed over here after having just gotten back from his trip. He's been with me ever since she came out of surgery. You're probably tired, too," he said to the young man.

"Tell you what," Justin replied directly to Vincent. "I'll take you home, and you can get a little rest so you'll be fresh and more relaxed when Carrie wakes up."

"That's a good idea, Dad," Maya agreed. "You go home with Justin. I'll stay with Mom and call you immediately if there's any change."

"Well…"

When Vincent hesitated, Draakar spoke up. He could see the fatigue on the man's face. "Your wife will be fine, Vincent. You have my word."

Maya's father nodded once, as though in silent acknowledgement of Draakar's pledge. "Okay, you all have convinced me. I can use a ride home. A friend gave me a lift to the hospital. I couldn't drive when I got the call."

"And a friend will take you home," Justin interjected. "When you're ready to come back, just call me. I'd be happy to bring you."

"That won't be necessary," Draakar and Maya said simultaneously. Draakar glanced at her before he continued. The sooner Justin understood his position, the better. "I'll have my driver pick him up when he's ready to return."

"Oh, it's no trouble," Justin insisted. "I'll want to check on Carrie, too. She does mean a lot to me, and she's also Maya's mother."

"Oh," Draakar said ominously. "What exactly is Maya to you?" Let the bastard make his claim to Draakar's face.

The air in the room dropped exponentially to match the chill in Draakar's voice. Maya moved to stand at Draakar's side, brushing her shoulder with his, calming him with her contact while presenting a united front. "A friend," Maya stated vehemently. "Justin and I are only friends."

Justin looked at her as though he would argue, but instead, he seemed to think better of it and sighed. Draakar hoped he resigned himself to her distinction. "Yes," Justin finally conceded. "We're friends."

Maya stepped forward to briefly hug the man. Draakar's dragon almost growled, but she immediately returned to Draakar's side and took his hand, calming him. "Thank you for staying with my dad and taking him home," Maya said. "Draakar will have a driver pick him up later. I'll call you tomorrow and let you know how she's doing. Maybe you could visit her then."

Justin stared at their joined hands for a moment before responding. "Okay. That's fine. Well, I guess I better go." He turned to Vincent. "Ready when you are."

Vincent leaned over the bed and kissed his wife. He whispered something to her. Everyone in the room, even without enhanced senses, could accurately guess what he had said to his wife of thirty years. 'I love you.' He rose from his chair and hugged Maya, who sat down in his place. He pumped Draakar's hand and squeezed his shoulder. "I'm sure I'll see you later."

"Yes, you will." He held out a card for Vincent to take. "My private number is listed there. When you're ready to come back, just call me and I'll have my driver pick you up."

"As long as this won't be an inconvenience," Vincent said, taking the card and glancing at it.

"None whatsoever, Vincent. It's my pleasure to be of assistance."

Justin placed his hand on the doorknob and paused. "Ah, will that guy out front allow us to leave?" Justin asked, half jokingly.

"Yes, he will," Draakar answered.

"Who is he anyway? Some kind of bodyguard? I've never known a doctor with a bodyguard," Justin complained.

"Some kind of something." Draakar offered no further explanation.

Justin nodded, maybe realizing his questions weren't going to be answered to his satisfaction. "Oookay," he said. "Nice to meet you, anyway. Maya, I'll talk to you tomorrow. Have a good evening."

Vincent kissed his daughter's cheek. "Bye, sweetheart. I'll only be a few hours, and I'll call the number when I'm ready to come back," her father said, waving Draakar's business card in front of her.

"See you soon, Daddy."

Maya and Draakar watched the door close behind the two men before turning to face each other.

A RUSH of emotion flowed through Maya's veins for the man in front of her. Her dragon surfaced, reaching out and connecting with his. She had truly forgiven him. *Thank you.*

You're welcome.

I may have misjudged...

Maya...Maya, is that you?

They looked down at her mother on the bed. Her sleep

still appeared a natural one, but she had clearly spoken in their minds.

Yes, Mom, it's me. I'm here.

Who...who's with you?

You know who I am.

Yes...yes I do. But I...don't really understand. I'm so tired, so tired—must rest.

Yes, rest. All will be well. Maya will stay and watch over you.

Yes, Mom, rest. I'm right here. You're going to be all right now.

CHAPTER TWENTY-TWO

*M*aya suddenly came to full awareness. She had no idea why, but something had pulled her from sleep. She opened her eyes and raised her head to check on her mother, who still appeared asleep. The disturbance hadn't come from her, and that's exactly what she had sensed, a disturbance…a discord in the environment.

She reached mentally for Ian. Draakar had left him to watch over her while he went to the house he had here. His use of power to heal her mother had weakened him. He needed the rest of the brethren to help him access the Stones from this distance. What he really needed was *her*.

Ian, she sent again. Only to be met with cold silence. She stood and had started for the door when it opened. A bright light blinded her vision. Maya raised her hand to shield her eyes from the glare, but it didn't seem to help much.

Maya, Ian is hurt. I am coming. The betrayer is there. Draakar's voice abruptly cut off in her mind.

Draakar! Draakar!

At last, Maya, at last you've awakened, and I have you. The sound of an unknown, yet familiar, voice vibrated in her head.

What? Who the hell are you?

You know who I am.

The betrayer. You bastard! What have you done to Ian?

Familiar masculine laughter flittered through her mind. *He thought to stop me from entering—again. This time, I was able to show him the error of his ways.*

What he said in her head didn't really make sense to her. *Did you kill him too, as you've killed others?*

No, at least not yet. To make sure it stays that way, you will come with me now.

Maya snorted and raised her chin up a notch. *I don't think so. I'm not going anywhere with you. Draakar is on his way as we speak.*

Yes, I know, but he will not reach you in time. Quickly, Maya. Come of your own free will or mine, but either way, you will come with me.

The betrayer opened up a limited mindpath, allowing her to see Ian. He lay on his back on the floor, apparently unconscious. She knew the image in her mind was real. Ian rested in what looked like a hospital room; he had to be nearby. She could see the wheels of maybe a hospital bed, but someone knelt over his still body. The person's face stayed hidden from her, but that someone held a gun to Ian's unmoving head. The gun she could see clearly before the image faded.

Well, Maya, do you come with me of your own free will, and I spare his life? Or do I take you anyway and kill him?

Bastard, she spat. *I'll come, but you have to let Ian go first.*

Maya winced as the betrayer established the link again, not bothering with being as gentle this time. A sharpness pinched her temples. She watched as the person withdrew the gun from Ian's brow and left the room. She still couldn't see a face, but from the back and the size, it appeared to be a man. He stepped on the elevator, and the lights above the door showed it descended, and then the vision stopped.

He is safe now and will awaken in a few minutes. I've kept my word. Now do you keep yours?

Hell no! If the bastard thought she gave in to him without a fight, he'd soon see the error of that sort of thinking. She just needed a chance to strike out with her powers at the piece of slime without endangering Ian.

Just as Draakar taught her, she raised her shield and built energy to send in the direction of the betrayer. She couldn't see him; the light still blinded her, but she could sense the outline of a man beyond the light. Maya let her rage grow and took a step toward him. She could feel the familiar burn in her eyes and knew what they looked like—golden fire. A second from letting loose a bolt of energy, she heard a choking sound coming from the bed behind her. Distracted, Maya risked glancing over her shoulder and her heart stood still. Carrie's eyes and mouth were open. Her mother's chest rose and fell as she gasped for breath. Only the whites of her eyes could be seen.

Ah, Maya, Maya, it's not going to be so easy. Drop that shield now or she dies.

Maya immediately dropped her shield and tried to reach for Draakar. She met a wall of silence, but he stood on the other side of that wall. She could feel him. It would only be a matter of time before he came for her; she had to believe that. Meanwhile, she would do what she could to help him. She stepped closer to her mother's bedside and grabbed the bed rail as she looked down at her.

"I'll go with you. Just leave my mother alone."

Of your own free will?

"Yes, damn you, of my own free will."

As soon as the words left Maya's mouth, her mother's breathing eased. Maya released the bed rail as darkness enveloped her. Losing consciousness, she crumbled to the floor.

The bright light blinked out. A man stepped out of the doorway, bent down and picked Maya up from the ground. He cradled her lovingly to his chest and kissed her forehead before walking out of the room and placing her in the waiting wheelchair in the hall.

Her mother on the bed opened sleep-glazed eyes in time to see a familiar figure cradling her daughter in his arms. Carrie smiled, then immediately frowned before her healing body claimed her in sleep once more.

ON HIS WAY back to the hospital, pain stabbed at Draakar's temple, a disturbance in the currents. He raised his head and scented the air. A stench filled his nostrils. The magicks of a silver dragon. The betrayer was near. An image of Maya exploded in his mind. *The hospital. He's at the hospital...Ian.*

Yes, Draakar. What...

Ian...

Silence, cold silence greeted Draakar's call, and it chilled him to his soul. At least he got a thought through to Maya before the wall descended. He would not get there in time. Maya couldn't face a silver dragon on her own, but to protect her mother, she would.

Hold on! He kept sending. *I'm coming!*

For the last five minutes, a wall of silence continued to meet him. He raged within himself even as he continued to try to breach the energy barrier, keeping him mentally from Maya.

If they were truly joined, he would be able to reach her.

Nothing short of death could separate them then. Even better would have been to have his powers at their peak, and he could will himself to the hospital. He couldn't even take his dragon form to fly there because he'd cause widespread panic in the streets. He wasn't strong enough yet to cloak his dragon appearance while he maintained the form. The Stones supported his powers as much as they could, but they could grant him no more. What he had would have to be enough until he mated to Maya. He would accept nothing else. Not this time.

He could, however, get there faster than the car. Draakar had the driver pull over to the side of the road and before the car came to a complete stop, he'd opened the door and had both feet on the ground. By the time the car did stop and pulled back into traffic, he was a half-mile away. Draakar raced at a speed so fast the human eye merely registered him as a shadow. He sent James and Robert to continue on in the car to get Maya's father, and Cass and Darryl raced behind him to the hospital.

Moments instead of minutes later, he stood in the hospital lobby, but he'd arrived too late. Maya was gone, and he couldn't get a sense of her. He went to her mother's room first to check on her. He could already feel Ian coming back to consciousness in the room across the hall where he'd been taken.

Maya's mother remained asleep when Draakar entered the room. As Draakar stood beside her bed, Ian stumbled into the room, pressing a hand against his bleeding head.

Lord, I'm sorry. I've failed you.

No, Ian, you have not. Draakar waved his hand toward Ian, stopping as well as cleaning off the blood and healing the blow to the side of his head. *It is my fault. I underestimated the betrayer. It will not happen again.*

Ian straightened up. *I will hunt this bastard with you.*

No. I need you to stay here and watch over Maya's mother. Cass and Darryl have just arrived and they will join you. I will take James and Robert with me when they get here with Maya's father. They should all be here soon. Do not let either of Maya's parents out of your sight. You all will have to remain in this room and at the door to keep vigilance. It isn't safe to move Maya's mother just yet. I need her close to human medicines just in case.

Do you know where he's taken her? Ian sent.

Not yet, but I know the bastard's scent. As soon as the others get here, we hunt.

"Who...who's there?" came a frail voice from the bed.

Draakar took a deep breath and reined his fear for Maya in; he had to remain calm for Maya's mother. She had been through enough. "Everything is all right, Carrie. May I call you Carrie? I feel as though I know you already. I'm Draakar Akgon, a friend of Maya's."

"Yes, Maya. But I...don't I know you?"

Yes, you do.

Yes, yes, I do know you. You're the Dark Dragon Lord. Oh, no... oh, God! Maya!

Maya's mother tried to sit up, and her body trembled in agitation. Draakar placed his hand on her shoulder, gently pressing her back on the bed and offering comfort. Carrie Trent placed her hand over his, and eyes with a golden tint looked into his. Draakar could feel her trying to will him to do as she asked, already knowing he would. "Draakar, you have to save her, please," Carrie cried hoarsely. "He took her, he took my baby—and I think he tried to kill me. What's going on? Where...where's Vincent?"

"Your husband is on his way now. But Carrie, exactly who took her? Who took Maya?" Draakar asked in a calm voice, but at the same time he looked into her mind. The scene unfolding in her memory caused his eyes to smolder while his entire body shook with the force of his fury.

The betrayer had fooled them, fooled him. He had stood no more than an arm's length from this creature and did not see him or sense him for his true enemy. How could this be? No Earth magicks could have cloaked the betrayer while in Draakar's presence. It should have been impossible, but it had happened. The betrayer had been right in front of him, and he did not know it. Now the bastard had Maya. If the betrayer could hide his true self so well, tracking him would not be easy. He would have to ask Mother Earth for help. His borrowed magicks were slowly draining and his distance from Maya wasn't helping.

"Draakar...Justin," Carrie choked out. "Justin took my baby. Justin, who has always been a part of this family, betrayed us. But what is he? What am I?"

Draakar paused a moment before answering her. He'd heard her husband's footfalls in the corridor. "Vincent is right outside the door. Let's wait for him and I'll explain to you both what has happened. We don't have much time."

Vincent pushed through the door and rushed to his wife's side, taking her in his arms. "Carrie, are you all right? What happened? Something's wrong." He turned to look at Draakar and the men and woman crowding his wife's hospital room.

I will explain everything, but it's best if I do it this way. It's also faster.

"What the..." That was as far as Vincent Trent got before his entire life irrevocably changed.

"Oh my God!" Those words about summed up how both Vincent and Carrie felt when Draakar finished with his explanations about the brethren. An appropriate response, Draakar thought, to the information about what they and their daughter were.

"This...this monster has our daughter!" Carrie Trent exclaimed.

"Yes, the betrayer has her."

"I can't believe Justin. *Justin* is the betrayer? How can this be?" Vincent asked. "How could we have known this man for all these years and not known he was capable of things like this?"

"He hid it well. He allows you to see only what he wants you to see. Even I did not know him for what he is."

"I think my mother suspected something," Carrie said. "She never liked Justin. Never trusted him from the first time she laid eyes on him."

"That's true," Vincent agreed. "Some people she took to, and others, no matter what, she never liked. We had all grown used to her quirks. Carrie and I only looked at the surface. Saw Justin as a successful, thoughtful person who adored Maya. No matter how much he showed those traits to Nana, she just never liked him. Never thought he was good enough for our Maya." Vincent paused and looked Draakar up and down. "We should have paid more attention to her intuition. Something tells me she would approve of you. Now what are we going to do to get our Maya back? Can you find her?"

"It may take time. The Stones, the source of my powers right now, are silent on her whereabouts, so I will have to ask Mother Earth to help me search for her."

"Can we help?" Carrie asked.

"You are still too weak, Carrie," Draakar said. "I cannot risk it. I can pull magicks from everyone else here to help me search." Draakar closed his eyes and a soft glow surrounded him, changing colors as the other brethren in the room began to glow in the color of their dragon. Suddenly, the glow around each of them stopped and Draakar opened his eyes, illuminating the already lit room in a bright emerald green.

"She is no longer in this realm," he said in disbelief. His

power slowly leveled off and the light in the room returned to a normal color.

"Realm? What do you mean by that?" Vincent asked, frowning. "Like another world other than Akgon?"

"Yes, something like that." Draakar raked his hand through his hair in obvious frustration.

"Well, can you find this other realm?" Vincent asked.

"The universe is composed of many worlds coexisting parallel to each other. The power the betrayer used to cloak himself from me was not of Earth's origin, but I do not recognize the signature source of the realm." He ran his hand over his hair again, frustration fueling his anger. "He must have found a way to tap into a power source from any of a hundred realms. It may take time to track the source down." Time Draakar knew they were rapidly running out of.

Father!

Draakar's entire body stilled. *Talon!*

Yes, Father. Look, I'm sorry I hid from you, but I know something is wrong. I felt Maya's anger and fear. Is she all right? I can't reach her.

No, Talon. The betrayer has taken her.

Everyone else in the room stopped talking or moving when they realized Draakar communicated telepathically with someone. He knew the others couldn't 'hear' the conversation, but they waited for him to finish and tell them with whom he communicated. His brethren Firsts knew it wasn't Maya. Her parents, on the other hand, hoped he communicated with her.

Even in his mind Draakar could hear Talon's hiss, and with the reestablished link he could feel Maya's distress through Talon.

Do you know where he has taken her?

Draakar hesitated before he replied. *No. I cannot sense her. I will have to return to the Stones.*

I think I can find her, Father.

No! Do not go after them on your own. Wait for me. I know where you are now, and you are near. I will come to you.

I await you.

Draakar looked at Maya's parents.

"What's going on? You were talking to someone in your mind," Carrie stated. "Is it Maya?"

"I didn't hear anything," Vincent frowned, "but I did kinda feel a tickle at the back of my neck. Did you reach Maya?" he too asked anxiously.

"Yes, I was communicating with someone, but not Maya. I spoke to my son."

"Your son!" Carrie exclaimed incredulously.

"My wife is dead," Draakar quickly added, knowing she thought he had a wife.

Immediately contrite, Carrie began to apologize. "Oh, I'm so sorry. Please forgive my thoughts. I'm just worried about Maya."

"No apology necessary," Draakar said, bowing his head slightly to her.

"Can your son help us?" Vincent asked.

"He may be able to. Vincent and Carrie, I must go now. I will bring Maya back with me." Draakar made it a statement with the confidence of a Dragon Lord. As her mate, he would settle for nothing less. Gesturing to the trio who stood silently against the wall, he said, "I will leave Ian, Cass, and Darryl to protect you." They bowed as he introduced them. "Please stay with at least one of them at all times and do whatever they tell you. James, Robert, you will come with me," he said to the two men who stood in front of the door.

"Do you really think we're in any danger?" Vincent asked.

"I am not willing to take any chances."

Carrie nodded. "We'll wait to hear from you then. Draakar, please hurry, and bring my baby back to me."

Draakar bowed his head to Maya's parents and left the room, Robert and James flanking him.

Where do we go, Lord? Robert asked.

It appears my son is acting as a student and is not far from here. He's at George Mason University. We'll have to take the car this time. I fear I will need to conserve all of my energy, as will you both, but I will still get us there faster than humanly possible.

CHAPTER TWENTY-THREE

*M*aya lay flat on her back, feeling as though her body carried no substance. She might have been floating on air and reluctant to return to consciousness, but something kept tugging at her, saying she needed to wake up.

Slowly, she opened her eyes. A fluffy white substance filled her vision. Maya blinked, but it remained. She could have sworn she looked up at a ceiling covered in clouds and lay cradled within the bosom of one. Maya turned her head from side to side. As far as she could see, nothing but swirling white vapor filled her vision. Not unlike being outside in the midst of a windblown snowstorm, but without the accompanying bitter wind and cold. Instead, a comfortable temperature surrounded her.

Her hands rested on her stomach. Maya lowered them to where she expected the ground to be. Instead, her hands passed through vapor, neither cool nor warm, until they touched something hard and grainy. She looked down at what she laid upon. It was some sort of raised platform, but she had a hard time seeing what she touched. The area appeared covered in a diaphanous vapor, which constantly swirled around her hands and body like nothing she'd ever seen before. Pushing against the hard surface, she sat up.

Maya tried to use her dragon senses, but they were— blocked. A psychic wall of energy prevented her from connecting to her brethren senses, and even her human senses had a hard time digesting what she saw and felt. Glancing around, she noticed something else strange about the place. The only discernable sounds came from the air exiting through her lungs, and what sounded like wind blowing against itself. Other than those, no other sounds reached her ears. No scent permeated the air, not even the freshness of moisture. Glancing around, she realized she could be in some sort of construct but no real way for her to tell yet. The place had a dampening effect on most of her senses.

She stood and turned in a complete circle. *Draakar, where are you? Where am I?* Nothing. She fished her cell from her jean pocket. A dark screen greeted her, yet it had been fully charged earlier. Pressing the power button changed nothing. Whatever blocked her from reaching her powers also interfered with her phone.

"Hello," she called out. "Is anyone there?" Interesting, no echo of her voice.

No one responded and, except for the vapor, nothing moved. She at least expected to hear the sound of the betrayer's taunts in her head.

Justin.

She still couldn't believe it. Justin. The betrayer. Murderer. All this time and she hadn't known what lay beyond the façade of the man. Never even suspected. What did he want with her?

She knew.

Deep down inside, she knew.

He had been her friend and then wanted to be her husband and lover, not necessarily in that order. Time and time again, she refused to let their relationship go beyond close friendship. She never could understand why. She had been attracted to him, had truly liked him. Most women would have jumped at the chance to enter into a commitment with the man Justin appeared to be: handsome, intelligent, charming, witty and usually fun to be around. At least, until she decided to take her trip to Ireland without him.

Yet, something always held her back from changing their relationship beyond friends. She didn't love him romantically. Maybe she had instinctively known to give herself to Justin would have been very wrong. Just as her family had been wrong to trust him.

A thought flashed through her mind. She suspected her mother's accident might not have been an accident. She shied away from thinking about her grandmother, who had never liked Justin and had always let Justin know of her disapproval of him. More than once, Nana told him to his face he sounded phony half the time. Maya had to come to terms with the fact Justin planned this for a long, long time.

Well, she would not sit around and wait for him to come for her. She needed to get out of here wherever here was. But how?

Ah, Maya, I see you are awake.

The voice in her head sounded near. Funny, the way she recognized it now. Maya looked over her shoulder in time to see him stepping through a tear forming in the clouds behind her. A black line stood out starkly against the white mist, about six feet tall then, expanded until it widened enough for his entire body to get through. It hadn't been there before, and it closed once he completely crossed over the threshold. Before it did, Maya caught a glimpse of rocky walls. Maybe the way out?

Quickly, she turned her body, so she stood in front of him. She wouldn't have her back to this creature. He could not be trusted.

"You bastard! Where am I?" She refused to speak to him mind-to-mind. It smacked of intimacy he had no right to. She would not voluntarily open herself any more to him than she already had. The more mind touch exchanged, the more likely a link could form between them. She refused to allow him to establish any manner of link with her. The less mental contact they had, the better. In fact, the less contact they had period the better.

Where you are is not really important, but I'll tell you, anyway. This is a between place. This is where I come to heal, rest, rejuvenate. Let time pass by, if you will. I discovered it quite by accident when I was injured once, but that was long before your time.

Maya took a wild guess. "Like when Draakar's mother tried to kill your sorry ass? It's a shame she didn't succeed, but don't worry, I'm sure her son will finish the job."

When his eyes fumed with silver fire, Maya knew she'd guessed correctly and hit a sore spot. Draakar's mother had hurt him. If he could be hurt, he could be killed. She never thought she'd ever plot to kill anyone or anything in her life, but if she could, she would kill this thing.

The glow from his eyes grew brighter. For the first time, Maya saw the true color of them, silver, just as she also saw him as his true self. Power fueled by envy, hatred and fear emanated from him, drowning her psyche. How could they have missed the fact he was dragon brethren? It seemed so obvious to her now.

You have no idea what you're talking about. I am stronger than Draakar and I will destroy him, just as I destroyed all the others. But let's not argue, you and I. I've wanted so long for you to be able to see me as I really am. To show you my power. No more pretending.

Maya turned her gaze away slightly and squinted at him. His eyes were so bright they blinded her against the white world. She grew tired of his ranting. "What do you want, Justin?"

"My true name is Anwar."

"Your true name is betrayer. Why am I here?"

You know why, Maya.

"Why don't you tell me, anyway?" She'd be damned if she gave him any leeway. He would have to spell it out.

Very well, I'll indulge you. I always have. You are mine. You always have been meant for me. You are my truemate.

Maya laughed; she couldn't help herself. The man, creature, clearly harbored delusions. Abruptly, Maya stopped laughing, and got angry instead. "You!" she scoffed, placing her fisted hands on her hips. "I don't think so! I have never wanted you and I let you know. Anything other than friendship between us was a figment of your overactive imagination, and frankly, so was the friendship part. You were never a friend to me. I turned down your marriage offer, but you don't seem to want to remember that. Well, get this through your fat head." She pointed a finger at her chest. "I am not yours. I have never been yours. I will never be."

Maya lowered her hand. She didn't shout her reply. She stated it in a low growl, making her denial carry the force of absolute truth along with her repugnance for him.

Justin threw his head back, raised his arms away from his sides, and roared. Blue flame erupted from his opened mouth, cutting a path about twenty feet high through the seemingly endless vapor.

The surge from his use of power crawled like an eight-legged bug down her arms. She shivered with revulsion. Maya scrambled back and tried to create her shield, but nothing happened. Mother Earth didn't respond to her request. No energy drifted up from the ground to empower her. She couldn't even feel her own internal energy of power. Something blocked her from connecting to her magicks as it blocked her access to Mother Earth.

Justin dropped his hands and stopped his display of temper. Only his eyes continued to glow. He laughed with glee at the shocked expression on Maya's face. Maya read his surface thoughts like a horror novel. The ripple along his skin told him she'd tried to use her powers and nothing happened. What he had done worked. Her powers were null; blanked in this realm, while his were as strong as ever and would get stronger still. All this she read.

Your powers don't work here, sweetheart. He chuckled. *You're not on Earth anymore, nor are you on Akgon.*

Stunned, Maya tried to hide her growing fear. If none of her powers worked here, did that mean Draakar's wouldn't either? She quickly shifted through her ancestral memories but could find no explanation. "Why…why do yours, then?" She frowned. "You're brethren of Earth and Akgon, so why do yours work?"

WOULDN'T you like to know? Justin laughed again. It worked; it worked. He wanted to dance and shout. The power source he had discovered here worked, but only for him. Only because he had the luxury of time to eventually figure it out. It merely took a couple hundred years of sporadic experiments. He had been trapped here after his battle with Draakar's mother.

Mortally wounded, he had stumbled into a cave. Drawn to a section of the cave wall pulsing with power, there he found a tear in the wall. A gateway leading to another realm, this one. His only thought survival. He had used the last of his strength to crawl through the portal and had fallen into a deep sleep. When he had awakened, he realised his wounds were healed but he couldn't access any magicks. At first, he panicked. He had no idea how long he had been there. After trying to repeatedly access his magicks and failing time after time, he finally figured out the secret to this realm.

While he had healed, his body had been placed in a semi-hibernation state by the realm itself, so he wouldn't starve. This state enabled him to maintain some level of conscious-ness and communicate on a basic level with the elemental existing in the realm. Eventually, he made his desires known. This realm held great power, not earthbound magicks, but magicks nonetheless. Magicks he now had easy access to since he no longer had full use of Earth magicks; Mother Earth and the Stones hampered him. But his access and use of the magicks from the mist made him very powerful.

Let's just say I had lots of time on my hands. He knew Maya would eventually, given enough time, figure out the puzzle of the realm. He had no intention of allowing her time.

He stopped laughing. Between one breath and the next, he stood close enough to grab her arms and tug her toward him. When she tried to push him away from her, he used his greater strength to pull her against his chest. Holding her so tightly to him, he could feel the beat of his heart vibrate against her chest. Arwan bent his head to kiss her, but she violently jerked her head away from him and brought her leg up hard, kneeing him in the balls. The blow came unexpect-edly. He had been aroused and the immediate and intense pain caused him to bend forward, automatically releasing her. She took several steps away from him as he straightened. Furious.

"Do not touch me!" she hissed.

He took a deep breath, and then visibly shook the pain off. *You took me by surprise, sweetheart. I promise you that will not happen again, but you need to understand something. I will touch you whenever I want to, wherever I want to. You are mine.*

"What? Are you deaf, too? Never! I will never be yours!"

Never is not a long time by dragon standards. Don't worry. I will be patient a little while longer, but mine you are, so get used to it. As soon as I kill Draakar, there will be nothing standing between us, and you will come to me of your own free will.

"Ha! Lie to yourself all you want. It's not happening. Draakar will come for me. He will kill you, and if he doesn't, I will." Maya knew she could and would kill this man, not only because if what she suspected he did to both her mother and grandmother was true, but also for all he had done in the past, and what he would do in the future. He had to be stopped.

His smile showed only teeth, and a coldness lit his eyes. *Oh, I want him to come after me. I've been waiting a long time to finish what I started. As far as who will kill whom, well, we shall see. No one will stand in my way. I will kill him as I have killed others.*

Maya couldn't help herself. She had to know. "Did you... did you have anything to do with my grandmother's accident? With my mother?"

The man she knew as Justin merely stared at her with those eerily silver eyes. No, not Justin, he never existed. It had always been the silver dragon. At first, Maya thought he wasn't going to answer her question, then she heard him in her mind and wished to God she hadn't.

I wasn't going to let anyone stand in my way. Your grand-mother was cleverer than I thought. She never trusted me. Most people do, you know. A year ago she came across some information, how I'm still not sure. Anyway, she began to ask questions about my background. She asked those questions of my business associates, and I believe she hired a private detective. He passed some of the things he learned on to your grandmother. Things that would have seemed innocent by themselves, but put together by the wrong person, had the potential to cause problems for me. Under such close scrutiny combined with her intuitiveness, it wouldn't have taken long for your nana to figure out my identity didn't hold up, and that some of my associates were not part of the law-abiding community. For some reason, my mind control could not work on her. She was able to see the truth and not what I wanted her to see.

"You mean she recognized you for the evil you really are."

His hands clenched at his sides and his chest rose and fell faster. *She recognized my power and feared it. So you see, I had no choice, really. She had the ability to turn you against me because, like her, I couldn't control you either. Somehow, she knew where to look, how to look to reveal some of my shadier dealings, and she would have revealed these things to you. So, as I said, I had no choice. I couldn't fool her; she was a threat and had to be removed. Conveniently, by accident, so there would be no suspicion of anything else.*

Maya took deep gulps of air before she could bring herself to say anything. "You...you killed my grandmother!" She suspected it, but to hear him so callously rationalize his thinking numbed her mind.

He held up his hands, palms forward. *It wasn't my hand that killed her. I would spare you that.*

"Bastard!" she screamed, balling her hands into fists. "Your hands carry her blood. It's because you wanted her dead. She is. Then you turned around and tried to kill my mother, too."

Actually, no. If I wanted your mother dead, she would be. I just wanted to make sure she was close enough to death you would return home. My plan was to restore her for you and earn your gratitude. His features scrunched up into a sneer. *Ah, but Draakar showed up with you. No matter. This just makes it easier to kill him. Away from the Stones, his powers will not be as strong.*

Done being numb by his revelations, blood rushed through Maya's body, giving her additional strength. She dug deep within herself, letting the anger guide her. She could feel her magick lying within but couldn't reach it, no matter how hard she tried. Maya sent a mental call again to Draakar and met silence. "Some way, somehow, I will kill you," she promised.

The beast merely smiled as though she told him something amusing. This just made her angrier. Her eyes blazed with heat, but no fire erupted from their depths to incinerate him where he stood. She took a step forward and raised her fist to punch the smirk off his face. Immediately, he raised his shield and shook his finger at her as if she were a wayward child.

Maya slowly lowered her hand, but made it clear by the tenseness of her body and her facial expression if she could hurt him, better yet kill him, she would not hesitate. None of which seemed to faze him one bit.

I have to leave you for a while, sweetheart. I have to lay the trail for Draakar to find you. Meanwhile, I've left you a little something to eat. Time runs a little differently in most of the realms, and you may be here for a while. As you will soon discover, there is neither food nor water in this place. You can't access your powers here, so you can neither summon food to you nor create it from matter. I don't want you to starve or go into a hibernation state. I need you awake and alert for when I return.

The betrayer raised his hand as if he wanted to touch her, but when she glared at him, he lowered his outstretched hand before he reached her. *I will always take good care of you, Maya, and attend to all of your needs.*

Obviously, Justin's power trip fried his brain. Before Maya could form a scathing reply, he took one step backward, and the tear reopened in the mist behind him. She again caught a glimpse of rocks and this time a dirt floor. Once his entire body appeared on the other side, the tear closed immediately.

It took a moment for Maya to move; when she did, she shook with anger and frustration. Walking over to the spot where the tear had appeared, she found nothing there but vapor filled space. She easily walked back and forth across the area, yet remained in the mist-covered realm. As she turned around, her foot struck something solid, and she looked down. Exactly where she had seen the bottom of the tear appear sat a wicker picnic basket that hadn't been there before.

She kneeled down in front of it and opened the lid, finding it stocked with enough food for a picnic for one. It included a bottle of water, a bottle of her favorite red wine, a baguette and lamb marsala—still hot. This was no picnic, though, far from it. She took out the bottle of water and closed the basket lid. Hungry or not, she couldn't bring herself to eat any of the food. She didn't trust Justin not to drug it, and she'd stay away from the wine. She would need her wits about her. Opening the bottle of water, she took a sniff. It appeared to be just water. She tested it by wetting her tongue. Cold, nothing strange, so she took a sip and enjoyed the sensation of the cool, fresh taste gliding over her tongue and down her throat. Still thirsty, she only took one more small sip; no telling how long she had to make the water last.

With the bottle in hand, Maya stood and walked away from the basket. She wanted to explore her surroundings, maybe try to get beyond the mist. Anything to evade Justin, or rather, the betrayer. She'd be damned if she referred to him any other way.

She'd been walking around long enough for the ice-cold bottle to turn warm from the heat of her grasp, but it didn't seem to matter which direction she went; it all looked the same. At first she tried walking in a straight line, as straight as she could without visual markers, and counted her steps as she walked. When she reached one thousand and nothing whatsoever had changed in the view, she stopped. She had once read somewhere the secret to most mazes was to always take left turns. This didn't appear to be a maze, but she didn't have any other ideas, so she turned left and continued walking.

She stopped counting after two hundred steps because she saw something up ahead. As she got closer to the object, Maya couldn't believe her eyes. She ran toward it, coming to a stop right in front of it. Dropping to her knees, she opened the lid of the basket, already knowing what she'd find. The picnic basket, just as she'd left it, minus the water bottle. How could that be?

She placed her head in her hands and groaned. "Well, shit!"

CHAPTER TWENTY-FOUR

$\mathcal{T}$he black Hummer pulled up in front of the Center for Performing Arts at George Mason University in Fairfax. It stopped beside a tall young man with ridiculously long blond hair standing on the sidewalk, obviously waiting for this ride. When the door opened beside him, he slung his backpack off his shoulder before climbing into the car. He hesitated briefly as his eyes met those of the man who sat in the back seat. The young man couldn't maintain eye contact and lowered his head. Slowly, he eased onto the plush leather seat and shut the door, placing his backpack on the floor between them.

Draakar shifted his head slightly. Talon watched as the emerald glow emanating from his father's eyes grew brighter, revealing a face similarly featured to his own. Minus the overt expression of anger. He had to concede his father had a right to be angry.

I'm sorry, Father, but you know why I had to do it.

I understand, but that still doesn't mean I'm not angry with you. You placed yourself in danger by cutting yourself off from me. There is a silver dragon loose in this world. He has already attacked our brethren, killed an innocent, and now he has taken Maya. He could just as easily have come after you.

I'm sorry, Father. I don't know what else to say. Uh, I did not know. I sensed something familiar yet foreign when I first arrived, but it didn't make any sense. How could there be a silver dragon aware on earth?

A good question and the Stones have been abysmally silent on an answer. But he is here and has been all this time. It's the betrayer.

That's impossible! Talon cried. *My granddam, your mother destroyed him.*

Apparently not.

DRAAKAR'S ANGER AND WORRY, at least for his son, dimmed as his eyes stopped glowing. Draakar welcomed Talon's silence, unable to bring himself to raise a discussion about the death of Talon's mother. Talon would have felt the loss of his mother's link and already know of her death. Draakar would wait for Talon to raise the subject of his mother. The devil lay in the details, though.

The car pulled away from the curb, heading past the campus entrance back onto a main road. The other occupants in the car had not been privy to the mental conversation between father and son. Draakar opened up the mind link so everyone could hear and introduced Talon.

This is Talon, my son. Talon, these are our Firsts. Robert is driving, and that's James next to him.

Robert only glanced at him through the rearview mirror and said hello. James twisted around in his seat and stuck his hand out to shake Talon's. "Good to meet you at last, laddie."

"Good to meet you as well." Talon spoke since James had spoken verbally to him. "Communicating like this is interesting. I'm enjoying using my vocal skills."

"Well, where do we go from here?" Robert asked.

Talon looked at his father. "I believe she's somewhere in the Blue Ridge Mountains, maybe close to Shenandoah. At least, that's where she was the last time I felt her."

What? Draakar sent. *What do you mean 'when you last felt her?'*

I have not been able to track her for some time now, but I know where she was before I lost her. I can take us there. He seemed to hesitate before he continued. *I could feel her anger, Father, and her fear.*

Silently, Draakar contemplated what Talon just told him. Anger at himself and fear for Maya ate at him. He'd left her alone, and she didn't know how to harness her full powers yet. He still had much to teach her. Draakar regretted with each breath he took, he had not immediately bonded completely with her. If he had, he would have been able to teleport; her life energy would have drawn him directly to her or in the right vicinity. At least now he had some direction. That, combined with the information Mother Earth had at last given him, would help him locate her. The betrayer no longer walked on Terra, which meant Maya may not be on Earth either. They weren't on Akgon; the betrayer was banned from entering the Circle of Stones to access the portal. Even if by some chance he did, he didn't have the power to open the gate.

I think the bastard may have found a portal to another realm. That's the only explanation I can think of why we cannot locate his life energy here and why we thought him dead. He's got a bolthole somewhere, and probably using powers he's acquired from another realm. Maya may no longer be on Earth, which is why Mother Earth can't locate her either, Draakar sent to everyone.

Father, how will we be able to find Maya if she's in another realm? I'm assuming it's not Akgon.

Draakar looked over at his son, at eyes so much like his own and coloring so like his mother's. *Not you, son. You only go as far as the portal when we find it. The rest of us will cross over.*

But Father—Talon began to protest. However, Draakar merely stared him down, using his power as Dragon Lord. His eyes glowed with emerald fire, so Talon understood he would not change his father's mind. Talon sighed. *Very well. I guess I've caused enough trouble. I'll wait for you.*

Beggin ya pardon, Lord, James sent, *but how could Maya be in another realm? I thought the Stones were the only gateway and that a lot of powerful magicks was needed to open the gate?*

There are many rips or tears in the fabric of space. These are places where dimensions can overlap or provide a connection to another realm. Powerful magicks can expand that rip, creating a portal or gateway between these worlds. Some portals, like the Stones, are gateways to many different realms. On Akgon long ago, before the first brethren came to Earth, we used lesser realms as places of banishment, but so rarely most don't have a memory of it. It was something only the dragon lords controlled. I am only aware of two portals accessible from Earth, but it is possible there are more. I think a lesser dimension is where the betrayer is holding Maya, and where he has been hiding.

Well, how will we find him? Robert asked.

If Talon can get us near where Maya was last on Earth, I should be able to locate the portal, and then I can open it.

Everyone remained quiet for a while, each in his own thoughts. When Talon turned to his father, he spoke to him privately. *After we find Maya, I'm not going back, Father.*

I know.

You do?

Yes. I understand.

I...I have to find her. I know she's close, at least she was, but I will find her.

Draakar debated whether or not to say anything to Talon about the child at the airport. He decided not to for now, unsure what it all meant. The girl was clearly a silver dragon, yet there had never been a female silver dragon in brethren memory. The Earth magicks had changed the old rules of power. He wanted to make sure no betrayer blood ran in her line. Even if she were of his line, he wouldn't know for sure until she got older if she would turn out like the betrayer. For now, she carried no hint of the taint of chaos. Until she matured, he would wait and watch, so he said nothing.

Meanwhile, I thought I'd get an education.

Draakar raised his eyebrows. *You already have knowledge beyond humans, Talon. Why would you attend university? You could teach the classes.*

I know, but it's one thing to have the knowledge handed to me. It's another to discover it on my own.

Draakar nodded his head. *I believe I understand that, too.*

I want to learn for myself and since my mate is human—at least human brethren—I want to know what it is like to live solely as a human on Earth. I want to be able to understand the things she has to go through so I may better understand her. Be better prepared to help her adjust to me, to our way of life. Does that make sense?

Yes, as a matter of fact, it does. I'm proud of you, son.

Talon's hesitation warned Draakar he would finally ask the question standing between them.

How did it happen? Did she suffer?

Draakar sighed. Time to tell him about his mother.

I think you know now she was not my truemate, but I did love her and I love you. He glanced out the window, barely seeing the passing scenery, then turned back to face his son. *You are the image of her. You have her coloring and her features.*

The only thing of me in you are your eyes and height. Maybe some of my bone structure, but you have both of our stubbornness. She used her powers to help sustain the life energy of the brethren and when she started to weaken, she maintained a balance by sheer will alone. Your mother died so the brethren could survive. She sacrificed her life for us all, and all brethren honor her.

Draakar looked into his son's eyes and lied through his teeth without an ounce of remorse. *Your mother did not suffer. She died peacefully in my arms, knowing I would find you and keep you safe.*

He gave his son the partial truth. After Sierran exhausted her magicks, she died in great physical pain. No way would Draakar tell his son that he and Akgon had literally sucked the life energy right out of his mother until only an empty shell remained. Finally, not even that.

What about Maya? Did Mother know about Maya? Did you?

Thoughts of Maya raised his anguish and sense of urgency. He had to find her. She had to be safe; he could not accept anything else. Draakar had let her down once; he would not do so again. If he could take to the air he would damn who saw him, but he had to conserve his strength if he were to face a silver dragon. He already had to draw on the magicks of everyone in the car to ensure they traveled as fast as possible. No traffic lights stopped them, and they drove well beyond the speed limit. Still, it all took time.

He forced his attention back to Talon's question. *Not at first, I did not know of her first existence until you were born, and afterward I turned that part of myself connected to her off.*

At least he had tried to cut the connection, but he never truly succeeded. She stayed always there on the perimeter of his mind. He could not cut himself off from the pain his truemate suffered each time she came into the world and each time she left it. He hurt with her, powerless to ease either of their suffering. At least he'd had Sierran and Talon; she had no one.

After you left, your mother confided to me she knew Maya existed on Earth in this time. She bade me find her and save the brethren.

What about Maya? How does she feel about all of this?

She felt betrayed.

Understandable.

But I think she's coming around.

I do like her, Father. She helped me. She has a good soul, and she's a Dam, a powerful one.

Draakar sighed. *Yes, I know.*

You haven't claimed her yet.

No. But I will.

I have every faith in you.

And Talon, you are right to wait for your truemate and to want to stay here to be near her.

Thank you, Father. Your understanding means a lot to me.

Robert glanced into the rearview mirror and caught Draakar's eye. "We're almost at the exit for the Shenandoah National Park. There's more than one. Which one should I take?"

Talon answered him. "Not this first one. Take the second and just keep going through that entrance. I'll tell you when to stop."

They drove for miles into the park. Climbing steadily in elevation past the beautiful scenery. No one had time to appreciate. Finally, Talon told Robert to pull over on a little patch of gravel on the side of the road, barely wide enough to accommodate the car. "We have to go on foot from here." Talon got out of the car first, his father right behind him. "Will they be able to keep up?" he asked his sire.

Both Robert and James heard him and answered, "Yes."

"We'll stay close to their pace," Draakar replied with a

small grin. "But I won't be able to cloak us all, so we'll hike at a normal human pace until we're out of sight of the road. Then you all will just have to keep up as best you can."

They had already changed clothing in the car to appear as though they were hikers, and quickly walked away from the road. Once the foliage engulfed them, they ran. Talon took the lead, Draakar right on his heels, and Robert and James several yards behind. They ran, creating their own path, constantly moving upward to the top of the mountain. Talon came to an abrupt halt. Draakar stopped immediately beside him. Shoulder to shoulder, they waited for the others to catch up.

This is the place I last felt Maya. She disappeared around here. I don't see anything and can only sense that she had been here recently.

Draakar walked around. *There may be an opening, a cave somewhere. Look around.* James and Robert hadn't reached them yet, but Draakar guided them and told them where to look. He gestured to his left to Talon. *Move the bushes aside, see if you find some type of opening anywhere.*

They moved off and tackled different areas, but Draakar found the cave. *Here. I found it and I can smell him. At last! He was here, but I don't believe he still is. The scent isn't recent. Let me go first. Talon, go back to the car and wait for us.*

Father, please...

No. I need you out of here. Draakar glanced up at the sky. An early evening blue sky with a star or two showing themselves lay over their heads.

If we're not back by dawn, go back to the city and find Ian at the hospital. Gather all of the Firsts together, as well as Maya's parents, and go back to the Stones. Ask Mother Earth for help. Together with her help, you all are strong enough to open a gate to Akgon. Return to Akgon, tell Valour what happened.

No, Father. I will not leave you.

I am your Dragon Lord and I command it!

Draakar watched the play of emotions travel across his son's features: anger, hurt, and finally, reluctant acceptance.

Yes, Sire, by your command. But may I just accompany you to the entrance to the portal so that I may see it for myself?

Draakar softened a little. *I need you safe, Talon. If I fail, you are Akgon's and Earth's only hope. When the time is right, return and claim your truemate. Together, you will be able to defeat the betrayer. We know who he is now.* Draakar sent Talon the image of Justin as well as a pulse of what his aura looked like, so he would know it.

CHAPTER TWENTY-FIVE

*N*o longer needing subterfuge, Arwan removed the glamour from around his eyes, revealing their true color. People who saw the handsome man get out of the car gave him a wide berth on the sidewalk, quickly looking away. Even if they didn't happen to catch a glimpse of his eerily glittering gray eyes, self-preservation automatically kicked in, warning they did not want to draw attention to themselves. Isaiah, waiting for him on the sidewalk, thought Arwan's eyes reflected the chill within his soul. A chill drawing him to the man.

"Well, what do you have to tell me?" Arwan asked Isaiah.

Isaiah, who could look any man in the eye and have him look away first, couldn't quite meet Arwan's. "I bin keepin' watch on the room just like you asked and staying out of sight. I holed up in the room down the hall from 'em near the elevator. Far's I could tell, they ain't left the hospital room, and Maya's father showed up here with two more body-guards while ago."

Isaiah saw no need to inform Arwan he had gotten bored and had fallen asleep for a bit. Man had to rest sometime.

Besides, he probably didn't miss anything important. He had above normal hearing and the sound of any footsteps in the hall woke him. And he made damn sure to clamp down on those thoughts.

"Excellent! I'll only need two of those bodyguards. How many of them are at the door?"

"Two, a man and a woman. The two who come with her father stayed outside. The other man who was guardin' before is inside the room with Draakar and Maya's parents."

"I'll take the two at the door and drain their energy, leaving Draakar fewer powers to call upon, but this time I'll leave a trail that even an uninitiated could follow."

"What about the others in the room?"

"We won't need to worry about them. Draakar can't sense me, and they won't know what's happened until it's too late. By the time they find us, I'll have everything arranged for them." The smile on Arwan's face reached his eyes, and they sparkled like a thousand pieces of silver. "This time I win. I will finally rule all humans and brethren kind here on Earth, and you, my friend," Arwan said, glancing at Isaiah, "have served me well. You will stand at my right hand as my First."

Isaiah had learned years ago the man, who called himself Justin or Arwan, was not a normal man, not completely. He had psychic abilities, the kind Isaiah had always sensed his sister and, more recently, his niece had. The kind of strength Isaiah craved and wanted desperately for himself, but only existed in him to a lesser degree. If Arwan wanted to use his powers to control the world, Isaiah had every intention of helping him achieve that end and be aptly rewarded for it.

Together, the two men entered the building. When they stepped off the elevator, Arwan stopped at the nurses' station. He spoke softly to them in a language Isaiah had heard him speak many times, yet could never understand. He knew Arwan made sure the nurses would not pay attention to anything they did by placing a mental suggestion in their minds. As far as they were concerned, the hallway stayed empty, and all remained as it should be.

ARWAN CONTINUED WALKING down the corridor with Isaiah by his side until they were abreast of the man and woman standing on either side of a door. He recognized them from the mountain, awakened human brethren. Because he had to use energy to cloak his presence, as well as Isaiah's, he couldn't tell who remained in the room, but it didn't matter. Draakar would come after him soon enough. Arwan turned his head and in the time it took for him to make eye contact with them, they were both slumping toward the floor. He grabbed the woman while Isaiah got the man, and quickly carried them to the empty room Isaiah had hidden in earlier.

Time was of the essence.

Placing them on the floor side-by-side, Arwan knelt between them and laid his palms on their foreheads.

Isaiah kept watch as Arwan's hands glowed brighter, then quickly stopped. He wasn't trying to kill them. Their deaths would have drawn Draakar immediately to him. He just took some of their life energy, enough to make sure they would be of no use to Draakar for a while. Arwan would need all the power he could summon to face the Dark Lord. The less power Draakar could access, the better.

When Arwan stood, Isaiah opened the door a crack and checked the hallway to make sure no one lingered. Both men walked to the elevator and quickly left the building. They got back in the car with Isaiah behind the wheel. Using the temporary powers from the stolen life energies, and the powers siphoned from the white realm, Arwan cloaked the car. It sped through the city and highway toward the mountains, but left a clear trail for Draakar to follow. Unfortunately, in spite of the cloak allowing them to travel faster than normal speed, they had to slow down. They came to a stop because of a traffic jam caused by an accident ahead of them. Fire trucks blocked all the lanes up ahead.

THE FOUR MEN entered the cave opening. They all had to bend down to get through the entrance, but once inside, the cave expanded and they were able to stand. There didn't seem to be any visual sign anyone or anything had been there recently. The dirt-covered floor held no footprints, and as caves went, there was not much to this one. It didn't appear to have a large interior. Although the inside remained dark, they could see all of it from where they stood with their brethren eyesight. The cave went no farther into the mountainside than thirty feet, ending at a rock wall.

Draakar inhaled deeply. "The betrayer was here and I can sense Maya now." He walked to the farthest wall and placed his palm upon it.

This is it. He sent to the others. *There is a portal here that leads to another realm.*

Can you open it? Talon asked behind him.

Yes, I can. Once we're through, Talon, go back to the car and wait for us. Draakar turned to stare at his son. *Remember, till dawn.*

Draakar returned his attention to the wall and called on Mother Earth. He would save his powers, if he could, and let Mother Earth use her powers to open the way. The gate sat on part of Earth, at least on this side; Mother Earth should be able to open it. She answered his request by infusing him with the power to open the gate.

Raising both hands, he placed them where she directed. At his touch, without a sound, the stone wall split apart. Directly in front of him appeared a perfectly straight line, as tall as he. On alert for any sudden appearance of the silver dragon, the others raised their shields. They anxiously watched the stones begin to shrink and the split in the rock widen enough for a person to get through. They could see nothing on the other side but thick white mist. Draakar placed one booted foot through the opening and, pausing briefly, sent, *James, Robert, stay behind me.*

Draakar continued his forward momentum, but as soon as his other foot cleared the opening, the portal sealed shut. He felt the tear close, but didn't bother to turn around. He barely heard his son's mental cry of anguish behind him. The wall closed, separating him from his brethren.

However, he held no concern. The woman who sat right in front of him captured all of his attention. Too late, he heard her mental warning, but it made no difference.

It's a trap.

Are you all right? He sent as he silently assessed her.

Yes. I'm fine. Oh, Draakar, I'm sorry. As soon as I felt your presence, I tried to warn you. This is a trap the betrayer set. Draakar, Justin is the betrayer. He calls himself Arwan. Our magic doesn't seem to work here, but his does.

CHAPTER TWENTY-SIX

If his can work here, then so can mine. He walked over to her and she stood. Before she could straighten to her full height, he had her in his arms and pulled her up against him.

Are you sure you are all right? Like a soft caress, Maya heard his whisper in her mind and felt his anxiety for her in his heart.

Despite their circumstances, Maya rejoiced. He'd come after her. He had not disappointed her, not this time. *Yes. I am now. But what are we going to do? How will...*

Those were all the questions she managed to get out before he assaulted her senses. His lips covered hers and he inhaled her.

The world tilted and she no longer held a separate existence. She'd become a part of him. Neither existed without the other. His breaths held her life. She took no breath he did not provide.

His arms surrounded her, cocooning her, while she slipped her hands under his cascading hair, wrapped her arms around his neck, and held him to her. Without releasing her mouth, she felt and heard his need in her mind, and it echoed through her soul. Time held no meaning for them. They were always meant to be. Their story carved long ago into the Stones. This one creature had been crafted for her.

As other truemates had done before them, she read his thoughts.

Draakar took a leap of faith. *Feed me your flame,* Draakar requested. *I need it for my fire.* He opened his mouth wider to receive her.

Instinct drove her actions. Needing to release what had been building up inside of her from the moment of her existence. Maya opened her mouth, pressed her lips to his even harder, and did as he needed. She was created just for him. This time she sucked the air right out of his lungs and released the flame born inside her. A flame that would only flare for this one man. She willingly gave him the breath of her life energy encased in living flame.

They exchanged the true bonding ritual between truemates, the breath of flame. The spoken words, as binding as they were, were a mere shadow of this bond. Only a truemate could be gifted with the exchange of flame, because only a truemate could call it forth and live through it. For him, the breath of life. For any other, the kiss of death.

This powerful man trembled in her arms as her magicks met and blended with his. Mouths locked in an embrace, nothing could break, their hearts thudding in unison, they both dropped to their knees. All the power he'd been born to as a dark dragon finally and truly awakened in his soul and roared to life, demanding to be fed.

More. I need more. He growled the command in her head.
I give you all that I am.
My mate. Yes, you will. As I will give to you all that I am.
Maya poured herself into him, never more alive than at

that moment. She was born for him as he for her. All her doubts seemed ridiculous in light of those indisputable facts. Excitement coursed through her veins to complete the bonding ritual between truemates. She had waited so long for him to claim her. She would wait no more.

Soon, beloved. Soon.

Draakar suddenly broke contact and raised his head as though he were listening to something.

"What? What is it?" Maya asked, looking around too. "Is it the betrayer?" She couldn't see anything but the swirling white vapor. Then she felt it. A light cool brush against her skin, whereas before she only felt the heat generated by Draakar. She dropped her hands from around his neck and rested her palms against his chest, where his heart beat steadily. She couldn't hear anything. But when Draakar's body stiffened against hers, it became obvious he communicated with someone or something.

What's going on? It took a few moments for his body to relax and for him to respond to her.

It's okay. Draakar eased his hold on her, but didn't release her completely from his embrace. "The entity that dwells here just made contact with me. It is also the power controlling this realm," he replied verbally. "It's the mist. The mist is a sentient being, an elemental possessing powerful magicks. It noticed the power we just generated and got curious. Connecting with me through this. It means us no harm, but it is a powerful being. It has been feeding power to the betrayer and providing him with a safe haven. I believe the betrayer is in for a surprise the next time he enters this realm."

"Why? What happened?"

"I shared some of my memories of the betrayer with the mist, and it is very distressed it aided such a creature. It doesn't know violence but understands the concept and will not be a part of it. The mist has promised it will not help the betrayer any longer."

Maya looked around, intrigued by the vapor curling around them. "The entire time I was here, I tried to use my powers, but never once thought to try to communicate with the vapor around me. What can it do?"

"At first, the power of the mist dampens our Earthborn senses, our powers, because it's trying to communicate with us. That's why your powers don't appear to work. Think of a positive trying to fit into a negative. They cancel each other out, but it has found a way to make contact. It's using its powers to augment our own instead of butting against it, so there can be two-way communication. Since it's had experience with the betrayer and I am familiar with the way other realms may work, it's easier for it to communicate with me."

"What about the powers it's given to the betrayer?"

"It can't take away any of the powers it's already given to him, but it will no longer help him when he returns. And he will return for you, I have no doubt about that, but you won't be here."

"How will we get out?" she asked. "Will the mist release us? I think his plan was to trap you here."

"Yes, but that's not going to happen. We are no longer trapped here. I can open the gate now at will."

"Even if we get out of here," she squeezed his arm, "when the betrayer returns, he'll just come after us."

"No, he won't."

"Why? What's to stop him?"

I will. It must end here.

Maya jumped to her feet. Wrapping her arms around her waist, she shook her head. She had just come to terms with her feelings for Draakar. She didn't like hearing the betrayer's powers had been enhanced. She couldn't lose her Dark Lord now. Reaching for him, she grasped his hands and replied mind-to-mind, needing the intimacy with him. It conveyed her feelings much stronger than vocalizing.

No. No. Either we fight him together or you come with me now. Like you said, the mist will no longer help him, so he'll be trapped here. There's no need for you to face him.

Draakar sat back on his hunches. *There is every need.*

The need for revenge?

Have you forgotten what he has done to your mother? That was no accident, nor do I think your grandmother's death an accident. I am also the protector of all brethren. Sentence was passed on the betrayer long ago. I cannot take the chance he will escape this place. So I will make sure he cannot.

Maya released his hands to raise both of hers in the air, as a sign of surrender. *So what? You will bring violence, death to the mist.* She knew she sounded unreasonable. Earlier, she wanted to take off the betrayer's head. Now faced with the reality of a betrayer who might be more powerful than Draakar, she did not want to risk him.

I did not choose the place he did. The mist understands this must be done.

Does it really? How can it understand, when it doesn't know violence?

It does.

What about your power? Maya grasped at anything here. On one level, she recognized her fears were unfounded, but she had finally found him and didn't want him facing danger.

I do understand your fears, Maya. But you have awakened all of my powers with your flame. You know this. Trust me. Trust us.

Maya's body stiffened, then relaxed. She nodded her head. The mist had been able to establish communication with her.

Draakar stood to face her, calmly waiting. Only a few moments seemed to go by before she could speak. "The mist says it doesn't know violence, but it also doesn't know love. It has felt the strong emotions we have for each other. It has never experienced anything like it and would like to know love."

He smiled and held out his hand to her. "I think we can manage that."

A skeptical Maya raised an eyebrow. "I don't know. I'm not sure I want an audience."

"It's not. Not as you understand audiences." Draakar opened the link between them, which helped her to understand the mist didn't really feel or see as their senses worked, but responded to power or magicks. It wanted the power love could generate to help mute the power of the violence it would soon experience if Draakar confronted the betrayer. Whatever energies released in this realm, it would absorb, and it needed something to counter the effect of the violence. It needed a balance.

"Ah, I understand." Maya took a step, bringing her close enough to place her hand in his. He tugged her nearer and lowered his head to hers.

My turn. Open for me, my Queen.

"Whoa, what's this, my queen, stuff?" Maya asked, holding her palms flat against his chest and this time feeling a rapid heartbeat. A heart beating in anticipation to match her own.

That is what you are, Maya. You know this.

I know I am your mate, Draakar. I've accepted that. How could I not? But I will not be queen.

You are my queen. You always have been and always will be. Draakar stopped. Maya read all of this in his thoughts. He planned to bond them completely first, then convince her later of her status as queen of the brethren.

"Was your first wife, Sierran, your queen, too?"

"No. I did not name her queen. I had the power to do so but could not, because I knew she was not mine. When we were bonded, Valour, my advisor, named her consort. Brethren queens are usually born as Dams, the strongest

females of our kind. We rarely accept females merely desig-
nated as queen solely because they are mated to the Dragon
Lord. Titles are granted by right of might. And most importantly, Sierran was not my queen. You are."

Draakar covered Maya's hand, lying on his chest, at the
same time he covered her mouth with his. *I need you to feel the
fire you created in me. As my fire burns for you, I need yours to
burn for me. Open for me. Let me feed you my flame.*

Without hesitation, Maya opened wider and thought she
would ignite where she stood. Every cell in her body flared
to renewed life while she burned from the inside. Just like in
her dream, but so much more. Strength she'd never known
infused her muscles, yet at the same time, the bones in her
legs felt like they had been sucked out of her body. If it
weren't for his arms around her, holding her up, she would
have fallen at his feet.

The flame died, but while Draakar may have stopped the
flame, the feeling of being consumed by fire from the inside
out did not cease. The heat remaining behind would never
entirely go away. This had been her dream, this burning
from within. Yet she'd lived through it and her powers had
come to life. Nothing to fear, but something to embrace.

Everything intensified tenfold. On a higher level, she
could feel the hardness of Draakar's body flush against her
own. She could feel the silkiness of his hair as it brushed
against her cheek. The roughness of his tongue as it invaded
her mouth, which she gladly greeted with her own as a
different type of heat built again within her core.

He lowered her body to a horizontal position. A good
thing he took control. Maya could no longer sense any part
of her body other than her mouth sealed against his, her
tongue wrapped around his, and her arms locked around his
neck.

Most of all, she felt the heat from Draakar and an unending need for more. She wanted to burst into flames.

Maya sank further into the comfort of the soft ground beneath her. Draakar, now as naked as she, covered her front completely with his larger frame. His hair hung around them like a dark velvet curtain, enclosing them in a world of two and blocking all else out. For the moment, they were in a world of their own creation.

He placed his hands at the side of her head, keeping most of his weight off her. Her senses, human and dragon, kicked in full throttle and she absorbed all of him at a level beyond mere skin. Every movement of rippling muscle. Every vibration from the rise and fall of his hard chest, the brush of his faint hair running from his navel to between his legs, rubbing against her stomach. Even he trembled as blood rushed to his pleasure centers. Draakar's earthy scent surrounded her. Most of all, the sensation of his hands moving on her bare skin had her blood rushing to her core. Thank God, he'd willed their clothing away, so she didn't have to stop or slow down to take anything off.

I know, beloved, that this is our first time—your first time—and I will try to go slow for you. But I ask forgiveness in advance if I am unable. I have waited so long.

Too long, Dark Lord, I command you not to take your time. To do what needs be done, for both of our sakes. We have waited enough time. I do not wish to wait any longer.

Draakar moved his lips across her face, placing firefly kisses on her closed eyelids. He moved to her nose, then briefly back to her mouth before continuing downward to her collarbone, where he paused and sucked for a moment. *Ah, but I find I need to wait for just a little bit longer while I get to know every inch of you. I promise I will make it up to you.*

Her hands ran through hair smoothly, gliding through

her fingers before moving to grasp his strong shoulder muscles. *I will hold you to that promise, Dark One.*

Sliding downward, he continued licking and placing kisses upon the very crest of both full breasts. Raising his hand, to lay it over one, then running his thumb back and forth across the pebbled surface. He watched, seemingly fascinated, as her already distended nipple peaked even more at his touch. Draakar moved his attention and mouth to the other breast, and opening wide, he took as much of her ample flesh into his mouth as he could and suckled—hard.

Maya bowed her back in reaction to the intense sensation centered on her aureole. The moan of satisfaction vibrating against the mist could have come from either one of them, but in actuality had come from both. When she thought she could take no more, Draakar raised his head. He moved his mouth to the other breast and lavished it as thoroughly as the first with tongue and teeth. Maya had her hands wrapped in his hair, trapping his head against her breast as she rolled her head from side to side in mindless bliss.

Draakar shifted his mouth from her breast and blew lightly over it in an attempt to cool her fire. When she tried to press him back to her, he removed her hands from his hair. "No," she whispered.

Shhh. We have time. I'm not going anywhere.

Her eyes popped open to stare into the blazing green glow of his. *Please, Draakar. Please.*

Mmmm, he rumbled. *And I will. Please you, as you already please me.*

So saying, he opened his emotions fully to her so she could share his pleasure in her before he began licking his way in a straight line down the middle of her body. Maya shut her eyes to completely immerse herself in the myriad of sensations. Her stomach muscles contracted and pressure gathered in her womb from the intensity of the pleasure he

246

slowly and diligently built up within her. The moment the tip of Draakar's tongue touched her woman's entrance, like the eruption of a sun, the force exploded, and her essence poured out for him to receive. He might have been a man starving for eons. He lapped up every single drop flowing from her core.

Before she could catch her breath, he growled against her sheath and the sound caused her body to vibrate as he then crawled up over her body. The gentle push of his hands to farther widen her thighs caused Maya's eyes to pop open. She saw their bodies surrounded by a colorful glow, warming her to her soul, before his eyes ensnared hers. Without pause he breached the last barrier between them and roared, claiming her for all time by deed, then by word.

Our life is one. Our soul is one. One cannot exist without the other. Ever we are intertwined, in this world and beyond, in this life and next. I belong to you as you belong to me. Even death hath no dominion over us.

Maya felt only a slight discomfort lasting the time it took to blink because by then he began to move inside her and other sensations bombarded her. Sensations so fierce, she could no longer keep her eyes open. All the better to bury herself in each and every one of them. The sensation of her mate inside of her was like coming home after a long absence. Every part of her reached to cling to him. Her body stretched to accommodate him and contracted to keep him there. Her soul no longer resided splintered and alone but joined with his, soaring to the heavens. Her mate wrapped around her, in her, with her, until they were both engulfed in the flames. Which blazed from the green fire she'd seen shooting from his eyes before she'd closed her own. Maya wrapped her legs around Draakar's waist and rode wave after wave, created by the inferno of their passion.

As Maya's inner feminine muscles clamped down on him, the rhythm of Draakar's movements increased. He could not contain his release any longer. With another roar, this one from the part of his soul always belonging to her, a cry of joy erupted. He spilled his essence and kept spilling into the cradle of his truemate. When the tremors throughout his body finally stilled, he rolled onto his back, taking Maya with him.

She laid her head on his heart and smiled as its frantic movement calmed. Without opening her eyes, she repeated the pledge of bonding back to him.

Our life is one, Maya told her mate as tears of joy coursed down her cheeks. *Our soul is one. One cannot exist without the other. Ever we are intertwined, in this world and beyond, in this life and next. I belong to you as you belong to me. Even death hath no dominion over us.*

Hot tears fell against his chest, and he felt the lingering sadness and joy in her heart. *Shed no more tears, beloved. I am here. I love you, Maya, I always have. From the day I was created, my sole purpose was to love you. I swear you will always come first. Nothing and no one will ever separate us again.*

Draakar raised her head and licked the tears off her face, but his actions made her cry even more. So he kissed her instead. That did the trick, and her tears stopped as she stretched her body fully over his. Then they both froze. They had run out of time.

He comes, Maya sent.

Yes. He's close. You still have time to leave. I can send you back to the hospital now. My powers are as they should be.

No. We are one. We do this together, Dark One. I am your mate, and as I told you once, I fight at your side.

He looked into golden eyes shining with tears, caring, worry, and love. Even though she hadn't told him the last, it shone in each look, each touch she gave. He brushed his hands against the sides of her face before raising his head to press his lips softly against hers. *Very well. We face him together.*

Draakar felt her reluctance to move. He shared it, but eventually she rolled off him. Before straightening, she dressed herself in black jeans and a rust-colored sweater. By the time she looked up at him, he'd already donned his customary all black ensemble, this time with a short black leather jacket.

"Oh, come on," she groaned and changed the color of his shirt to match the color of her sweater. "Better, and don't go changing it."

Even knowing the confrontation with the silver dragon remained imminent, he took a moment to smile at his mate. "As you wish. Your powers are coming easier to you. You didn't even give it thought."

She beamed. But then Draakar saw the short lived bubble of euphoria she had been riding abruptly pop when she remembered what they yet had to face. "Draakar, what are we going to do?"

"We're going to kill the betrayer."

"I understand that we have to. But how?"

CHAPTER TWENTY-SEVEN

"What the hell happened?" Talon asked, not really expecting a ready answer.

"I don't know," Robert replied. "The wall just closed up on us."

"What should we do?" James asked. "Can you open the portal, lad?"

"No. Even with you both helping, I still can't open it. Maybe if we combined all the powers of the First, we might be able to open it."

"So, should we contact everyone at the hospital and have them meet us here?" Robert asked.

"Not yet. Let's give my father some time," Talon stated. "We wait till dawn, just as he wanted."

"Well, lad, I believe he'd want us, Robert and me," James said, indicating himself, "to wait. He wanted you to go and wait at the hospital."

Talon shook his head. "No. He wanted me to wait until dawn, so that's what we'll do. If he's not back by then we'll all head back to the Stones, and we'll open a gate to Akgon."

Talon.

Father! What happened? Are you all right? Did you find Maya?

Yes. We're both fine. I need you to listen. Take Robert and James and leave now. The betrayer is on his way.

But Father...

No buts, Talon. Go. Go now. Return to the hospital and get everyone back to the Stones. Have Ian go on ahead and get the jet ready. Maya and I will join you at the Stones.

All right, Father, when should we expect you?

Time moves differently in the realms, Talon. We know that. So I'm not sure. But if we do not join you in a couple of days, use the power of the Stones to help you put out another call to our human brethren. Return to Akgon with as many as you can gather.

I will not abandon you, Father.

You have no choice. There are mates among the human brethren who can help save our world. If I fail, you are the brethren's only hope. Save as many of them as you can. Use the power of the Stones and ask Mother Earth for any help. They will help if they deem it a time of great need.

What about my mate, Father? I cannot leave if she remains and is in danger.

Although she is young Talon, she is strong. A call, such as the one you may have to send out, will guide her to you. Now go. You don't have much time.

Talon turned to his father's Firsts and quickly told them what he had said. They all understood if the betrayer prevailed, those with brethren blood would be the first hunted and destroyed. Chaos would ensue. They hurried out of the cave and down the mountain to their car in pitch darkness. Not even a sliver of moonlight split the overcast night. With their dragon sight, they could see clearly enough to get down the mountain to the car still parked at the side of the road.

"I'll drive," Talon said as they approached. "I'll try to cloak our presence as much as possible." Talon paused as he opened the car door and looked up at the darkened, deserted road. "I can sense the betrayer now. There is a distinctive odor of chaotic magicks on the edge of the wind. Come, we've got to hurry. Since my cloak isn't strong enough to protect us if he passes us on the road, we'll leave in the opposite direction I sense he's coming from. Hopefully, I can manage so he won't be able to sense us or the car from a distance."

"I don't know, young Lord," Robert said as he got into the car. "It just doesn't feel right leaving Draakar and Maya to face this bastard on their own," he continued as James got in behind him and Talon pulled away from the curb.

"He's right," James agreed.

"I understand how you both feel. I feel the same way. But if my father and Maya together cannot defeat the betrayer, we'll probably need all of us to even stand a chance."

"So what are ya saying, laddie?" James asked.

"We go back to the hospital and get everyone. I'll send Maya's parents with one of you on to Akgon castle in Ireland, but the rest of us will come back here. We will be there if he needs us. I may need your energies. I cannot draw them like my father can, but you both can feed me yours."

Both men nodded. They understood.

The black Hummer hadn't rounded the first curve when Talon looked in his rearview mirror and saw headlights coming up the mountain. He called on Mother Earth to boost his magicks. The Firsts in the car also channeled their powers to help him shield their presence from the powerful being in the car behind them.

Talon didn't see the car pull over to the side of the road and the two shadowed figures get out. By the power of Mother Earth, they didn't see him, but one stopped and looked in the direction the Hummer had gone.

"What is it? Is something wrong?" Isaiah asked as he came to stand beside him.

"I'm not sure," the man he knew as Justin said. He turned and looked at the mountainside in the direction of the cave. "Come on. Let's get this over with. Draakar should be here soon. He may be closer on our heels than I thought, but it doesn't matter. I'll still have enough time."

The two men stood before the stone wall in the cave, and Arwan opened the gate. The second he crossed over, it slammed shut behind him.

Isaiah, stranded on the other side, called to his Lord but got no response. He didn't panic since they had prepared for this. He knew what he had to do. Isaiah made his way back to the car and returned to the city to execute his Lord's wishes.

ARWAN KNEW IMMEDIATELY he had been tricked, even though he could neither sense Draakar nor see him. The mist appeared thicker than usual and, try as he might, he couldn't communicate with the being of the realm. The gate didn't respond to him, and he could no longer call forth the portal. He reached for his magicks, enhanced by the power of the mist, and found it still there. At least he still had those powers.

He surrounded himself with it until his body generated a silvery glow. Bolstered, he took a few steps forward and the tendrils of the mist moved with him. Where before its touch soothed now, it turned bitterly cold, and Arwan could not block the cold from seeping into his body. Shivering once, he blocked his discomfort from his mind, then came to a stop.

I know you're here, whelp. What did that weak, sniveling fool of a brother call you? Ah yes, Draakar. I remember. Draakar, so you continue to use that name. Well, let's get this over with. Show yourself.

I am here, betrayer.

Arwan slowly turned to face Draakar.

Where's Maya?

"I'm here." The mist cleared beside Draakar to reveal Maya standing at this side.

You belong next to me, Maya.

"Not in this lifetime, betrayer, or the next." She raised her hand from her side and Draakar took her hand in his.

Ah, but you will be mine. No matter what the whelp has told you. You are my mate. And my true name is Arwan.

"I don't really give a shit what you call yourself. And my mate is beside me."

Arwan looked at them with his dragon senses and knew they were mated. He growled. *Not for long.* He raised his hands and shot a bolt of silver lightning straight at Draakar's heart.

Draakar and Maya immediately raised their shields.

CHAPTER TWENTY-EIGHT

Is that the best you can do? Draakar didn't wait for a reply but shot an energy bolt from his eyes right back at Arwan, who didn't react quickly enough. The bolt hit him squarely in the chest, knocking him off his feet and into the air. The betrayer landed on his back, some twenty feet away from the couple. The mist cleared a path directly to the body, giving Draakar a clear view of the unmoving creature on the ground.

Draakar didn't move. He simply turned his palm over and sent more energy fire to his enemy. But Arwan's body started to glow again. Even though he appeared unconscious, his shield remained raised and Draakar's bolts couldn't penetrate it.

He released Maya's hand and moved toward Arwan, but he hadn't gotten very near when the glow surrounding Arwan's body grew brighter. The betrayer's body shimmered and his shape expanded and elongated, transforming into his dragon form.

Draakar initiated the change to his dragon to meet the silver dragon rising before him. Arwan completed his shift faster than Draakar and took to the air while Draakar's dragon form remained incomplete. The silver dragon spread his wings, hovering above the Dark Lord. He opened his jaw and spewed silver and blue fire down on Draakar's still shimmering partial change.

MAYA WATCHED in horror as flame surrounded her mate.

Acting purely on instinct, she raised her hand and a bolt of golden energy shot forth, hitting the silver dragon in one eye. The vibration from the roar of pain erupting from Arwan's throat caused the ground beneath her feet to shake. She had brought Draakar the time he needed to recover and complete the change.

A dragon reflecting no color raised his enormous wings. It shot up off the ground to meet the silver in the air, raking his talons across the betrayer's chest as he flew past. Thick red blood oozed from the eye Maya's energy bolt had hit and also ran from the chest of the silver dragon to stain the mist swirling beneath the battle in the sky.

Draakar soared higher above the wounded dragon. The betrayer still hovered in the air, a little closer to the ground now. His wings appeared to barely hold him up and his head hung down toward his chest. Hurt but still dangerous. The Dragon Lord turned in midair, pinned his wings to his sides and dove straight for the betrayer to finish it all. He was at the point where he could not stop his downward momentum when Arwan suddenly turned. He tucked his wings against his body, propelling straight up into mist, faster than Draakar could react to stop him.

By the time Draakar turned to follow, Maya couldn't see the other dragon.

He shot into the mist, Maya sent to him as she watched from the ground.

Flying in circles, Draakar replied, *Yes, he came this way because he left his scent as well as a trail of blood behind. There is another portal here. That's how he's escaped.*

How could that be?

Draakar landed before her in dragon form and changed before responding to her question. *Portals can exist anywhere,* he sent as he walked toward her on human legs clad in black jeans.

It took Maya a moment to respond as she raked her eyes over him, still in awe of the change from dragon to man. She would never get tired of staring at the beauty of Draakar in either form. She shook her head. This was not the time. They were in a battle, and she had to focus.

Maya sent her thoughts to him. By the smile lighting up his face, she could tell he had already heard her wayward thoughts.

As I am in awe of you, beloved.

Are you all right?

Yes, thanks to you.

When he stood in front of her, she had to touch him. Maya reached out and ran her hands up and down his muscular arms, just to make sure for herself he was all right. He pulled her toward him. She placed her hands on his shoulders and looked up at him. Maya still had questions, and knew if she succumbed to his embrace, she would forget everything but him. *Why wouldn't the mist warn us?*

The mist didn't understand it was a portal. To the mist, it appeared as just another place in its realm. It controls the one we came through, but apparently not this one. It opened from the other side.

The betrayer must have a link to wherever it leads. That's the only way he could have opened it. I do not believe it leads back to Earth. I would know. Very few power sources are strong enough to open to more than one world, and the Stones no longer respond to him.

Well, do you know where it does go? Surely not Akgon?

I don't know where it leads, but it doesn't go to Akgon.

Can you open it?

I have tried, but its magicks are unknown to me.

Well, what are we going to do? We can't let him get away.

You're right. He may still be able to get back to Earth. We will have to return to the Stones and see if they can be of any help in locating the betrayer or opening this portal. If not, when I get back to Akgon, I can consult with my seers. They may be able to come up with something.

Maya moved out of his embrace. *Come on then, let's go. Can we seal the portal at least from this side so he can't use it?*

Hmm...yes, but then no one will be able to ever enter this realm again from that portal. With the help of the mist, I can close the one above, but that would mean the mist would be isolated for eternity.

Maya's body suddenly became rigid. When her body relaxed, she spoke. "The mist wants you to bind the portals with your magicks, Draakar. It said not to worry. The energy, both positive and negative, we generated here today will enable it to keep both portals closed to the betrayer, but your powers or your emissaries would be able to open it. Now that it knows about the portal to another realm, while it can't control the opening from the other side, it can control who enters this realm. The betrayer will not be allowed."

"That's good. I would not like the mist to always be alone."

"It would like us to send other brethren here from time to time so that it may learn more about us."

"That's possible."

"Oh, and by the way, did you know the entity is male?"

The lines on his forehead crinkled into a frown. "A male? I don't believe it's either male or female as creatures from either Earth or Akgon understand it."

"Not true. I get the sense it's definitely male. Call it Dam intuition."

He smiled. "If you say so, beloved." He took her hand and kissed her palm.

The mist parted in front of them to reveal a dirt floor and a rock wall on the other side. Draakar let Maya cross over first, but then they both paused to say farewell to the mist before moving into the cave. The slit in the wall closed behind him.

Draakar turned to face the rock surface and lay his palm upon it. Maya heard him call upon both the powers of the mist and Mother Earth, and then he sealed the portal so no one the mist did not wish to enter could. He took Maya's hand again. *We must return to your parent's house. That's where Talon and the others are. I've let Talon know we're headed there and to wait for us.*

Where's my mother?

She's there as well. I told you she's fine. Apparently, Sherri and Paul have arrived. I have some good new. Sherri finished the healing on your mother, I began.

That is good news. Wait. What about Paul? Is he well enough to travel?

Yes, he's fine.

What happened to his wife's body? Is it still in Ireland? I didn't even think about it or about funeral arrangements when we left.

You had other things to think about, but all is well. It has all been taken care of. We've actually been away for two of your earth days, Maya. During that time, Sherri and Paul brought his wife's body back with them. She had no family of her own, so they had her buried earlier this morning in Florida, where they lived.

Poor Paul. I'm sorry we weren't there for him. Was Sherri at least with him?

Yes, so he wasn't alone. I'm sorry too that we couldn't be there for him. Another death that bastard has to answer for.

Maya sighed, sadness still present in their small victory. *Well, what are we going to do about Justin, or Arwan, or whatever his name is? We've got to find him.*

We have to go back to the Stones. I would also like your parents to come with us.

My parents! I don't know about that. Besides, my mom still needs more time to recuperate.

She's fine, her dragon has awakened, and I think they will want to come.

Maya stepped away from Draakar, and he released her hand, silently watching her. "I'm not sure if I can return to Ireland with you just now," Maya said. "My vacation is almost over and I have a business to run. I've already been gone for some time and I have people who are depending on me."

He smiled at her. "Those are not the reasons why you don't wish to return with me. You forget, Maya, I am in your thoughts as you are in mine. I know what you fear."

She shook her head. "Do you? Well, explain it to me because I'm not sure I fear anything about you anymore."

Draakar laughed. "You never did." He closed the space between them and wrapped his arms around her waist. At the same time, she raised her arms to wrap them around his neck. "Hmm...I'm beginning to find I don't like having you out of my arms for very long."

She kissed his cheek and smile. "Me either. Will it always be this way?"

He nodded. "I fear I will always have this need to constantly be near you." He rubbed the top of her hair with his chin. "I promise we will work this out. But for right now, no one is safe, especially you, if I can't figure out where the betrayer has gone. We severely wounded him, but this is not the first time he's escaped justice. I won't be fooled into thinking we killed him or that he won't be back."

She raised her head up to look at him. She knew she was being stupid. Her fear, not of him, not even of going back to Ireland but returning with him to Akgon held her back. Yes, she was brethren, but she was human too. "I know you're right, but…"

"No buts. I need to get to the Stones as soon as possible, then we will try to locate the betrayer. For now, he won't be able to gain access to Earth's realm through the mist. But wherever he's gone, he may still be able to get back to Earth directly from there, so we must try to find him. The other alternatives would be to try to block all the portals here on Earth."

Maya understood the betrayer had to be stopped, but he didn't really need her to find him. She frowned as another thought occurred to her. "How many portals are there?"

He ran his hand through his hair; she'd come to realize he did that when he was frustrated. "I don't believe there are many. I know of only one other, besides the one for Akgon and the mist and I suspect there are others, but the Stones will know of them all. And some portals may be used to enter more than one realm, such as the Stones. If that's the case, they may be almost impossible to close off."

"You mean the portal at the Stones can take you to other worlds?" She had not considered that.

"Yes. That was one of the dangers we faced when we used it the first time. The portal at the Stones is a true gateway to other worlds."

She stepped out of his embrace and placed her hands on her hips. "Wow! How many other worlds are we talking here?"

"I do not know." He began to pace. "We've only ever used it to access Akgon, and the main portal on Akgon only leads to Earth. The three others lead to lesser limited realms."

"So even though you can use the portal here on Earth to go almost anywhere, it doesn't mean the ones in other realms work the same way."

He returned to stand in front of her, and she lowered her arms to her sides. "Yes, that's correct. It's also why I'm positive the betrayer won't be able to get back to here through the gate at the Stones. To use that entry, the Stones must accept you. Just as the mist will be able to bar access to its realm, the Stones can bar access to Earth. And the betrayer was banned long ago."

"Okay. Good to know, but since there may be other portals on this planet, he might still be able to return."

"That is why we have to try to find him first, or find all the other gateways and try to block the essence of the silver dragon from using a portal. Even then, some of the gateways will have to be constantly monitored." He raised his hand and caressed her cheek. "Come on, let's go. As soon as we get everyone, we'll return to Ireland and begin our search for both other gateways and the betrayer."

"How long will it take?"

"I don't know. I suspect to close all the portals might take a few days, but finding the betrayer may take as long."

He was right. Of course, he had to go, but she still needed to make arrangements for her business, since she could be gone for a while. "Not me. At least not yet. I'm going to need a few days to tie up some things here before I can leave. You go ahead and search for the betrayer. If you find him, I'll join you."

He took her hand and shook his head. "No. It is still too dangerous for you to be alone."

"But I thought the betrayer was hiding someplace..."

"I will stay with you and send Talon and some of the others back to the safety the Stones will provide. Talon can generate the necessary power to get the information we require from the Stones." From the strength in his voice, she knew she couldn't argue about this with him. In truth, some of her reluctance stemmed from her fear and confusion about leaving Earth and all she knew behind. But she also wanted to take care of the people who depended on her business for a living. Because when it came right down to it, when Draakar returned to Akgon, she would go with him.

She nodded. "Ah, how are we going to get to my parents' house? Are you going to call someone to come and pick us up?"

He grinned, then kissed her hand. "No need. My powers are at their peak. I can take us there."

Before Maya could question further what he meant. A soft green glow surrounded their bodies, and he kissed the question right out of her mind. The sound of Cass's voice finally got her attention.

"THERE YOU ALL ARE! Thank God! Are you all right?"

Maya turned out of Draakar's embrace and found herself being hugged by Cass. They were no longer in the cave, but stood in the middle of her mother's living room with the rest of the Firsts surrounding them.

Her parents stepped through the circle of brethren to hug both Maya and Draakar.

"Thank you, Draakar," Maya's mother cried as she hugged them both. Reaching only up to Draakar's chest, she had to tilt her head back to look up at him. "Thank you for returning our baby to us."

"She will always be safe with me," Draakar stated.

"Mom, how are you?" Maya asked, hugging both of her parents. "Should you be on your feet so soon? Shouldn't you be in bed?"

"Oh, shush. I'm fine," her mother replied. She removed the arm she used to hug Draakar with and gently patted his check. "Thanks to this one here." Then she glanced over her shoulder until her gaze found Sherri. "And Sherri, who arrived only a few hours ago and, well, here I am. The doctors are calling it a miracle. And so it is. You're all miracles." She included everyone in the room.

Maya hadn't noticed Sherri before, but she noticed her now. "Thank you," she said. Paul stood next to her and when Maya glanced down, she saw he held Sherri's hand. She stepped away from her mother and moved toward them. Draakar moved beside her. Maya hugged Sherri first, then Paul. "How are you feeling?" she asked as he hugged her back.

Paul briefly glanced at Sherri before meeting Maya's eyes, then looking at Draakar. "Better," he said, sounding like the Paul she remembered.

Maya could see his skin looked healthier than the last time she'd seen him, but his eyes told a different story. Still a beautiful shade of ocean blue, but while before, they always seemed to sparkle with laughter, no laughter lurked there now. The eyes staring back at her were old, drained. The spark missing. "I'm sorry, Paul, so sorry." Maya decided to address what happened directly to Paul, but for everyone to hear. Draakar had already communicated to the group the betrayer had escaped, but Maya told them of the sentient being, the mist, and of the fight.

"He's wounded, Paul. Draakar doesn't believe he killed him, but he sure as hell hurt him."

"We hurt him. And Maya took out his eye," Draakar supplied, pride in his voice.

"What!" her parents gasped in unison.

"I got lucky."

"Well, if it sheds enough blood, it can die." Talon stepped into the circle in the living room.

Maya swung her head around at the sound of a familiar voice. "Talon!" She rushed over to him and hugged him. "Am I glad to see you. It was you who led Draakar to me."

"Yeah. So see, the link I formed between us did some good," he smiled sheepishly.

"I'm still not sure I'm ready to forgive you for that," Maya said in a serious voice, but winked to let him know she wasn't angry with him.

"Tell ya what. Forgive me or I'll start calling you Step-Momma."

"Oh, no you don't!"

"Talon," Draakar warned.

"Step-Momma?" Maya's mother said, followed by her father's, "What!"

"Do you have something to tell us, honey?" her mother asked.

"Yes. Do you?" her father agreed sternly.

Draakar stepped forward and cleared his throat. "Actually, yes we do."

He dropped to both knees before Maya, who gasped as she watched him.

I only do this once, beloved.

He took her left hand in both of his. The air left her lungs, and she placed her free hand on her cheek as her parents stood on either side of her. Talon stood beside his father. The rest of the brethren looked on.

"Maya, in the life that came before this one, in this and in the next, I have loved you, will always love you. You have always held my heart. I am here to claim yours now until a time that has no end. Will you walk beside me to the end of our days and beyond? In the manner of your culture, will you marry me?"

I only do this once, beloved, Maya responded to her mate.

As brethren, they were already mated, husband and wife. Now he would honor her using earth's custom. Maya dropped to her knees before Draakar, releasing his hands and placing her own at the sides of his face. "Yes. In this life and the next, yes. Under brethren law or human, under any law, yes. I love you so very much."

They sealed their promise, this time with a kiss. But Draakar pulled away once their lips had done nothing more than touch. "Wait. One last thing." He placed his hand in his pants pocket, withdrew a small square black velvet box, and opened it. A marquis cut onyx stone surrounded by diamonds lay nestled inside. Draakar took it out and raised Maya's left hand, placing his ring on her finger.

"I belong to you as you belong to me. Now all will know this."

He pulled her face toward his own and this time, when his lips touched hers, they stayed a little longer. But not long enough to suit either of them. The sound of a cork popping out of a bottle drew their attention. Hand in hand, they stood and looked around the room as everyone smiled and raised a glass to them.

CHAPTER TWENTY-NINE

*A*nother cab pulled up in front of the passenger departure section of Reagan International Airport, and a single traveler got out. He didn't need help with his luggage nor was help offered. He only had a carry-on strapped across his shoulder and a weekend bag in his hand, not at all a remarkable occurrence.

He barely got a second glance from security as he made his way through the airport. The guy, while about average height, stood bulky with muscle and emitted an aura of menace. Yet no one bothered to really notice.

The man should have been stopped at the security check-point before boarding the plane. His one-way ticket, enough to warrant closer scrutiny. Along with the fact, he was a convicted felon wanted for questioning in two states as a person of interest in a murder investigation. The one guard, who checked his ID, stared at him hard but turned away once he met his eyes and allowed him to pass. No one even bothered to glance at the monitor as his bags went through. If someone had, they would have seen the five hundred-year-old sheathed ceremonial blade in his bag. A blade still as sharp as the day it was forged by dragon fire.

He made it to his gate without once being questioned, just as his flight to New Orleans boarded. But the land of jazz was not his ultimate goal. From New Orleans, he would rent a car and drive to his final destination: Window Rock, Arizona. If all went as planned, he would meet someone there. He was not sure how long he'd have to wait, but wait he would. For as long as it took.

MAYA SHOULDN'T HAVE BEEN SURPRISED to find herself walking down the aisle some forty-eight hours later in a little chapel not far from her parent's house. After everything that had happened in her life, nothing should surprise her. But this did.

Her mother held her arm on one side with her father on the other while the brethren stood before them. Cass stood up as her bridesmaid and Talon was Draakar's best man. There were no other friends or family present, mainly because they'd rushed everything. Also, Maya didn't want to bend the minds of her friends and family to help explain Draakar and her new family. They sent everyone announcement cards instead. Besides, they didn't need anyone else to witness their marriage; their bond was already stronger than any marriage ceremony. At least she didn't have to shop for a dress; she wore her grandmother's. Cass and Sherri helped her make alterations so it fit perfectly, and Sherri wove a garland of dark purple and green flowers to crown Maya's hair.

In one day Draakar had helped her turn over her business

to the general manager. Robert would remain behind to keep an eye on Talon and things. Draakar, along with her parents' help, arranged the wedding. Amazing what money and brethren willpower could accomplish.

Draakar.

He stood above everyone else in the room, and strength radiated from him—literally capable of moving mountains. Draakar wore a black fitted suit with a gold-colored silk shirt underneath and a bronze tie. His hair lay pulled back away from his face and fell in a long braid. His beauty brought tears to her eyes. This time, when she looked into those emerald eyes from her dreams, she found endless love within their depths.

You are my heart, Maya, and now you know you always were and always will be.

As you are mine, beloved.

Their wedding may have seemed rushed, but she had waited lifetimes for this day, a wait finally at an end. As soon as the ceremony concluded, the entire wedding party would head for the airport to return to Ireland. Maya took several deep breaths, unsure how she felt about leaving, and not just the country. Soon, she'd have to leave her world too, but she couldn't allow herself to think about it right now. This was a happy day. The music began, and she walked into the room. She placed her small hand in Draakar's larger one. Together, they turned to face the minister. They had already been mated under brethren law. Now they would be married under human.

As the limo drove up the mountainside, Maya neared the end of her long journey, the last leg home. Funny the way things happen. The first time she'd hiked the trail to the Stones in ignorance. The first time she traveled the road beside Draakar, she was in denial of herself and her relationship to him. Not anymore. She wondered how many more times she'd travel this road.

She nestled against his side. His arm lay across her shoulder and her head rested on his chest, listening to the steady rhythm of his heart. She'd left this place, unsure of her destiny, but returned as Draakar's truemate, Lady of Castle Akgon and Queen of the brethren.

As they got closer to the Stones, she could feel their call welcoming her, them both, home. She tilted her head to stare at Draakar.

Yes, I feel it too, he sent. *The Stones are pleased.*

I know, but there also seems to be a sense of desperation in the currents.

Yes. The silver dragon. We'll be at the castle soon. Hopefully, we will be able to find him by combining our powers with the power of the Stones.

I have a strange feeling, Draakar. Like we missed something and are now working on his time.

The sun dipped beneath the horizon when the car silently came to a stop at the bottom of the stone steps. Another car carrying the rest of the brethren and Maya's parents pulled up behind them. Ian opened the door to their car and Draakar stepped out. He turned to help Maya out of the car but never gave her a chance to stand on her own two feet. Bending down, he placed his arms under her thighs and lifted her to his chest. She wrapped her arms around his neck and laid her head on his shoulder.

Together, they watched her parents climb out of the limo.

"Welcome to our home, Vincent and Carrie," Draakar

said. "Ian will show you to your room. Please excuse us. We'll see you at dinner." Their audience smiled at his command. Without another word, Draakar turned with Maya cradled in his arms and effortlessly climbed the dozen or so steps.

The heavy front door opened before they reached it, and he carried his bride across the threshold of the brethren stronghold, the place of power. Never releasing his hold on Maya, he didn't head for the stairs leading to the bedrooms. Instead, he headed for what lay beneath the castle, the Circle of Stones.

As soon as they stepped into the circle, the Stones began to glow and softly hum. Draakar put Maya down in the center of them. They stood face-to-face, fingers entwined and their foreheads touching, while the Stones bathed them in their light, rejoicing in their union. Draakar raised his head and looked down at his wife, his truemate. "I love you," he said aloud, but the sound vibrated tenfold throughout the cavern and burrowed its way into her soul. Before Maya could respond in kind, she found herself standing in a shadow-filled room, lit only by moonlight shining through the opened window.

"What...where?" she began. She turned her head to see where she was. Draakar had sent them to his room.

Our room... He spoke in her mind.

She looked up at him, smiling as he lowered his head toward her, but he turned his aside before their lips could touch and nuzzled her neck instead. A sound erupted from deep in his throat. The man didn't purr. Oh, no. Nothing so tame. This was no kitten. He hissed and growled as he licked and nipped at her earlobe.

Hmm, what would it take to tame a dragon?

"I can hear your thoughts," he whispered. "To tame a dragon is a dangerous thing. Are you sure you want to?"

"Oh. Yeah."

He turned his face to her again so she could see his response. His eyes flashed emerald fire with his need for her. Placing her hands on his shoulders, he used his to softly touch and trace the features of her face.

"I love you," she said.

HE STILLED one hand at the side of her neck but began to move the other. One lone finger ran lightly down her collarbone and skimmed over the buttons on her blouse. As it touched a button, it immediately came undone, and still his finger continued its descent toward its ultimate goal.

Long, blunt tipped fingers skimmed past the top of the calf-length skirt she wore. As his hand moved downward, the skirt moved up until the bottom edge settled around her thighs. Never taking his eyes off her, he rubbed one finger back and forth across the barely there front of her bikini cut underwear. He'd found what he sought. He inhaled deeply, filling his lungs with her woman's scent and filling his soul with the scent of pure Maya.

His.

Soon he would fill her...but not quite yet.

Continuing to maintain eye contact, he halted the hand under her skirt and moved his other to her mouth. Rubbing his thumb back and forth across her mouth once before sticking it inside when she parted her lips. She sucked on it hard, causing him to growl again.

Mine! The thought came from both.

While her tongue sucked and swirled around his thumb, he removed his hand from underneath her skirt and placed his finger, now saturated with her juices, into his mouth. He kept his mouth open so she could see his tongue as he swirled it around his finger before closing his lips around it.

"Mmm," he rumbled. *I like.*

Like a runaway train, he could sense Maya's heat rising up from her core. She opened her mouth, releasing his thumb, and orgasmed right then and there. If he hadn't reached out to catch her, she would have sunk to the floor in a puddle of her own fluids.

"So passionate. And all for me," he said, kissing her forehead while at the same time ridding her of all of her clothes.

Draakar picked up a naked Maya and placed her on the bed. Following her down, he covered her with his body, but kept his arms beside her head to hold his weight. He used his magicks to release his hair from the braid. It fell over his shoulders onto her arm, causing electricity to spark wherever the strands touched her bare skin. She raised her hands and grabbed fistfuls of his mane as she pulled him down to her.

As their tongues joined in a universal ritual, she could taste herself mixed with the dark rich flavor of Draakar. Better than the richest dessert.

With a thought, she removed his clothes, and skin rubbed against skin. Two sets of hands were everywhere until there only remained one place they hadn't touched. But not for long. Gliding her hand over his chest, past his navel, Maya's hand grasped her objective and guided his sex where she needed him most.

They both growled at the contact of him firmly encased within her. Draakar found her mouth with his own and the rhythm of his tongue matched the rhythm of his hips as he thrust and withdrew from his mate. At first his movements were slow and languid, then he stopped all together and rolled over, taking her with him without breaking contact. He helped her sit up and straddle him by placing her legs alongside his hips. Then he bent his knees and placed his feet higher on the bed, spreading his legs slightly to better cradle her.

Ride me, Maya. Tame your dragon.

She grabbed two fists full of hair, and ride him she did. Her inner muscles clamped around his shaft as she pumped up and down. He met her thrust for thrust, hitting her sweet spot each time. The heat built between them until they were surrounded by the glow of their joined magicks. Maya threw her head back and flew. Her body released from its physical shell and exploded into a thousand pieces. And Draakar, her truemate, caught each and every piece and put her back together. As one, they came down from the heights. Maya dropped forward until her head rested on his chest, and he placed his arms around her.

"I love you," she told him. "Since the day I was born, I love you."

He kissed the top of her hair. "I love you, too." Wrapped in each other's arms, they finally found the peace together that had always eluded them apart.

LORD. My Lord.

Draakar, who is that? Maya woke abruptly from a sound sleep in Draakar's bed.

Valour and his sisters, I think. They are trying to reach me. They must have tapped into the power our mating generated to be able to call to me now. Come, we must go to the Stones. I should be able to communicate with them better from there.

"But…what's going on?"

"Come, we must hurry." Draakar had them in the center of the Stones before the last syllable left his mouth.

Maya looked at her mate, who held her hand and stood naked beside her. She looked down at herself, just as naked. "Oh, no! Wait a second." She immediately clothed them both in matching golden silk robes.

Draakar smiled. *They cannot see us, my love. I am the only one who shall ever see you, thus.* Then his facial features relaxed into a more serious expression. Holding Maya's hand, he closed his eyes, and the Stones glowed brighter than they had the last time they were there. An aura of light reflecting all the colors of the rainbow surrounded Draakar and Maya. She closed her eyes, instinctively knowing she needed to join her powers to his. The colors blazed brighter with their combined magicks.

Thank the Claw we reached you.

Valour. What happened? How did you know you would be able to communicate across the portal?

Greetings, my Lord and my Lady. My sisters and I knew you had found your mate, Lord. Our casting showed it so; we knew your powers would be strong enough to hear us through the portal if we tried at the Center of the Stones on Akgon.

I suspected as much. What's wrong?

You must return, Lord. Sierran was only the first. Since then, others have weakened physically.

Have any died?

None yet. But it is only a matter of time.

Bring those so weakened to the Circle of Stones, Valour. I think their healing power will help until my return. I cannot come back just yet. There is danger here, too.

Maybe Sherri can help, Maya interjected.

Draakar looked at his mate. *Yes. Maya is correct. Sherri is one of the human brethren and she is a natural healer. She will be able to help sustain those who are ailing until Maya and I can return.*

Is the power there strong enough then to open the portal more than once, so easily? Valour asked.

Yes, the magicks here are very strong and I am at full strength. With Maya's help, I can open the portal to Akgon at will. And with the help of the brethren I've awakened, we can all cross over any time.

Very good. But Majesty, what is this danger and how soon will you follow the healer?

Maya understood Valour merely tried to understand why his Lord didn't return straight away. After all, he had found his mate. And with the longstanding of a trusted friend and advisor, he had no fear of asking, so Draakar replied. *There has been a complication here on earth. The silver dragon, the betrayer, is still alive.*

Maya could hear the shocked gasp of Draakar's advisor in her mind.

But...how can this be? Your mother killed him after he murdered your father.

I'm not sure how it happened, but he is alive. There's another complication. Time moves differently here. How long have I been gone from Akgon?

Ah, I should have realized that. You've been gone for six of our cycles. How long is that on Terra?

I have been gone a long time. I have been here about two Earth weeks. It is referred to as Earth now. But I cannot leave until the betrayer has been found. He's gone to ground in another dimension.

Do you know which one?

No. But there can't be many portals that link to Earth.

That's true, I do not remember there being many.

We will call on the Stones for help to show us where all the portals on planet are located. If we can't find him, then we'll seal all we find, so no one may enter Earth's realm without my leave. This may take a few days.

Yes, the Stones would be aware of all the portals. The betrayer must be stopped. He would not be satisfied with destroying Earth. Akgon would be next.

I know. I will send Sherri, one of our Firsts, to you shortly, and I expect her to be treated accordingly. But she is still learning the full extent of her powers.

Have no fear, Lord, all shall be made aware of her rank and I will help her harness her magicks as I've helped you and Talon. Besides the healer and my Lady, how many others have you been able to awaken?

There are many here, Valour, who carry the blood.

So it's true? The brethren bloodline still exists there?

Yes, Valour, it's true. There may be truemates here that can save our world.

Praise to the Claw and Mother Earth for keeping us within her bosom. I look forward to finally meeting the forgotten ones, forgotten no more. I will pass this on to the others.

My Firsts are seven of the strongest awakened brethren.

Seven is a number of power.

And they are very powerful. The Earth magicks have been changed somehow. You'll see when you meet them, and I have a surprise for you.

I already know you've found your truemate.

Ah, but she's so much more. You'll see. "He's going to weep with joy when he see's you're a Dam," he whispered to Maya.

"Why?" Maya whispered back, confused.

"Because at long last, the brethren would have a queen. And a powerful one."

I look forward even more then to meeting my Lady, at last, Valour sent, interrupting their verbal exchange.

And I you, Valour, Maya sent.

Maya touched Draakar's arm to get his attention. "I think

277

Paul should go with Sherri, so she's not in a strange place alone. Besides, I'm not sure you can separate them."

"I think you're right," he replied. *Valour, Sherri, will be accompanied by another one of my Firsts, Paul, but he has been damaged. The betrayer killed his wife in front of him and then tried to drain his life energy. I've restored his balance, but it will take time for his spirit to heal. To that end, I believe Sherri helps him.*

Are they a mated pair, Lord?

I'm not sure. I think it's too early to tell.

I might know when I see them.

I shall send Sherri and Paul through within the hour; have a place in the palace prepared for them of human proportions. They have not learned to take their dragon form yet, but you can teach them how when they get there. The magicks here are very strong and prevent them from changing. And Valour, please do not greet them in dragon form. I don't want to scare them for the first time in an unfamiliar place.

Don't worry. My sisters and I will take good care of them. What about Talon? Will he be returning with you?

We'll see.

Draakar cut the connection, and the Stones lost their brilliant glow.

"We'll gather everyone here," Draakar said. "But first I'll speak to Sherri and Paul to let them know what's happening on Akgon and why they must go ahead of everyone else."

"I think we should speak to them face-to-face," Maya said. "It will not be easy for them to leave their lives here on Earth, but at least they'll be together." Maya spoke through her own concerns about leaving her world and entering another. As queen, no less. She found the prospect daunting and something she chose not to think about. Instead, concentrating solely on being with Draakar. The brethren needed him on

Akgon, and Valour's comments proved how much. Her place lay by his side.

They found Sherri and Paul in the green room, one of many sitting rooms in the castle, already seated side-by-side on an original Queen Anne sofa. Their fingers entwined. The room had a plaque at the entrance titling it the green room, even though the only thing green in there was the sofa. Maya and Draakar turned to briefly stare at each other before returning their gazes to the couple before them.

They immediately stood. "Lord, Lady. Congratulations again," Sherri said with a smile in her voice. "We didn't expect to see you so soon, at least not until a little later when we were to gather at the Stones."

Maya blushed slightly at Sherri's words. "Ah…we have some news from Akgon."

"Yes," Draakar confirmed, taking her hand. "Now that my full powers are engaged, my advisor was able to communicate with us. There is trouble on Akgon."

"Oh, no!" Sherri and Paul exclaimed in unison.

"You know our world is weakening, and the brethren, as a result, are also weakening. Some have fallen very ill. I cannot return yet. I must try to find the betrayer first, or at least prevent him from returning to Earth by sealing the portals of the other realms."

"How may we help, Lord?" Paul asked.

"Sherri is a healer, like me. In fact, she is stronger at it. I need her to return to Akgon and help the brethren there."

Sherri frowned. "But I don't understand. Are they physically injured in some way?"

"Not exactly. Over time, their life energies are being drained, so the body functions more slowly until it completely shuts down, resulting in death. But this can take a very long time. Unfortunately, we've reached the time when the decline is happening faster in some of the older, less powerful dragons."

"But…how can I help? What can I do?"

"The same thing you did for Paul and Maya's mother. With the help of the Stones on Akgon, you can help keep the energies of those brethren who have begun to fail balanced until I can get there."

Sherri turned to look at Paul. Maya could read the worry emanating from Paul for Sherri and the uncertainty in Sherri's eyes at the thought of leaving Paul.

"I…"

But before Sherri could finish whatever she wanted to say, Paul spoke up, continuing to stare at Sherri. "She'll go and help anyway she can, but I'll go with her."

"Of course you can go with her," Maya said quickly. "We didn't mean she was going to go by herself. It's always better to have someone you know with you in a strange place."

Signs of relief appeared on Sherri and Paul's faces.

"Then we'll go," Sherri said. "How soon will we leave?"

"Right after we attempt to locate the betrayer, we'll open the portal to send you both to Akgon."

Paul hesitated. "But if we do locate him, won't you need us here to help kill the bastard?"

"No. I can take care of him by myself now."

"Don't worry, Paul," Maya stated. "Draakar will not face the betrayer alone and you will be avenged."

Paul nodded his head in agreement.

"Why don't the two of you go and pack?" Draakar said. "Take whatever you want and then join us at the Stones."

"Will we be able to create things there, Lord, like we can here?" Sherri asked.

"Hmm, I'm not sure. When we first arrived on Akgon, Earth was still in a primitive state, and we had no trouble creating the things we needed using our powers on Akgon.

But electronics, computers, as you know it, I don't know. However, you can create whatever you want here and take it with you, and you can certainly test the limits of your powers on Akgon."

For the first time since his wife's death, Maya read the glimmer of interest flaring in Paul at the prospect of testing his powers. He had been an engineer, so it would be interesting to see what he came up with.

CHAPTER THIRTY

*P*aul and Sherri arrived in the cavern, a large suitcase in each hand, a few minutes after everyone else, and took their places around the circle. Maya's parents were not there. Even though Maya's mother could harness magicks, Draakar didn't want her trying to expend any energy until she had been trained. So her father kept her company in their room.

Draakar and Maya stood in the circle and called on the power of the Stones. He held her hands and laid his forehead against hers. The current of energy in her answered the call of need in him. The familiar glow of magicks surrounded them, getting brighter and brighter. Together they harnessed the strength of the Stones but, no matter how much power they generated, they were still unable to locate the betrayer. Mother Earth couldn't help because he had escaped through a portal not of her world, but one that merely had a gate anchored here.

At least now they knew the locations of all the portals on the planet. There were five in all. The Circle of Stones portal already had its own protection and barred the betrayer from the area, as well as the portal to the mist. That just left three. They had to close, but all the portals would always be watched.

"Will we be able to close the other portals from here?" Maya asked.

"Unfortunately, no," Draakar responded. "Since the portals are only partially on Earth, as the anchor, I will have to be physically present at each of them to ensure they are closed from this side."

"Then we all will go with you, Father," Talon said.

"That will not be necessary, Talon," Draakar replied directly to his son, hoping from his tone Talon would know his Lord spoke to him and not his father. He noted Talon wisely decided to keep quiet, even knowing what came next. "I will not need everyone to go with me, but I will need everyone's help for something else. We will open the portal to Akgon. I can open it myself now, but you all will need to know how to open it if I'm not around."

Draakar understood what Talon wanted to know and what he feared. He did not want to go through the portal until he found his truemate. His father watched as Talon silently listened, so he sent directly to him to ease his apprehension. *No Talon, you will not be returning with us.*

Talon breathed an audible sigh of relief. *Thank you, Father. Thank you, but why? Why did you change your mind?*

Draakar turned to look at Maya and squeezed her hand. *Because I know what it's like to be apart from your truemate. I've found mine. I have no choice but to allow you to find yours. Besides, when Maya and I return to Akgon I will need someone here to watch over things. You will stay here at Akgon castle, run Akgon Enterprises and oversee the Earth brethren and the brethren of Akgon who come looking for their mates.*

Talon walked over to his father and hugged him. "Thank you."

When he turned away to return to the edge of the circle with the others, Draakar stopped him.

"No, stay." He linked his hand in Talon's and Maya's, and she linked her hand to Talon's. The three of them formed a circle within the Stones and combined their energies. A slight sulfur scent carried within the cavern just before a gray swirling mass formed in their center.

Sherri and Paul. Draakar looked at them. *You will have to enter the circle to enter the portal, but do not break or touch the contact of our joined hands. Enter between Talon and me; we will raise our hands to allow you through.*

Sherri and Paul each picked up their suitcases, and after nodding to each other, they stepped under the raised hands and entered the gray mass in the center. The sound of thunder filled the cavern, then a flash of blinding light. Once the light blinked out, the cloud disappeared, as had Sherri and Paul.

"Are they through?" Maya asked.

"They're through," Draakar replied. "Don't worry, they'll be fine. Meanwhile, we have portals to close. Now, did everyone pay attention on how opening the portal was done and the energy necessary to manipulate it?"

"Yes, Father. I think we got it." Talon grinned.

"Good. Closing the portals will be a similar process."

"Who will you take with you, Draak?" Ian asked.

Draakar smiled at his First among Firsts, so far the only one to shorten his name. "Talon will stay here. But I will take you, Darryl and Cass." He turned to face James and Robert. "You two will remain with Talon until we return."

"But, Father," Talon interrupted, "what about my mate? How will I find her if I'm stuck here?"

Draakar sighed. For a four-hundred-and-some-year-old brethren, he looked and sounded like a human teenager. He glanced over to see Maya grinning at him.

"You know she's not of age yet, Talon. When she is old enough, you will be able to find her. For now, she is probably safest not being with us and drawing attention to herself."

His acceptance didn't come immediately, but finally he agreed. "Alright. But I will find her, Father."

Draakar nodded in agreement. No one told Talon they'd already seen her, leaving Draakar to let him know. And Draakar still wasn't sure what to do. But he'd decide before he left if to tell him about the girl they'd seen at the airport or not. "You will," he said to his son. "Meanwhile, I think you had the right idea wanting to study human ways. So go ahead and enroll in the university here. Make a place for yourself in this world. With Akgon's resources and your abilities, you will do well here until it is time for you to return home with your mate. It will take a little time for all of the knowledge Mother Earth has already imparted to you to make sense. Robert and James can also be of great assistance in helping you to adjust."

"Sure," James said. "We'll have a grand time."

"That's correct, young Lord," Robert replied.

"Okay. Cool," Talon said. "How soon will you guys leave and when should we expect you back?"

"We leave as soon as Ian can get the jet fueled, and I'm not sure how long it will take. A lot depends on the strength of the magicks of the portals."

"Draakar," Maya said, "what about my parents? They'd probably want to come with us, but I'd prefer my mother stay here and rest."

"Yes, it's the safest place for them. I don't want any of you leaving the parameters of the wards until we get back and the portals are closed. The betrayer is still out there somewhere."

"Don't worry so, we'll be fine." Talon hugged Maya. "I'll

take good care of your parents, and you take good care of my father."

"You know I will."

"And I'll start your mother's training," Talon offered.

Maya smiled. "She'll love that."

CHAPTER THIRTY-ONE

*T*he plane touched down in Massachusetts at Logan airport. The first of three cities, Draakar, Maya, and their Firsts, had to visit to look for the dimensional portals. A rental car awaited them at the curb as they walked from the terminal.

The driver got out and Ian palmed him with a tip for his trouble. The brethren continued their journey to Salem. There they hoped to find a long forgotten grave on Winter Island, the gravesite a gateway to another world. After a short trip from the airport to Salem, they arrived and Draakar had no trouble finding the marker of power currents he sought.

This is the place, Draakar sent as he stopped before a mound of dirt facing the harbor.

The wind buffeted them as they stood upon the cliff, and Maya pushed the hair away from her face as she looked around. She could not locate a grave marker no matter where she looked, only a swelling in the grass-covered ground in front of their feet.

Understanding dawned. *What? This pile of dirt? You're kidding?* She asked incredulously.

No, I'm not. Open your senses. Feel.

Maya closed her eyes and reached out with her brethren senses. *My God! You're right. There's something here. I can feel it. Like a gap, a kind of break in the earth.*

Yes. Cass agreed. *I feel it, too.*

They all glanced around. They were not alone. This time of day, a lot of tourist frequented the area. *Ah,* Darryl sent to them. *How are you going to go about this? Will these people be able to notice anything when we shut this gate?*

No. They will only see us standing as we are now admiring the view. A few who are sensitive to magicks may feel a slight twinge. No more than Maya's father would feel, but that's all.

What if there's someone near with stronger brethren blood? Maya sent. *Won't they be able to detect more?*

If there were anyone near with that much power, I would know. Come, we don't have much time.

Okay, what do you need us to do? Maya asked.

I need everyone to stand around the mound and clasp hands.

Although not very large, the mound appeared just wide enough for all of them to stand around it holding hands. Draakar drew on his powers, the powers of the brethren and Mother Earth, to seal the portal. Like a beating heart, the mound pulsated as though the magicks of the connected realm were trying to fight against the seal. But as Draakar's magicks and will were stronger, they set the seal firmly in place.

The Dark Lord opened his eyes and released Ian's hand, but maintained Maya's. *This portal is now sealed, but we're not done. This one was easy, but let me warn you, it is the weakest of the three portals that must be closed. It only led to one other realm. The others wield stronger magicks and will be much more difficult to close.*

Draakar, Darryl sent, *why seal the portals? How come we don't just cut the anchors holding them here?*

If we cut the anchors, the portal is gone forever. Also, to cut the portal would require destroying a part of Earth magicks. That is also part of the anchor, perhaps harming Earth in ways we cannot foresee. Besides, these portals were created for a reason, even if we no longer remember, but Mother Earth allowed the anchors to be placed, and we must honor her wishes. The other reason is someday we may need these portals.

"Are we going to stay the night here, Draakar?" Maya asked, trying to hide a yawn behind her hand.

Draakar smiled at her. *You're tired.*

Maya returned a weary smile to him. They were drawing on and using massive amounts of energy. It had been a long, trying last couple of days, but they could not rest, not quite yet. "No. I'm sorry, beloved," Draakar replied, placing a kiss on her hair. "Let's head back to the airport. We can sleep on the plane."

They returned to their car and as Ian got behind the wheel, he asked, "What's our next stop?"

"Egypt!" Cass exclaimed.

"Yes. There is a portal at the Temple of Isis on the island of Philae," Draakar said.

"But I thought Mother Earth said there was another portal here in the U.S.," Maya replied.

"Correct, but that one will take a lot of energy and I think it's best we try to close it last. It is another true gateway leading to many different worlds, much like the Circle of Stones. It will hold considerable magicks and we will have to meld with the power of the Stones as well as Mother Earth in order to seal it."

"What about the one in Egypt?" Cass asked. "Is it like the Stone portal, too?"

"Not quite."

"What do you mean, not quite?" Maya asked curiously.

"It is the Temple of Isis. It leads directly to her realm and from there she can, if she wishes, send you anywhere."

"Oh my God!" Maya cried. "You mean she's...real?"

Draakar laughed. "As real as dragons that once flew in these skies."

"Have you ever met her?"

"Yes, just before her ascension. That is one portal we will not have to close, but I must warn her."

"Ascension?" Maya asked, frowning. "What exactly do you mean?"

"Her mortal body died, but her energy was reborn to stand watch over the portal."

"So what the Egyptians believed was true, about life after death?" Cass asked, fascinated.

"In a manner of speaking," Draakar replied. "Long ago there were some humans who were more sensitive to magicks, but who did not have brethren blood. Isis was one such human, and Mother Earth granted her ascension to this other realm, but she can never return to Earth because she would die here."

"Are there others like her?" Maya asked. "Who have been allowed this ascension?"

"Very few. But yes, there are others, and some even populate this realm."

"Wow," Maya said, at the same time wondering if heaven was where one ascended.

Draakar, ever present in her thoughts, must have heard her silent query. "No, Maya, it is not heaven, not even close. But there are many things existing outside of the Christian heaven and hell that are both part and apart of this realm. Think of the temple as a gateway and Isis as one of the last of the gatekeepers."

"But what or who are they keeping out?" Darryl asked.

"There are many other worlds in the universe and beings who inhabit them. Some of those beings are a danger to Earth. If they were aware of this place, their only interest would be in conquering the realm and subjugating its inhabitants."

"Like the betrayer," Maya said.

"Exactly. Mother Earth knows her children are still too young to have to deal with these beings from other worlds and has taken steps to keep them out. So until the time comes that her children are of age, she will do everything in her power to protect them, including controlling access to and the very knowledge of the portals. Frankly, there may never come a time when the portals will be common knowledge."

"But other than the brethren, are there others that have been allowed access here?" Cass asked.

"None that I know of. Ancestral memories only show our need was great, and Mother Earth adopted the first brethren as her own. By using her magicks, our ancestors were able to take human form."

"Well, why aren't there gatekeepers at the portal we just sealed or back at the castle?" Maya asked.

"There is no gatekeeper here or the portal at the mist because they only lead to one realm, and Mother Earth had no fear of the beings from those realms. The brethren are the gatekeepers for the portal at the Stones. Although, the mist may also be a sort of gatekeeper. The last place we'll head to should've also had a gatekeeper, but it doesn't, not anymore. The people of the land were supposed to stand guard over the portal. But they stopped believing a long time ago, so there is no longer a gatekeeper."

"Wow." Darryl grinned. "Well, Egypt, here we come."

THEY HAD BEEN CONSTANTLY TRAVELING for the last five days. The group sitting in the car on its way to Window Rock, Arizona, felt a unanimous relief to reach the last portal they had to close.

Maya leaned against Draakar's shoulder. He rubbed his face against her hair, inhaling her unique fragrance. She'd found the visit to Isis the most awe inspiring. He'd promised her one day they would return and spend more time amongst the pyramids of Egypt and enjoy the hospitality of the temple longer. Unfortunately, on this trip, time mattered; they had a silver dragon to stop, and they had to return to Akgon. As the car slowed down, Maya raised her head off Draakar's shoulder to stare out the window.

"Wow," she exclaimed.

Draakar glanced over her shoulder. Before them lay another magnificent sight. A graceful red stone arch rose up from the ground, but it didn't look as though it belonged to the earth. It appeared rather like a very large hole in a rock. Large enough for a dragon to fly through. Nonetheless, it was a mystical place, timeless and ageless. It reminded him of some of the men and women of the Navajo nation they'd seen as they passed through the reservation. The arch stood on their land.

"Wow!" Cass echoed Maya's sentiment. "It's beautiful."

"Yes," Ian agreed. "But it's really open and on display. How're we going to do this?"

Even as he spoke, a freak storm rolled in. Out of nowhere, lightning cracked across the sky and thunder rumbled overhead. Thick gray clouds quickly hid the afternoon sun as people ran for shelter before the rain released in torrents from the sky. In the span of five minutes, the day went from brightly colorful to gray as sheets of rain poured from the sky, obscuring everything around them.

Draakar stepped out of the Jeep. *Come.*

Maya and his brethren followed him. Rain fell all around the group, but a waterproof shield surrounded them. The water didn't so much as slide over them, as it never touched their bodies at all. Even their shoes never sank into the mud puddling beneath their feet.

They walked to the rocky path, then climbed up the side of the rock into the center of the hole.

Draakar looked down at the ground and frowned. *Blood has been spilt here recently. And the place carries the stench of the silver dragon. This is the realm to which the betrayer crossed.*

The magicks of this place is strong. Maya take my left hand, Cass on my right, and Darryl and Ian in-between the women. They joined hands as they had done before and Draakar called up his powers, as well as the others. A multicolored glow surrounded them all. Anyone watching the arch would have seen strange colorful lights flickering through the storm in the center of the rock formation. Although, no one would venture near to see what caused the bizarre occurrence. This was, after all, a mystical place, so maybe the lights were not so strange and none of their business.

As Draakar built his power, he formed an energy seal to close the portal to Earth. But…something…something very old and very powerful on the other side of this portal fought the combined powers of the brethren. Voraciously fighting the seal forced on the portal connected to Earth. A guardian, perhaps, stood on the other side and wrestled with them for control.

The Dark Lord called brethren he sensed in the area. He called to Mother Earth, and on the power of the Stones for help in sealing this side of the gate because their powers could go no farther into the other realm. And still, the power on the other side resisted the seal.

The center of the hole grew brighter and brighter until no one could look directly at it. But Mother Earth would not be denied; she ruled here. The sound of a sonic boom rent the air. The bright light went dark and so did the brethren, leaving only the falling rain bathing their faces as they lay on the ground.

Draakar, the first to regain consciousness, lay on his side. He raised his head to check on Maya, who rested beside him, her breathing even and steady. She stirred and her lashes opened as he watched. He placed his hand on her arm to help them both stand. *Are you all right?*

Yes, yes, I think so. What...about the others? What happened?

They turned to look around them. They found Darryl against one side of the rock arch and Cass on the other. Both were coming around and didn't appear any worse for wear. They could hear Ian before they saw him, staggering toward them a few feet away from the arch.

What happened? Maya asked again.

Whatever controls this portal has strong magicks, maybe as strong as the magicks of the Stones. Thank the Claw it does not work on this side of the realm. We were able to close the portal on this side of the gate using Earth magicks. The magicks of the realms may be equal in power, but no one on the other side will be able to open the portal.

Can it be opened on this side? Maya asked.

Only with Earth magicks and only by someone strong enough to wield a lot of power. We'll have to keep an eye on this area. I will open a branch of Akgon near here. I have already called upon brethren in the area to watch over this place. But I'll have to find one strong in the blood to run the operation here.

I'll stay, Lord.

Draakar turned to Darryl and grasped his shoulder. "You don't have to. I would like you to come to Akgon with me."

"It's fine. I'll get to Akgon eventually, but for now, I'm the most logical choice. Besides, one of my great, great, great grandpas somewhere down the line claimed Navajo origins, or at least that's the story I was told. I could do some digging about that." He grinned, showing straight white teeth. "Get to know the people around here. It would make it easier for us to keep an eye on this portal. Maybe even find out what happened to the people who were supposed to guard this place."

"Are you sure? I can get someone else to do this. I sense another not far from here who has potential."

"I'm sure. You need one of us with power."

"And you do have power. What worries me is although the stench of the silver dragon is around this portal, he did not return to Earth. I think this is where he left and he may have had help from this side. That would explain the blood; a sacrifice in an attempt to open the portal."

"Is the betrayer the one that tried to stop us from closing the portal?" Darryl asked.

"No. That wasn't his magicks at work. It's the magicks in the other realm. But it doesn't matter; he will not be able to break the seal. Not from the other side."

"But it can be broken from this side."

"Yes," Draakar replied. "Using Earth magicks, but it would have to be very powerful magicks."

"Then it's even more important one of your Firsts stays to keep an eye on things, at least for a while."

"All right," Draakar reluctantly agreed. "We'll drop you off at the hotel. By the time we get there, I will have everything in place. Tonight there will be two others who will join you who are strong in the blood. Train them. If you need help, call on

Talon. He'll remain in Ireland for some time and run the brethren worldwide business. But I'll have you head the Akgon Enterprises here in the U.S. and you can report to Talon and have full access to all the necessary resources. Also, there maybe other brethren on Akgon who would like to cross over and you can help them here. Whenever you're ready to come to Akgon, get to the Stones and either Talon or I will bring you across."

They said their goodbyes in front of the hotel and returned to the car, waiting to take them to the airport and back to Ireland.

"Do you think he'll be all right?" Maya asked after they'd boarded the plane.

"As long as the seal holds, and it will, he'll be fine. Even if the betrayer finds someway to breach it, Darryl is very powerful and will be able to hold it in place with the help of the brethren I've awakened until additional help can get here." He paused and took her hand. "Come, my love, let's go home."

"Back to Akgon castle?" Maya asked.

"No." Draakar waited to see if she would put voice to what he already knew worried her. When she remained silent, he kissed her fingers and continued. "It's time to go home. I must, and I need you with me. I want to show you Akgon."

She squeezed his hand. "I know. And I want to go with you. It's just…"

"I know, beloved, and understand. But you have nothing to fear."

Maya released some of her anxiety, knowing he understood. "It's just hard to leave my world."

"We'll come back from time to time. And I know your

parents will come with us when we leave, and they're more than welcome."

"Yes, at least for a while. I can't see my dad leaving his volunteer charities or my mother leaving her friends for any significant amount of time. But don't worry, we'll take it one step at a time. Just know when you leave, I will be by your side. That's where I want to be. I just hope the brethren accept me."

Draakar pulled her closer to his side. At last she'd admitted the real issue. Maya still didn't understand. Not only would they accept her, but she would be their queen. Her very existence on Akgon would save their world. They would love her for that alone, but they would love her even more for herself—her warmth and her caring, generous nature.

SHE HELPED his son with no thought to herself, and she had been willing to help him when she hadn't been sure of him. He opened himself fully to her, and let her hear his thoughts and examine his feelings so there would be no doubt in her head or heart of her place in his life.

"Thank you," she said. "Have I told you how much I love you?"

"Not since last night."

"Well, I love you. Let's go home."

CHAPTER THIRTY-TWO

"*A*re you sure you won't come with us?" Maya asked Talon for the third time.

$ Draakar sent to Maya through their bond. "Do you think I'm right not telling him we'd seen his truemate at the airport?"

"Yes, for now. You haven't been able to locate her since then and we only know she's left the country." The same way Maya had initially blocked her presence from Draakar, Talon's mate also seemed able to block Talon as well as Draakar.

"I think she blocks me partly because she's a child and had not completely awakened to her powers yet, and perhaps also as a defense mechanism."

"That makes sense. She's protecting herself from any other magicks searching for her, including the silver dragon."

"But I've established a connection with her, so if she calls to me, I will be able to find her. When she gets older, so would Talon."$

"Maya," Talon replied, smiling. "Yes, I'm sure. I have to be here for her if she needs me." He spoke of his truemate. Maya smiled, glad for him.

"I know you have to stay, it's just that…" Maya's voice trailed off.

Talon hugged her. "You'll be fine. You'll make a great queen. Tell Valour I said so."

Maya smiled. "I guess I can't put this off any longer."

"No," Draakar said, coming to stand behind her. "You can't." He wrapped his arms around her and she leaned back into his embrace.

"Well then, what are we waiting for?" she said. "I've kept the others waiting long enough. Let's go."

Draakar transferred himself, Maya, and Talon to the circle. Maya's parents were already there; each held a suitcase. Cass stood next to Ian. Robert and James stood apart from the others but approached as their Lord and Lady appeared.

Maya stepped out of Draakar's embrace to hug James goodbye.

"Take care, lassie," James said, kissing Maya's cheek. "And don't worry about a thing. Everything will be fine."

"That's right," Robert agreed, also kissing Maya's cheek and shaking Draakar's hand. "We'll take care of everything at this end."

"I know you will," Draakar stated. "There will be other brethren crossing over. As my Firsts they will answer to you and Talon. Help them to adjust and whenever you all wish to cross over, I will know." Draakar looked over at Maya. "It is time."

"Wait," Cass said. "Where are your bags? Aren't you taking anything with you?" Cass held two bags in her hand and one of the suitcases Ian held also belonged to her.

Maya smiled. "I already have everything I'll need." Maya had decided she would live as the brethren lived. She dressed from an image Draakar had provided for her of the types of garments the women on Akgon wore. A very sheer, sleeveless, ankle length side slitted gown, woven with golden thread, but you could not see through it. It reminded Maya of a Roman toga, but this dress wrapped around her curves and moved as she walked. Maya felt beautiful in it and by the look in Draakar's eyes when she first showed it to him, he agreed.

Around her throat she wore a torque Draakar had given her the night before. He also now wore a matching one around his neck. Hers was made of onyx in the shape of a dragon with emerald eyes, whose tail wrapped around her neck. Draakar's was bronze, with a gold-tipped tail, and his dragon had golden eyes.

Maya briefly wondered if their daughter's eyes would be the color of her father's or her mother's. She had to stifle a sharp intake of breath, and her hand flew to cover her stomach. *She was pregnant.* How did she know? She just did... and...it was a girl child. She smiled.

Their first time together in the realm of the mist she had conceived. She glanced quickly at her mate. He didn't know, but he was a little busy just then. Maya would tell him once they were on Akgon. Their child would be born there.

Once again, Draakar shone when he called his powers and the magicks of the Stones to open the gate.

When the gray mass appeared, Maya gasped. "You...you did that alone!"

"Yes. My powers have actually been growing. I can open the gate alone now, and I think so can you. Now help me get everyone safely across." He raised his hand, and she placed her palm in his.

She had forgotten about the bond. The moment he touched her, he knew too. *We're having a child, a daughter.* His voice sounded hoarse in her mind. She nodded at him in confirmation. His smile matched the golden light surrounding them as they watched her parents, then Ian and Cass, walk into the gray cloud.

Together, beloved. Shall we?

Let's.

Maya wasn't sure what to expect when she stepped into the cloud with Draakar. However, it was not the sensation of her body moving forward. Her legs remained standing still, but her feet no longer stood on solid ground. Draakar remained beside her, his hand clasped tightly in hers, but she couldn't see him. Maya could see nothing but bright light. Then suddenly the brightness dissipated and she could see color, the colors of the rainbow, and her feet rested on solid ground once again.

She blinked to adjust her sight and saw they stood out in the open. Surrounded by what appeared to be a circle of stones, like on Earth, but looming just beyond the circle, a fortress rose, made of stone of gigantic proportions. She looked up. The sky would take a little getting used to. A light purple, and not the blue her mind kept insisting it should be. She turned around to examine the width of the fortress, but her eyes slid past it and she kept turning in a half circle. Her lips parted.

The circle of stones and fortress stood on top of a plateau. But it no longer claimed her attention. She walked beyond the perimeter of the stones and looked down. Before her, on bended knees, were thousands of brightly dressed brethren in human form.

"What…what's going on?" a stunned Maya asked. "What are they doing?"

"They are paying homage to their Queen, to you," Draakar replied in a husky voice.

"Did you…did you tell them to do this?" she gasped. "Do they know I'm pregnant?"

"No, how could they? We only both just realized it. They do this on their own, for you."

Draakar kissed her hand before raising it above their heads. *My brethren, I give you your Queen, Maya.*

Several thousand heads raised and their voices chanted "Maya" to the purple heavens of Akgon.

Maya looked down through the tears in her eyes at the happy, excited faces and felt as though she had come home. She saw her parents in the front of the crowd, along with their Firsts beside them.

I've come home.

The noise the brethren made at her declaration rose even stronger.

Yes, you have, Maya. Yes, you have.

NINE MONTHS LATER...

The cry of the child could be heard throughout the realm. A new brethren had been born to the Dark Lord and his Queen. The dragons raised their heads and roared in celebration. Within the walls of the castle, Draakar's advisor beheld the female child for the first time. Clutching at his heart, he stumbled backward before fainting.

An exhausted, fearful Maya cradled her child closer to her breast as Draakar and Valour's seer sisters bent to take care of Valour.

"What's wrong with him?" Draakar demanded. "What did he see?"

"I do not know, Lord," the oldest of the three sisters replied. "But he saw something."

Sherri came running into the room; she had stepped out

for a few minutes after delivering the child. Draakar had summoned her before Valour even hit the floor.

She rushed to his side and Paul stood framed in the doorway. They were never far apart. "What happened?" Sherri asked.

Draakar answered, "We're not sure, but I think he had a vision."

Maya spoke in a soft voice from the bed. "Sherri, he was looking at the baby when he just kinda staggered away, and his eyes rolled back into his head before he passed out."

"Ooooh…"

All heads turned toward the sound of the groan. Valour moved, raised his hand toward his head, and opened his eyes. "Oh my, what…what happened?" he asked.

Sherri kneeled closest to his head and answered him. "You gave us quite a scare. You fainted."

Valour tried to sit up, and Draakar immediately moved to help him. "Easy, old friend. Just stay still for a second."

His advisor looked at him before glancing over at the bed. He quickly returned his attention to his Lord. "I…I will be fine."

"Did you have a vision?" his eldest sister asked.

His mouth opened and closed twice before he spoke. "Yes. Like none before." His eyes swung back around to Maya and the child, who lay on the bed wrapped protectively in her mother's arms.

"What…what is it, Valour? You saw something about the baby, didn't you?" Maya's voice wobbled. In the nine months since she had been on Akgon, she and Valour had become more than close friends. He became her teacher, her mentor, and she trusted him like a brother. She couldn't think of him as elderly. With his long brownish hair, smooth skin, and lean physique, he seemed only a few years older than she. He was, in fact, even older than Draakar, but she preferred not to think about the age thing. It blew her mind. If what he saw caused such a reaction in him, Maya didn't want to know about it. Her body trembled.

Valour crossed to stand beside the bed. Draakar followed and sat on the other side, engulfing his mate and child in his arms.

"What is it, my friend?" Draakar said. "Tell us."

The advisor looked down at the child. Maya noticed her daughter turned her head so she could gaze trustingly up at him with vibrant green eyes, surprisingly clear and alert for a newborn.

"Wow! Look at that!" Sherri exclaimed. "It takes most newborns a few days before they can turn their heads; she has very strong neck muscles."

"That's not the only thing she's strong in," Valour said. "I am sorry, Your Majesties. I...I did not mean to scare you. It was such a shock. I didn't know such a thing could ever happen. But we should have known, so much has changed on Earth and the forgotten brethren have been surprising us every day." Valour shook his head in seeming exasperation. "I did indeed have a vision." Then he smiled and his smile told Maya everything. She had nothing to fear.

"Your child, this child," he continued, "will be the next Dragon Lord, ah Lady, ah Queen." He took a deep, excited breath. "I'm sorry. There is no precedent for this."

"What are you talking about?" Draakar said as each of Valour's sisters gasped at Valour's words. Maya glanced at them. They wore shell-shocked expressions.

"But...but I thought only brethren males could be Dragon Lords," Maya said, clearly confused, "because only the males are strong enough to wield that much magicks?"

"That's true," Draakar replied.

"With all due respect, Lord and my Lady," Valour said with a slight bow of his elegant head. "Apparently not. This child is clearly female, and she is the next Dragon Lord. Her powers are clear. Open yourself to her and you will see what I saw. Ah, but that's not all."

"What, there's more?" Draakar asked sarcastically.

"She will be a Dark Dragon."

This time, Draakar gasped. "But…that's impossible."

"What about Talon?" Maya asked. "Talon is Draakar's heir. He's the next Dragon Lord."

"That's not the way the ascension works, Your Majesty. The strongest in power leads the brethren. This child could grow to be stronger than even her father."

"What?" Maya exclaimed. "But wait a second, wait a second. How can this be?"

Valour raised his eyebrows. "I do not know. Only what is."

Maya knew Draakar quietly delved into the soul of their child before speaking again. "Valour is correct. Our daughter is indeed a Dark Queen."

All eyes looked at the smiling child.

EPILOGUE

*T*alon walked down the narrow stairwell and stepped into the bowels of the dark smoke-filled nightclub. He had no trouble seeing in the gloomy, crowded room. Bodies stood, rubbing shoulders and thighs everywhere. They were even closer on the dance floor as couples or threesomes moved in a simulation of the sex act to the pulsing beat of the latest craze passing for music. But no one touched Talon's six-four frame as he moved through the crowd toward the private tables raised on platforms in the back.

No one dared.

There were some in the crowd who noted his passing. They saw he wore the face of an angel, with a waterfall of golden hair cascading around one broad shoulder to lie across his leather-covered ribs. But for all his beauty, an air of danger or difference surrounded him. It could be seen in the flash of golden fire erupting from the depths of his eyes. Clearly proclaiming him a fallen angel.

People automatically moved out of his way, yet all the female eyes and some males in the place tracked his movement. Only one set of eyes tracked his approach with both anticipation and dread.

You came. Talon sent into the void.

You knew I would. So you are real. The voice in his head sounded soft, feminine and husky, causing cells already sensitive to her growing nearness to vibrate even more.

Yes. Very much so. But you always knew I was.

It had taken him twelve years, but he had finally found her. All the time he had been here on Earth, he had dreamed of her. Catching fragments of her life in shared dreams— emotions, really. At times, he could see her as though through a mirror, looking back at him between the frames. Once, for one incredible moment, both of their auras met on the plane known as sleep and they had made love. But it wasn't real, and he woke up with tears in his eyes because she did not lie beside him, and he did not hold her in his arms. The dream propelled him even more to find her, although he never could—until now.

A lone woman sat at a table against the far wall, the farthest from the stairs and the dance floor. She sat in the shadows, and no one approached the table or bothered her. He could not see her face. Even now, she cloaked herself from him. It didn't matter. Every cell in Talon's body knew her.

Would know her anywhere.

Her gaze on him burned through the cloth covering his body and seared into his soul.

Mine!

He paused with his foot on the bottom step to the raised platform. Ruthlessly, he stripped the glamour she used to protect herself and then enfolded her in the protection of his own powerful magicks. She bowed her head as though to hide from him still. But there was nowhere she could go now he would not be able to find her. They were linked. And soon they would be bonded. Finally, when he had called to her, she answered. Or rather, she had called out to him for help.

Danger followed her. *His mate.* He would kill to protect her.

His father had placed his faith in him to protect Earth and the brethren here while he returned to Akgon with his queen to restore the balance there. His little sister would rule Akgon someday, leaving it up to Talon now to protect this realm. The silver dragon still lived. Somehow Arwan had broken through the seal Draakar placed on the portal at Window Rock and ran loose in the world once more. Now the bastard stalked his truemate, but Talon had found her first. He breathed a sigh of relief.

His footsteps took him to the back of the platform, stopping only when he stood before her. Slowly, she raised her face toward him, and at last he could see the silver glow of her eyes shining up at him. His truemate.

He held out his hand to her, and she placed her smaller hand in his. A glow surrounded their joined hands before expanding to enclose their bodies.

Complete!

At last!

Thanks for reading. If you enjoyed this work or any others, please consider leaving a review. Because without you, our writing is just words on a page.

DRAGON'S BLOOD BLURB

Can you hear my dragon roar?

After losing her mother at a very young age, Arianna's world changed when her father came to get her. He took her across the Atlantic Ocean, away from everything she'd ever known and loved. But once again she's forced to cross the Atlantic, this time leaving everything she'd grown to love behind. Running from the thing that had killed her remaining parent, running for her life. And fleeing from the being she'd dreamt of for half her life. Nothing could save her, she didn't believe in myths and fairytales. Didn't believe in the man with the eyes that flashed gold. She could trust no one. Not even the voice whispering inside her head she recognized as her own.

Talon had come to Earth searching for his truemate. Knowing she was near but still so very far away. Only able to reach her when they both closed their eyes, but waking up to find it had all been nothing but a dream. Until one day he heard her cry of pain and felt the crippling pang of fear that invaded her mind. She needed him, but he couldn't find her. Not until she released her block against him. He just hoped it would not be too late. Because an ancient enemy roamed Earth once more and hunted his truemate. It was a race as to which one of them would find her first. Talon would not lose.

This is not an erotic romance but it does contain sexual content and violence suitable for 18+

READ TALON'S STORY

ABOUT THE AUTHOR

LaVerne Thompson is a USA Today Bestselling, award winning, multi-published author, an avid reader and a writer of fantasy, paranormal, contemporary, and sci/fi sensual romances. She loves creating worlds within and without our world. She also writes romantic suspense and new adult romance under the pen name Ursula Sinclair also a USA Today Bestselling Author.

She is a certified chocoholic and is currently working on several projects. Some might even involve chocolate. But writing helps maintain her sanity.

Sign up for her newsletter for sneak peeks and advance info on new releases as well as a few freebies to subscribers. http://bit.ly/1hA7C9W

lavernethompson.com

ALSO BY LAVERNE THOMPSON

PARANORMAL/ROMANTIC FANTASY/URBAN FANTASY

SERIES

Story of the Brethren

A romantic fantasy

Dragon's Heart Book 1
Dragon's Blood Book 2

Redemption

An urban fantasy

Angel Rising Book 1
Angel Rising also on audio
Angel Hunter Book 2
Angel Guardian Book 2.5

Lost Gods

A romantic fantasy

Zeus Book 1

Ledo Book 2

Linc Book 3

CHILDREN OF THE WAVES

A romantic fantasy

Sea Bride

Sea Storm

Sea Witch

Sea Child

The Children of the Waves Collection Books 1-3 in KU

CROXROADS

An action adventure urban fantasy

Wild Child

Wild Fire

Wild Magic

CroXroads Box Set

THE ELEMENTALS

A medieval fantasy

Journey of the Princess of Ice- A graphic Novella Edition

The Beast Within World

A paranormal fantasy romance

The Beast Within

The Beast Within also on Audible

The Hidden Series

A dark paranormal romance

Dark Mist

Dark Shadow

STAND ALONES

Day of Death-Rise Of The Dreads

A dark fantasy romance

The Princess Bed

A fairytale fantasy romance

The Glass King

A fantasy romance

The Christmas Spirit
A holiday romantic fantasy short

Day in the Sun
A futuristic sc/fi romance

Come To Me
A contemporary romance

Hold On
Contemporary romantic suspense
Also available on audio

Chances Are
Contemporary romantic suspense

Promise
Contemporary romance

Masquerade
Contemporary romance

Writing as Ursula Sinclair

Fantasy/Paranormal/Sci/fi/Contemporary New Adult

Paranormal Fantasy

The City of Sin

After Midnight- City of Sin

When Dawn Comes- City of Sin

The Eventide Hour- City of Sin

Contemporary

The Ballerina Series

Contemporary new adult

The Ballerina & The Fighter- Book 1

Also available on audio

Maze- The Ballerina Series Book 2

Also available on audio

The Dancer- The Ballerina Series Book 3

The Ballerina Series Collection- Books 1-3

Young Guns

Contemporary new adult

The Prison Guard's Son- Young Guns Book 1

The Martini Lounge

Contemporary new adult (can be read as stand alones)

Shaken- The Martini Lounge (also Young Guns Book 1.5)

Stirred- The Martini Lounge

Frozen- The Martini Lounge

The Guardian Agency
Romantic suspense

White Wedding- The Guardian Agency Series Book 1
Something Blue- The Guardian Agency Series Book 2
Wine and Roses- The Guardian Agency Series Book 3
Guardian Agents Boxed Set

Sci/fi

Shadow Wars
Sci/fi new adult

Shadow Wars Homebound
Also available on audio

Co-Written

The Maji Series co-written with Phoenix Daniels
A paranormal romance

The Cigar King in KU

Defiant co-written with Kassanna writing as Ursula Sinclair
A new adult contemporary romance

FREE ON PROLIFIC with Sign up

Tears On A Rose

Tatianna

Coming 2024/2025

Soul Collectors full length

Alien Sons

Quiet Strength- Defiant Series Book 2

Dark Soul- The Hidden Series Book 3

Choose Me- The Ballerina Series Book 4

The Otherworlders- Wolfen (Ursula Sinclair)- New Adult

Shadow Wars Ronin Riders (Ursula Sinclair)- New Adult

Living On The Edge- The Clan

Skye High

Kissed By A Rose

Lexi's Journal

The Ice Man Cometh- The Elementals Book 2

www.ingramcontent.com/pod-product-compliance
Lightning Source LLC
Chambersburg PA
CBHW051237260626
47162CB00002B/471